GRIM

ISBN: 978-0-9971650-5-0

New Rise Press
1818 Martin Luther King Jr. Blvd.
Chapel Hill, NC 27514

www.afterpsychotherapy.com

GRIM

Dark Fairy Tales
for the Psychologically Minded

by

Joseph Burgo

New Rise Press
1818 Martin Luther King Jr. Blvd.
Chapel Hill, NC 27514

ALSO BY JOSEPH BURGO

<u>Non-Fiction</u>

Why Do I Do That?
Psychological Defense Mechanisms and the Hidden Ways They
    Shape Our Lives

The Narcissist You Know
Defending Yourself Against Extreme Narcissists in an All-
    About-Me Age

<u>Fiction</u>

Vacillian (Book One of the Illuminariad)

The Lights of Barbrin

CONTENTS

CINDERELLA

ONE

Sometimes at night, curled up on her pallet beside the cooling hearth – the musty smell of old straw in her nostrils, in her ears the sound of mouse claws scratching on the stone floor – Cinderella felt as if she *belonged* amidst the ashes. She always felt dirty, though she kept her hands fearfully clean, washing them many times each day before cooking or serving, before changing those linen sheets upon Griselda's bed or helping her sister to dress. As for her own clothes and body, she could do little but brush away the ashes then scrub her face and arms with old dishwater. Mother left her no time for proper bathing. By the time she'd finished carrying water in steaming pails from the kitchen cauldron to Griselda's tub – up and down the stairs seven, eight, nine trips – new chores awaited her. Sweeping, mopping, cooking, sewing.

Cinderella did her best with these chores but her best never seemed quite good enough. Her stitches lacked refinement, her cooking was too bland; she inevitably missed dirt in the corners when she scrubbed the floors, or left streaks of grease on the dinner plates when she returned them to the cupboard. It sometimes seemed as if she could do no right and her sister no wrong. No matter how badly Griselda played the piano – Cinderella wincing below stairs at the wrong notes, the plodding tempo – Mother called it "delightful." However indolent or pettish, Griselda never heard an unkind word.

Reading Mother's face, listening to her differing tones of voice when she addressed them, it was obvious she felt blessed with one perfect child and burdened by the other.

9

Sometimes at night when Cinderella thought back on her life, a surge of bitterness made the kitchen shadows go deeper; she heard the skittering mice and wanted to smash them with the frying pan. Their hairy skins would split open, spilling blood and guts onto the stone floor. After another long day void of kindness, with the warmth of fading embers at her back, she would imagine a *different* mother, one who might love her in spite of her ugliness. She felt ashamed of having such a dream; she would never have told a soul about this imaginary mother, even if someone had cared enough to take an interest in her dreams, her thoughts, what passed unnoticed within her.

The lovely image would flood her thoughts with light. *My fairy godmother* – that's what Cinderella called her. Dressed all in white – a pearlescent white aglow with kindness – she would smile from the corner where Cinderella had conjured her. Fairy Godmother never spoke, but the way she *beamed* – the way she fixed her smiling eyes on Cinderella's face and never looked away – seemed to tell her, *You are beautiful, too. As beautiful to me as I am to you.*

Occasionally, on mornings after Fairy Godmother had come and lingered long into the night, Cinderella could almost believe it to be true. Catching a glimpse of herself in the looking glass upon Griselda's dressing table, she'd think, "Perhaps I really am beautiful!" She compared the lines of her own figure with her sister's physique, seen and felt each day upon dressing, and briefly believed her own form lovelier, more pleasing in shape.

If her father hadn't died when she was so young, life might have turned out differently. She had few memories of Father, and not one of his face. She did recall his hands, their massive size, the feel of them. She remembered sitting on his lap and the look on Mother's face when she saw them together.

"Leave the girl alone." That's what she remembered Mother saying.

* * *

One morning, as Cinderella stepped onto the upstairs landing, her arms laden with fresh linens for Griselda's bed, her sister was coming down the hall toward her. As she came close, Griselda stepped to the side, as if to give way; from the smug look on her sister's broad flat face, Cinderella guessed that she'd come up with some new way to torture her, another one of her "pranks," as Mother called them. She probably intended to stick out one of her enormous feet so that Cinderella would trip and drop the laundry then insist afterwards that those "filthy" sheets be washed and pressed anew.

Before Griselda had time to act, Cinderella pretended to stumble, falling sideways so her elbow jabbed sharply into her sister's breast. Her aim was true and Griselda let out a sharp shriek of pain.

"I'm so very, very sorry!" Cinderella carefully held the sheets away from her sister, out of reach. "What's wrong with me today?!"

Griselda glared back, clutching a hand to her breast and rubbing it. "You clumsy fool, that really hurt!"

"What's the trouble?" Mother's voice boomed from her bedroom down the hall. "Is everything all right?"

"It's my fault," Cinderella called out. "I tripped and fell into Griselda. But I think she's all right." She shaped her features into innocence; she rounded off the edges in her voice and lifted its notes still higher. "I didn't really hurt you, did I, sister dear? Not badly anyway." She gave Griselda a smile meant to convey concern.

"You little witch," Griselda hissed. "I'll get you for this." With heavy ungraceful strides, even heavier and less graceful than usual, she hurried along the hall and down the stairs. Cinderella held her breath; she didn't have long to wait for the sound of glass shattering, loud and piercing even at this distance. She tried to imagine what her sister had broken. In her stupid rage, Griselda might actually have broken something that she herself cared for. Afterwards, she'd tell Mother that Cinderella was to blame. Mother believed whatever Griselda told her. Cinderella was always to blame.

Minutes later as she was fitting the sheets to Griselda's bed, Cinderella felt awash in shame. As unlikely as it seemed, Griselda might actually have intended to let Cinderella pass in the hallway. Even if she did have another one of her pranks in mind, why couldn't Cinderella learn to accept things as they were? Why couldn't she be good? Today, she took special care with the counterpane, folding it down and arranging pillows in just the way her sister liked. Usually, she got it wrong on purpose, smiling to herself below stairs when she heard Griselda curse.

Cinderella startled at the sound of Mother's voice. It came from behind her, near the doorway. "When you're finished with my room, there are some errands in town I need you to run. I'm out of face cream and my new hat should be ready at Morton's."

The butcher had lately taken to scowling whenever Cinderella came in, muttering about the unpaid bill; how could they afford face cream and a new hat?

"Yes, Mother."

Cinderella turned, gazing at her mother's buckled shoes and the hem of her dress – the green silk, one of the few remaining pieces in her wardrobe that hadn't yet begun to show its age. She and Griselda must have plans to make a social call.

"Why are you just standing there?" Mother's voice was tight with scorn and impatience. "Aren't you finished here?"

"Yes, I'm finished." Cinderella finally glanced higher, into her mother's eyes, and felt stung for the thousandth time. She felt ugly.

"Then get started on my bedroom. And leave my dressing table alone. I've told you a thousand times – I don't like you touching my things."

Only a child so hideous as to be unlovable could make a mother grimace with distaste – the way Mother did as Cinderella passed by – or glare after her with hatred for no apparent reason. She *had* to be ugly.

* * *

The other families of equal stature – the ones with carriages and large houses, who came for evening parties and in turn hosted Mother and Griselda – they had *servants* to do their chores. On days like today when Mother sent her into town on errands, Cinderella saw them in the shops, or pushing barrows they used to carry what they'd bought. Her lot had always been thus; she took it for granted, and yet it didn't seem just. Though she did the same chores and went on errands like any other servant girl, she wasn't actually one of them. She knew she wouldn't be welcome to join the other girls giggling and gossiping inside the shops.

It sometimes seemed as if these other girls with their clean while bonnets and starched aprons were sneering at Cinderella (always clad in the same tattered gray dress) or whispering behind her back in line at the butcher's. She thought it possible that she'd only imagined their contempt; she hated them for it anyway. She longed for friendship, to join in their gossip, but felt too ashamed to speak. Most times when Mother sent her into the village, Cinderella tried to draw as little attention as possible. She pretended that she was invisible and could almost believe it to be true.

The girls mostly ignored her but lately, now that her breasts and hips had grown larger, the boys enjoyed teasing her. Sometimes one of them would whistle as she passed, or make rude kissing noises that caused the other boys to laugh. Today, one of the local peasant boys secretly followed her away from the village. He came suddenly up from behind, put his hand under her skirt and touched her in the soft dark place. He tried to kiss her neck. Cinderella felt unable to move.

He wasn't a large boy but somehow, he felt oddly massive behind her ... his hands so large and powerful she'd never break free. His fingers pressing into her, hard then gentle. She hated him for the way he made her feel, the pleasure of it.

She finally broke free and ran all the way home, crying tears of rage, thick with shame. Dirty and even uglier than before.

The dingy old carriage with its pair of white geldings stood in front of the house as she came running up. Mother and Griselda were just coming out, the front door held open by the coachman. She longed to tell Mother what the peasant boy had done, to confide her sense of humiliation, to receive some comfort. Tears were streaming down her face.

"Why don't we have a maid and a cook like the other fine families?" Cinderella cried. She knew she'd made a mistake but couldn't stop herself. "Why must I do the work of a servant? Am I not your daughter, too?" Her voice was ragged with tears.

Cinderella had never seen Mother's face go so red, her mouth distort with such hatred. Her palm struck with enough force to knock Cinderella to the ground ... the sting of grit in her hands and knees. Mother's buckled shoes passed by and stepped into the carriage. Griselda tittered and climbed in behind her. The coachmen snapped his whip, made a clucking noise to the geldings, and the carriage moved off.

In the kitchen, Cinderella felt so beside herself that she couldn't bring herself to carry on with her chores. She paced back and forth across the stone floor, from scullery board to fireplace, whimpering softly in tones that brought her comfort. She tried without success to call up Fairy Godmother's loving face. She felt the boy's large hand again beneath her skirt, felt sick with excitement. With lye soap and the bristle brush, she scrubbed her arms until the skin burned. Then she stripped down and scrubbed all over. Even harder along her thighs, near to where'd he touched her. Nothing would ever make her feel clean again.

The hard bristles scratched red lines onto her skin. Seeing them on her arms and legs, feeling the pain brought Cinderella unexpected relief. One very sharp bristle sliced open her skin and the vivid sight of swelling blood felt deeply soothing. By the time she stopped bleeding, after she'd dressed herself again and wiped away her tears, she felt ready to resume her life. If she hadn't managed to clean at least the main drawing room by the time they returned, Mother might fly into a rage.

She'd just begun the dusting when there came three slow raps from the brass door knocker. One … two … three. So portentous in pace, ominous even. When she opened the door, a short fat man in gilded livery stood on the threshold. With his powdered wig and pointed shoes, he looked so curious, so thoroughly unnatural that Cinderella almost laughed. No doubt he belonged to some terribly wealthy nobleman, or maybe the palace! What could he possibly want? Behind him stood a groom, clutching a lead rope tethered to a pony. Even the groom had fine clothes.

The short fat man gripped a round salver, beaten silver that glinted in the sunlight, with a rectangle of lettered white upon it.

"By order of the King and Queen, all unmarried ladies of the land must attend." He jiggled the tray impatiently, as if to say, *Take it!*

Attend what? Why did the command refer to *unmarried* ladies in particular? She had a feeling the message had started out much longer and shed words as the day wore on. Delivering the same speech to every household in the land would be tedious. As she reached for the card, the red lines on her arms, the crusty red-brown of the bristle scar seemed to glare anger. The fat man didn't notice.

> *On Friday fortnight, a ball will be given in honor of Prince Charming's 21st birthday. By order of the King and Queen, all unmarried noblewomen under the age of 30 are commanded to attend.*

15

By the time she'd finished reading the card, going over it twice to make sure she understood, the messenger was preparing to mount his pony. Though the beast was not tall, no more than 12 hands, the groom had laced his fingers together and made a step of them, bearing the fat man's weight as he hoisted himself upward.

"*All* unmarried noblewomen?" she called out. "Are you certain?"

"No exceptions!" he snapped, throwing his leg over the pony's back. "Just exactly what it says." And with lead rope in hand, the groom led the pony and rider away across the courtyard.

She lowered her gaze once more to the invitation.

The Prince was coming of age, of course – time to select a wife from the eligible prospects, all of them commanded to appear for inspection in less than three weeks. The very idea that she, too, might have to attend the ball filled her with dread. All those people! She saw herself in her usual drab rags, there on the palace steps, everyone else in radiant finery. The scorn and amusement in their eyes. When she thought of Prince Charming, the chance that she might actually have to dance with him, she felt almost sick. She felt better when she realized Mother probably wouldn't let her go. Mother never let Cinderella appear anywhere in public if she could help it. She'd find a way to evade the king's command and save them all from embarrassment.

Cinderella placed the invitation on the mantel, propped in the gap that had been left behind when Mother sold the blue porcelain clock to pay taxes. Father's clock, in the family for generations. She was down on her knees, scrubbing the black-and-white entryway tiles when she heard the gravelly rattle of wheels, the hollow clop-clop of hooves in the courtyard. Moments later, Griselda hurled the door open and came rushing in, red-faced and out of breath. Her large nostrils flared wider.

"Where is it?" she snapped, glaring down at her sister.

Cinderella made her face a blank. She dropped her brush into the bucket, passing the back of her arm across her brow. "Where is what?"

"The invitation, you idiot! We saw him on the road, the messenger. So where is it?"

"Oh that. It's on the drawing room mantel."

Hoisting her skirts, Griselda hurried into the drawing room and snatched up the invitation. Mother came in, closing the door behind her, and crossed into the drawing room. Though she moved slowly, Cinderella could feel the tension in her steps.

She kept a surreptitious eye on her mother and sister while continuing to scrub the floor. Griselda looked unhappy.

"It says *all* unmarried noblewomen." She must've intended it as a whisper, meant for her mother's ears only, but anguish made the sound carry.

"I don't see why it's limited to women over thirty. I may no longer be able to bear children, but still …"

"Don't let her go!" Griselda moaned. She sounded so anguished Cinderella almost felt sorry for her. "You can't let her go! If she's there, then everyone will …"

"Hush!" Mother cut her short. "We'll discuss the matter *later.*" That meant in private, of course, where Cinderella couldn't hear.

Alone with her afternoon chores, she puzzled over Griselda's words. Did she mean that everyone else – their neighbors and the nobles at court – would see that Griselda had a sister to be ashamed of, an ill-favored girl fit for nothing more than scrubbing floors and doing laundry? That had to be what she'd meant. In a shy corner of her mind, Cinderella entertained quite another possibility. She thought of the way Griselda sometimes stared at her tiny feet (so much smaller than her own loafish ones) as if she hated the very sight of them.

In the days that followed, she often felt Mother's eyes watching her, not angrily, not resentfully in the old way but with a new sort of interest. If Cinderella caught her glance, Mother didn't turn away with a grimace as she usually did. She kept looking back, her eyes full of questions. As much as she'd always longed for her mother's attention, this change made Cinderella uneasy. If Mother didn't hate her ... then who was she?

One morning as they passed in the upstairs hall – Cinderella on her way to empty the chamber pots and Mother smelling of bath salts, dressed for breakfast – Mother stopped and said, "Should you like to go to the ball, Cinderella?"

She couldn't remember when she'd last heard Mother use her name. The sound brought tears to her eyes; she clenched her teeth hard to stop from crying.

"I'd die of shame," she answered. "I couldn't bear it."

"You're unused to society, that's all. I'm sure you wouldn't mind it if you had something fit to wear." She didn't say it kindly, but neither did her voice hoarsen in familiar disgust.

Cinderella had no idea what to think. The world felt in flux around her.

"I'd rather not go unless I have to."

"If it would make me happy? Would you go then?"

She lowered her eyes. Mother had to know the answer to that question. Had she asked it to humiliate her? "Of course I'd do anything to make you happy. Only ... if I don't have to ..."

"The invitation did say *all* noblewomen. We can't disobey the king's command."

"I'm not a noblewoman." She felt the angry tears welling up. "I'm only a servant girl."

Mother bristled. She must've heard the rebuke. "We won't discuss it further. And if I say you are to go, then you will go. Do you understand?" Her petticoats rustled in irritation as she strode away.

* * *

If Griselda seemed to hate her still more these days, Mother seemed to despise her less than before. Her attitude fell short of affection. Cinderella felt as if her status were being re-evaluated: there might be some more effective way to make use of her. Twice that week, Griselda tracked mud into the entryway just after Cinderella had mopped it – one of her favorite pranks. The third time, Mother called Griselda "stupid fool," a term customarily reserved for Cinderella, and asked whether she could really be so simple that she couldn't remember to wipe her shoes before entering. Griselda looked shocked, her mouth sagging open; she burst into tears and ran off to her room.

Later that day, Cinderella knelt trembling outside Griselda's door, ear pressed to the keyhole, while Mother and Griselda argued inside. They expected her to be downstairs, polishing the glass candlesticks as she'd been told, but still, they kept their voices low. Cinderella strained to make out their words.

"It makes no difference which one of you saves me from the poorhouse," Mother was saying. "Bringing your sister along will double my chances."

"But everyone will *see*!" Griselda whined. "Put her next to me and … and they'll *see*."

"Everyone already sees, Griselda. People have eyes of their own, you know." Then, when Griselda began to whimper in self-pity, Mother's tone softened. "Now don't fret. I've made up my mind. She's going. With my luck, nothing will come of it anyway. Then it's back to the cellar. Stop you're crying, Griselda. Who's my favorite? Please stop, darling. Who has always been my favorite?"

That night, Fairy Godmother glowed with special brilliance from her corner. *I always said you were the beauty.*

Maybe going to the ball might not be such an awful experience. It would be worth enduring the dread and anxiety if her presence would make Griselda suffer as much as she seemed to fear.

Next morning, two men with a wagon carted off the grand armoire from the entry hall, yet another of Father's heirlooms traded away for gold; in the afternoon, the dressmaker came with silks and satins, ribbons, bows and measuring tapes. He was a wiry, bony man who gave off a faint smell of old cooking oil. He carried a flat valise with worn leather handles.

Mother stationed him upstairs, in the yellow room with its canopy bed and three-sided mirror, just across from Griselda's bedchamber. Cinderella brought him a stepstool as Mother directed, along with the brandy he asked for. When he took the glass from her hand, his fingers brushed against hers and she tried to still a shudder of disgust. The contact hadn't lasted for more than a second or two, but something unwholesome seemed to penetrate from his skin into her body. Her eyes kept traveling back to his long fingers, with their thickened knobs at the joints and tiny red scars all over, no doubt from the pins-pricks and needles.

Griselda demanded the first fitting. While the dressmaker took her measurements and helped her choose fabric, Mother ushered Cinderella into her own changing room; she gave her clean undergarments and an old dressing gown ... grudgingly, as if she resented sharing a single thing that belonged to her.

"Put them on," she said. "You can't very well be fitted for a ball gown wearing those filthy rags." She took in Cinderella's tangled, oily hair and handed her a ribbon. "Just tie it back. There's nothing to be done about it now."

From down the hall came Griselda's peevish tones. No words, only the unmistakable rumble of grievance, punctuated by high notes of disdain. She was obviously giving the dressmaker grief. By the time Cinderella's turn came, he was in a foul mood, scowling at his tasseled slippers as he gestured her onto the step-stool. Mother stood behind, arms crossed over her bosom, image reflected in the mirror's side panel. Holding very still, Cinderella clutched her dressing gown tightly around her.

The dressmaker muttered unhappily in a foreign tongue as he spread drawings from his valise across the bed. Years ago, before they began to run out of money, Griselda used to have a French governess. Cinderella thought the dressmaker might be a Frenchman. He tugged with irritation at one curling end of his moustache.

Catching sight of her in the mirror, he said, "Please, you will take it off." He meant the dressing gown, obviously. The way he said the word *it* sounded more like *eat*.

Cinderella dropped the dressing gown from her shoulders and Mother came forward to take it, retreating to her post of observation. The dressmaker turned, measuring tape at the ready, and physically startled when he actually looked at her. His hands (grotesque and fascinating) began to pass the tape around her body – first her hips, then her waist, then higher still around her bust. Did he find her ugly? The trembling in his hands told her otherwise. His taut, uneven breathing made her light up between the legs. Mother's reflection in the glass looked unhappy. Her eyebrows came together, creasing the skin between them.

She'd felt as if she'd lived this moment before – the man's hands touching her body, Mother vigilant behind her.

The wiry little man made notes in pencil, writing down the measurements he'd taken. Cinderella forced herself not to stare at his fingers. What would he do to her if Mother weren't here in the room? Try to touch her, the way the peasant boy had done a few days ago? He might want to put his fingers inside her, he might try to force her. She felt herself growing wet.

* * *

On the day before the ball, the dressmaker returned for a final fitting. Once he'd finished with Griselda – first again, of course – he helped Cinderella into the blue silk dress he'd made for her. He peeled it apart at the back, all the way from shoulders down to the waistline, and she stepped into the opening when he lowered it. Mother had gone to console Griselda, who was unhappy with her own dress. Mother wasn't watching today.

As the dressmaker pulled the dress higher around her body, she passed her bare arms through the sleeves. Cinderella stared at but didn't see her own reflection in the mirror; he stood behind her, slipping button after button into their holes. The silk itself, the inner lining and then her underclothes – so many layers between his fingers and her back. The unwholesome feeling seemed to penetrate right through. She felt disgusted by the smell of old cooking oil that came off of him. She didn't want to feel the way she'd felt the other day, the heated wetness between her legs.

It took some time before she could bring herself into focus – there, in the mirror, that girl wearing a pale blue dress, a satin sash round her waist in an even deeper blue. Her face and body were clean today. Mother had finally told her to bathe. What Cinderella saw now in the mirror … she couldn't quite believe her eyes. The dressmaker was fussing about her, pulling and adjusting the fabric around her waist, at her shoulders, across her breasts.

Just when she thought he was going to touch them, to cup and press them, he stepped back to appraise her, raising his knobby fingers to his chin. He was reflected in the mirror, behind her and to one side. The knuckles of his hands seemed so large.

The door opened and Mother came in, took a few steps forward and then stopped. Cinderella felt herself appraised from both sides, the dressmaker reflecting in the left-hand side of the mirror, Mother on the right. The dressmaker didn't matter now. All she cared about was the expression on Mother's face. She kept waiting for it to change, waiting for that special look to tell Cinderella that at last she was beautiful. Mother's gaze traveled up and down her body. She nodded slowly.

"You've done very well, Henri," she said.

He made a breathy, dismissive noise, as if he found her praise inadequate. "It is among my greatest creations. This dress will be talked of and admired by everyone at the ball. And next season, all the ladies of the court will be sending for me."

Cinderella wished he would keep his mouth shut. She kept watching Mother's face. Its expression never changed.

She sensed rather than heard movement at the door. Her sister was peering through a narrow opening, just wide enough for her face. That look of envy and malice in Griselda's eyes – Cinderella understood what it meant, the implication of beauty, but it wasn't what she wanted.

* * *

Mother left Cinderella's dress in the yellow room, locked in the wardrobe, carrying away the key as they escorted the dressmaker to the door. Mother had seen that look in Griselda's eyes, too, and knew better than to leave Cinderella's dress unattended. Cinderella had hoped she might actually be allowed to sleep in the yellow room – she had bathed, after all, and sleeping downstairs in the straw, as usual, would only make her unclean again. Nothing was said about where she would sleep. Mother still expected her to make and serve the evening meal, wait at table and clean up afterwards. As she was carrying away the last of the plates, Mother said, "Tomorrow is an important day for us. Make sure you get to bed early."

"Yes, Mother."

Though very tired, she had a hard time falling asleep. As the owls hooted outside and the mice scurried across the kitchen floor, she tried not to think about the ball – so many opportunities to humiliate herself! A little spasm of dread took hold when she imagined herself in conversation. What subject could she talk about? The weather? Crops in the field? The pumpkins were finally ripe, with their hairy vines and dull orange skins crusted with dirt. What more could you say about pumpkins? Did other people save the seeds and toast them over the fire, or only hungry servant girls who never let food go to waste?

She brought her mind to quiet and focused on her breathing. She counted backwards from a hundred. Just as sleep nearly engulfed her, an image of the dressmaker's large knuckles waked her up again. The thought of his knobby fingers made her throb in a way that excited and disgusted her, down there, below her waist where she didn't like to feel. Then she thought of the tiny scars where he'd pricked himself. Before her mind's eye, the blood began to ooze from a new cut, this one larger and longer, a fine line inscribed by his razor. The blood gathered into shiny drops, slipping from his arm into a tin basin below. He'd put it there to catch the drops. Then the arm was her arm. She drifted off to the sweet tones of blood pinging against metal.

She slept long and hard, awakening with a knot of dread in her belly. She soaked crusts of old bread in milk and fed them to herself in tiny bites, as if she were a baby. She made breakfast trays and carried them upstairs one at a time, first to Griselda then Mother. Griselda yawned and stretched with a self-satisfied look on her face, like a cat arching its back in the sun. "It's going to be a glorious day," she said, to no one in particular. Certainly not to Cinderella. Mother told her to finish her morning chores and then wash her hair. "Be sure to rinse away all the soap. The hairdresser will be coming in the afternoon. He'll tend to you in the yellow room then you can dress."

Wrapped in the old dressing gown Mother had given her, hair wet and clinging to her cheeks, Cinderella climbed the stairs. She turned the knob, stepped inside and stifled a scream. Her dress lay in shreds upon the floor – jagged rents in its pale blue silk, long tears in the satin sash. The wardrobe door was ajar, the wood around its lock gouged and scarred. Griselda might've used the letter opener from her desk, or a poker from the fireplace. Cinderella howled at the injustice, a lifetime of injustice; as she let the sound out, she felt it shredding the delicate moist flesh in her throat.

Mother hurried in moments later. "For heaven's sake, what is it?" She sounded annoyed more than anything else. When her gaze fell to the ruined dress, she said, "Oh."

"She did it," Cinderella hissed. "She didn't want me to go, you know she didn't. Now this." She felt her eyes fill up. The tears were so hot they might have burnt furrows into her cheeks.

24

"Whatever is the matter?" In her embroidered dressing gown, Griselda stood at the threshold. Neither subtle nor smart, she couldn't keep the note of glee from her voice. She couldn't erase the smile from her broad piggish face.

Mother looked at Griselda and for one moment, Cinderella thought she might actually become angry. Then it passed and Mother sighed.

"I suppose it was a foolish idea, anyway. All that money – what a waste! We'll speak of this later," she told Griselda, without rancor or intent. To Cinderella, she said: "Clean this up and then get on with your chores. Keep below stairs – I don't want any further mishaps. You're not to go anywhere near Griselda's dress, is that clear?"

Griselda shot her a triumphant glance before turning away. Mother needn't have worried. The revenge Cinderella had in mind did not involve Griselda's dress, but rather her face. She'd use the same letter opener or poker from the fire, the tool her sister had inflicted on the wardrobe. In the end, she'd take her eyes out.

* * *

All day long, an incipient scream lodged at the base of her throat. She had to keep hold of herself as she went through her chores because the temptation to shatter something delicate – the glass candlesticks or one of Mother's cloisonné bowls – was strong. Unlike Griselda, she didn't entirely lose her mind when anger took hold. Breaking something now, however relieving in the moment, would only hurt her later.

After Mother and Griselda set off for the palace in the coach, Cinderella paced the kitchen floor, beset with a rage that wouldn't abate. Last night, she'd been afraid of attending the ball, but now the thought that Griselda might soon be dancing with the Prince made Cinderella want to shriek again. She took off all clothes and went to work with the bristle brush. She wet it with old dishwater and began to scrub.

As they scratched into her flesh, the bristles set her skin on fire. The pain from her arms and thighs brought immediate comfort, but not enough to make her stop. Even more pain, that's what she wanted. She pressed harder and felt the skin snap back in places where the bristles cut. Fear didn't enter into it. She seemed to see one of those incisions opening wide, opening wide the way her ball gown had opened when the dressmaker held its sides apart and told her to step into it. From within her body, an imaginary hand seemed to reach out through the gaping incision. Not her own hand. Someone else's.

It will take whatever it wants, she thought. She felt triumphant, as if she could dance upon the moon.

The sight of blood seeping from the cuts finally brought her calm; the shriek at the base of her throat finally relented. That's when she first noticed the light – a corner of the room was aglow behind her. Perhaps Fairy Godmother had been with her for some time already and Cinderella hadn't noticed. All at once, she felt awash in Fairy Godmother's light, cleansed and uplifted by it.

On every other visit, Fairy Godmother had remained in the corner, glowing her message of love from a distance, but this evening she came close to Cinderella, who felt no shame in her own nakedness. Fairy Godmother held a wand in her right hand. As she brought its tip to the cuts on Cinderella's body, one by one they healed. First her arms then her thighs. The blood pulled back, her cuts closed up and virgin flesh remained. Cinderella used to believe that Fairy Godmother was a comforting dream, an imaginary mother born from unhappiness in the lonely night. Now she knew she was real.

Fairy Godmother had no need of words; Cinderella understood each detail of the plan and rejoiced in it. First, she captured the mice with an inverted saucepan. In her haste, she smashed one of the scurrying creatures and broke its back. As the poor animal writhed in pain, Cinderella felt a horrible flinch of sympathy all over her body. She brought the saucepan down again, hard, putting the broken mouse out of its misery, and went back to work. Soon she had six, trapped inside the coal scuttle with a cutting board over its opening to keep them from clambering out.

The rat took a little more time. He was swift and wily. Cinderella shuddered with disgust when she finally seized him by the tail; he thrashed about and tried to bite her before she dropped him into the scuttle with the mice.

Following Fairy Godmother, Cinderella carried the scuttle outside to the vegetable garden. Her breath made frosty blooms in the night air but she felt no cold. Nothing could touch her now. She chose the most perfect pumpkin she could find, brushed away the mud that encrusted its flesh and set it in the place Fairy Godmother had indicated. Cinderella crouched down beside the coal scuttle, holding the cutting board in place, awaiting her cue. She felt the dirt between her toes. She could hear the rat and mice scrambling with terror. When Fairy Godmother nodded and raised her wand, Cinderella lifted the board away, tipped the scuttle over and stepped back.

She felt a momentary panic as the writhing clutch of hairy rodents darted away from the scuttle. They might rush toward her, try to bite her. Fairy Godmother twitched her wand before they could cover much distance and they froze in place. The transformation didn't happen all at once. It was repulsive to behold. She didn't mind the mice so much, bloating and swelling into six cream-colored horses, but it disgusted her to see the rat's tiny claws lengthen into human hands and feet, still attached to its plump fur-covered body. Only when he was fully formed and upright did the coachman begin to shed his fur. Naked skin emerged into the moonlight.

Cinderella gaped at the coachman's genitals. She'd never seen the male member before, at least she thought she hadn't, but it looked just as she would've expected. She pressed her knees and thighs tightly together. Then his clothes began to take shape and cover him up. Full livery in gold and green. She felt more self-conscious now, shielding her breasts and genitals with her hands. As it grew, the pumpkin looked as if it might explode, the way tomatoes sometimes did when you dropped them into boiling water, then it puffed out nicely and sprouted wheels, finally solidifying into a coach, a pumpkin-shaped coach enameled in white. The coachman set to work, harnessing the six milky horses.

At last, Fairy Godmother turned to Cinderella, who could feel that they shared the same excitement, each of them giddy with it. Fairy Godmother whirled her wand in circles above her head, as if to gain momentum. She looked almost crazed, her eyes unnaturally wide and bright. Faster and faster, the wand spun above her head. Then she pointed it toward Cinderella, shooting sparks from its tip. Gossamer threads shot out in all directions and began to congeal across Cinderella's flesh. They tickled. Her hair came undone and began dancing higher, shaping itself atop her head. The ball gown finally wove itself into shape, white satin and lace, elaborate and ornate in its detail.

Cinderella felt like an overly decorated cake, with too many candy roses and other embellishments. She couldn't disguise her disappointment; even if she didn't give voice to it, Fairy Godmother read her thoughts and knew that she'd hoped for something different. It was the only time Cinderella had seen anything but love and acceptance on Fairy Godmother's face. Her expression closed up for a moment and her lips seemed to pout.

Cinderella closed her eyes and concentrated hard, sending the picture within her mind across the air between them. When she opened her eyes again, the momentary irritation on Fairy Godmother's face had passed. She emitted a soundless laugh and put her wand back to work. Whirling, whirling. The threads began to unravel and reweave themselves. The new dress took shape. Still white, still delicate, but unencumbered with too much detail.

Cinderella wanted a looking glass, not just any looking glass but the three-sided mirror from the yellow bedroom. Fairy Godmother used her wand to bring it. When Cinderella saw herself reflected three times in its panels, she thought she might burst with happiness. It wasn't an entirely pleasant experience. Breathing deeply helped to calm her. Digging her toes into the soil made her feel more grounded.

What about shoes?

Fairy Godmother spun her wand and pointed it once again. Tiny glass slippers took shape, molding perfectly to her feet. Simple and unique. Had anyone ever worn glass slippers before? For one moment, she worried that they might shatter as she walked, shredding her toes and slicing open the bottoms of her feet. Blood everywhere. And the pain! She flinched and shut her eyes tightly at the thought of it.

But of course, Fairy Godmother's glass would have to be unbreakable.

Thank you, Fairy Godmother! Thank you for everything!

It's nothing but what you deserve! Don't forget – be home by midnight! You must be home by midnight or ...

Fairy Godmother didn't need to finish the thought.

The coachman held the door open for Cinderella. As she stepped into the coach, she couldn't help but glance down at the puffy fabric around his crotch, remembering what she'd seen there. The image of it.

TWO

The coach hurried her toward the palace. Cinderella felt herself moving faster and faster, with more speed than was humanly possible. Her thoughts, too … like a shooting star across the night sky.

As she hurtled along, she seemed to be shedding layers, stripping away her old self. By the time she found herself at the top of the stairs, waiting in line as the herald announced guests ahead, Cinderella felt herself to be a different person entirely – no longer that ash-ridden girl but someone pristine and new. It wasn't just the dress and glass slippers. Something inside her had suddenly changed. From below, the hum of ballroom chatter mingled with music. Yesterday, the prospect of dance and conversation had terrified her. Now, thanks to Fairy Godmother, she felt possessed of some inner magic that would see her through.

As she stepped forward, the herald inclined his bewigged head toward her, waiting to hear how he should announce her. With supernatural speed, the syllables of her familiar old name came apart and began to dance within her mind, rhyming and changing places, elongating and adding new sounds.

Rella … bella

Cin … saun

She felt like an enchantress, working her magic. She heard each transformation, each link connecting to the next in the chain until finally (only a few moments later), her new name took shape.

Miss Isabella Saunders.

She said it into the herald's ear.

First she heard the blare of trumpets then her new name, the perfect name, repeated. As she took hold of her skirts and went down the broad staircase into the ballroom, she willed the assembly to take note. What a feeling, to wield such power! *I'm here* – all she need do was think it! Heads turned, chins lifted. Dance partners on the floor came to a stop and looked up at her. At last, the orchestra on the dais fell silent. The entire room held still in suspense as she descended the staircase.

She reached the bottom and he was moving toward her, the Prince. He seemed to materialize from the crowd like the fulfillment of a wish. He was all in white, from his doublet and hose to his embroidered tunic, the fabric shot through with filaments of gold. Shorter than she'd expected, barely an inch or two taller than she was. Exceptionally well groomed. His skin glistened and he'd put something on his blond hair so that every strand stayed in place. She felt almost certain that the tiny beauty mark on his chin had been painted on.

She bowed her head and curtseyed, lowering her gaze. "Your Highness," she said.

She could feel the magnetic pull she exerted on everyone in the room, the spell she cast making it impossible for anyone to look away. The Prince gave her his hand and helped her to rise.

"Please," he said, "you must tell me your name. I didn't hear it when you arrived." He obviously knew how to use his voice, how to make it resonate in his chest and bring out the most affecting tones, almost as if he were singing.

"Isabella Saunders." The name felt natural to her now, only the second time she'd said it.

"Isabella," he repeated. "Lovely. I hope you'll call me Charming."

A laugh began rising in her throat and for one scary moment, she thought she might lose control of it. *And I hope you'll never give me reason to call you anything else* – that's what she wanted to say. It would be a crazy thing to do. If she were to laugh just now, right in his face, it would ruin everything.

"As you wish," she said, lowering her eyes, biting her lower lip. "Charming."

He offered her his arm, nodding to the conductor, and when the music resumed, they began to dance.

She'd never danced before, not with a real partner, but the glass slippers knew the steps. She gave herself over to the Prince, who led with grace and precision. As they waltzed, the other dancing couples kept a respectable distance. It felt as if she and Charming were in their own private world sealed off from everyone else, enclosed within a giant crystalline bubble. The other young ladies, the prospective brides, stared with envy into the bubble and wished they could be inside.

Where was Griselda? Until that moment, Cinderella had forgotten all about her sister. She imagined her broad flat face, those cumbersome feet – Griselda standing at the sidelines feeling hopeless, ugly, unwanted.

Griselda this time, not Cinderella.

She felt completely at ease in Charming's arms, but she didn't like his questions. *Where do you come from? Why haven't I met you before?* It was easy to deflect his attention, though. All she need do was change the subject, focus on him instead. He seemed eager to talk, and one well-aimed question was enough to set him rambling. She found she had a great many questions in want of an answer.

What does a prince do with his day? Do you have specific responsibilities or can you do more less what you like with your time?

Do you enjoy being a prince or is there something else you'd like to do with your life?

Do you have any sisters or brothers?

What about pets?

Have you ever seen a dragon and do you have any inclination to slay one?

Asking questions also kept her mind off the grain of sand caught between her right big toe and the smaller one next to it. Just before Fairy Godmother conjured up the glass slippers, she'd caused all the dirt to vanish from Cinderella's feet, except for that one irritating piece of grit between her toes. She felt it digging into her flesh.

Of course there were other questions Cinderella could not ask, though she did feel curious. About what he did to make his nails shine so. How often he bathed. And was it true, what one heard about the way noblemen took advantage of their servant girls?

The King and Queen were seated upon their thrones at one end of the room, just at the edge of the dance floor. Each time the Prince spun her by, Cinderella felt his mother's gaze upon her. It seemed to Cinderella that the Queen didn't like them dancing together and disapproved of his hands upon her body, but it might just have been her imagination. The King wore a silly expression on his face, as if he were drunk or dim. Rumor had it that he'd lost his wits and spent his days playing mumblety-peg with the gamekeepers' son.

Charming seemed to have forgotten about his other guests, the many young ladies waiting their turn to dance with him. He insisted she remain his partner for the gavotte, the chaconne and the gigue. She could feel anger and discontent festering on the sidelines. Each time she glanced into the crowd, she found a new pair of eyes glittering with malice. It made her so happy. As Charming whirled her past the meats table, she finally spotted Mother, who looked a little unsteady on her feet. Economies at home made wine a rare treat; tonight, she was clearly taking advantage of the free champagne. She looked straight at Cinderella with no sign of recognition

But Griselda recognized her. Not far from Mother, she stood agitating a fan toward her reddened face. Cinderella couldn't tell whether she read fear or anger in Griselda's eyes. It didn't matter – either one was good.

She brought her attention back to Charming, who was nearing the end of a long story about a horse he'd bought that had gone severely lame soon after it was delivered to the royal stables. Cinderella was surprised to hear there was such a thing as an *equine apothecary*, someone skilled in the application of herbs and poultices for an ailing horse. The most able of such men had been called from every corner of the land, but to avail. At last the horse had to be put down.

"And so," Charming concluded, "there was nothing else I could do. I had the horse trader put down as well, a warning to anyone else who might try to cheat me."

"Put down?" She couldn't keep the surprise from her voice. "Do you mean, you had the man killed because he sold you a lame horse?"

Charming pulled himself up in offense; she could feel his hands tighten where he gripped her. He nearly lost pace with the music. "Are you suggesting I shouldn't have done so? May I remind you that I'm the Prince."

Cinderella laughed and leaned into him, briefly pressing her breasts into his chest. "No criticism intended, your Highness. On the contrary. I'm filled with admiration. To think you have the power to order up death simply because someone displeases you!"

If she were a princess, could she command someone to cut off Griselda's ugly head? Would they let her do that?

The Prince beamed at her. He sighed. "I still can't believe we've never met! Isabella, my dear – it seems like I've been waiting for you my entire life and didn't realize it till this very moment."

He might not have the most intelligent face, but Cinderella liked the way he gazed at her, as if nothing else in the world mattered for him. She liked the way he professed to adore her. She was certain now that the small beauty mark on his chin was painted because it had blurred around the edges.

In the distance, she heard the clock chime, a lovely musical tone that seemed to speak of happiness, of dreams come true and getting everything you deserved. First one bell, then another

– resonant tones that filled the ballroom with their vibrations, penetrating her torso and limbs as Charming whirled her about the floor. A third bell. She felt as if she were in a dream, that the entire evening had passed as if in a dream. She had no idea how long it had been since she'd arrived. No more than an hour, surely.

"What's the time?" she asked.

"Midnight, I think. He craned his neck toward the clock, a massive gilt-faced clock built into the far wall. "Yes, it's just midnight." He gave her another adoring smile. "We have the whole night ahead of us."

Cinderella awakened from her dream with sudden sickening dread. "Midnight!" she cried. "I must go!" She placed her hands on his chest and pushed way but Charming held her more firmly. The arm around her back locked tight.

"Don't be silly. The ball won't end until dawn."

"You don't understand!" Her heart beat an alarming rhythm in her ears. She felt herself caught in a trap, flailing to break free from its iron jaws, those merciless hands of his. "If I don't go now …"

"I'm the Prince and I want you to stay. I *command* you to stay." He said it with a smile but his grip on her hand began to pain her. The clock chimed out again – how many times had it sounded now? Four? Five? In her panic, she saw she had no choice. Lifting her right foot, she brought it down hard on the front of his slipper. When he screamed out in pain, he sounded like a girl. He released his hold and Cinderella broke free. She hurried across the room, her shoes clicking rhythmically against the floor.

Nobody wanting speed could run across a ballroom floor and up a marble staircase wearing glass slippers. She quickly stepped out of them, hooked her fingers into the toe boxes and ran on. Another chime. She took the stairs three at a time. From behind her, she heard Charming call out, "Somebody stop her!

She broke my toe!" In her ears, the drumbeats of her heart were loud and urgent.

At the top of the stairs, the herald put himself in her way. As she leaped onto the landing, she thrust out her elbow and knocked him down. He fell to the ground, his wig fell off and she had one brief glimpse of an entirely bald head. The glancing blow she gave him dislodged one of the glass slippers from her grip and it clattered onto the marble floor. No time to go back for it.

Another chime – she was out the palace door and leaping down the stairs toward the line of carriages out front, the grooms and coachmen clustering in a group ahead of her. She sprinted past them, their faces alight with surprise. She quickened her pace toward her own pumpkin-shaped coach, further down the alley of plane trees that led away from the castle. Yet another chime and she felt tickling against her flesh as the dress began to unravel.

Ahead of her, the coach briefly swelled, took on an orange tint and then began to shrink. The coachman standing next to it fell writhing to the ground. Cinderella felt an abrupt chill against her bare skin. The six cream-colored horses began to change shape, grew huge mouse ears and sprouted whiskers. Her chest hurt and she felt painfully out of breath but she kept running until she was beyond the palace gates, encased in total darkness on the country road. With one hand on her chest, she came to a stop. She was naked in the night, panting heavily, heartbeat booming in her ears. Her breath came out in frosty gusts, gradually slowing as her body calmed down. She felt cold.

Once she could breathe normally, she whispered, her voice tight with bitterness, "However can I thank you, Fairy Godmother!" What a ridiculous spell! If Fairy Godmother could perform all this magic, why not give her clothes to wear in place of the vanished ball gown? Why cut short her time at the ball when the evening had barely gotten underway? Even Cinderella, who'd never been to a ball, knew that nobody ever left the party before the clock struck three. Perhaps she would've done better with a different Fairy Godmother, one who might've given her more time with the Prince and left her with a shawl, at the very least, when it was all over. She shivered as her body lost heat.

And why had everything else disappeared but not the glass slipper dangling from her fingers? The inconsistency annoyed her. She wondered if the other glass slipper still existed, too, back in the palace at the top of the stairs.

Now and then along the road home, naked and shivering, she'd whisper ironic thanks into night. "I'm so deeply, deeply grateful, Fairy Godmother." The third time she said it, a mass of fabric fell out of the sky onto her head. Cinderella stifled a cry of surprise. When she unraveled the material, it turned out to be a cloak. The way it had dropped without warning, all in a clump, felt hostile, or sarcastic at the very least. As she wrapped the cloak about her, Cinderella felt chastened, though she still didn't understand why Fairy Godmother had left her naked so long upon the road.

It took her hours to make her way home. The sliver of moon didn't help much to light her way but at least there were no turnings to miss – one straight road from the castle, into town (mercifully dark, the streets empty) and then out the other side toward home. After all that dancing, and then miles upon the rutted road, her feet throbbed with pain. She tried to comfort herself with memories of the ball, especially the admiring look in Charming's eyes, but she couldn't shake the feeling of grievance, as if she'd been cheated.

By the time she turned into the gravel courtyard, her feet were raw and bleeding. She was in such pain she could barely walk. In the kitchen, she stirred the embers and kindled a new fire. She found her tattered dress, still in a heap on the floor, right where she'd left it when she stripped down and took the bristle brush to her skin. As the fire warmed her body, Cinderella found her resentment easing. She had a lot to be grateful for, after all.

Not everyone had a Fairy Godmother who would send her to a palace ball and help her to captivate a prince!

Just as she was about to drift off to sleep, she remembered her glass slipper, the one she'd brought back with her. Startling awake, she crawled across the floor toward the table where she'd left it (the agony in her feet made walking unbearable). She glanced around the kitchen, searching for the best place, and finally hid the slipper at the bottom of the rag pile.

* * *

Early in the morning, with dawn breaking through the window, Cinderella was awakened by something nudging her in the rib cage. Her eyes felt so heavy they seemed crusted shut. She pried them open, squinted in the raw light and saw Griselda standing over her, still wearing her ball gown. They must've just returned from the palace. Once more Cinderella felt a nudging in the ribs – Griselda's toe, that big clumsy foot pressing into her.

There was a rosy, exhausted tint about Griselda's eyes and nostrils. Her mouth turned down at the corners. "Where were you last night?" she said.

Cinderella stretched her arms, yawning; her body ached with exhaustion. Fairy Godmother had come again in the middle of the night, clearly, because the pain in her feet had vanished. She knew without looking that the raw flesh had healed.

"Here in the kitchen," Cinderella said. "Where else would I be?"

"Liar!" Griselda snapped.

"So where do you think I was, then?" Cinderella couldn't keep the note of contempt from her voice. "You say I'm lying – where was I?"

Griselda's nostrils flared and turned even redder. "Just watch your step or I'll tell Mother," she said, turning to go.

"Tell Mother what?"

Griselda didn't answer. "Bring me my breakfast tray at once!" she commanded. "I'll have coffee this morning. None of your weak tea!"

As Cinderella struggled through her chores that morning, she now and then repeated Griselda's final retort in mocking tones – to herself, under her breath. "None of your weak tea! None of your weak tea!" For the first time in their lives, Cinderella felt as if she were winning. She, not Griselda, had turned heads at the ball. She, not Griselda, had danced half the night with a prince. She, not Griselda, had captivated him. An elated sense of triumph burned through her exhaustion.

She couldn't keep it up. As the morning wore on, she began to ask herself what difference it had made. She might have danced last night with the Prince but this morning, she still had to empty the chamber pots. Last night, she might have found herself at the center of an envious crowd, but this morning, she was once again alone, hated by her sister, forced to slave without thanks, without the rights of a daughter. Charming might have preferred Cinderella to every other girl, but Griselda was still Mother's favorite.

Nothing had changed.

Why did you open my eyes to such bliss, only to return me to this misery? Why?!

Last night before the ball, Fairy Godmother had seemed so very, very good – perfect even, a benign sorceress eager to grant each and every wish. After the ball, and even more so today, Cinderella's belief in that goodness seemed to come and go. At moments, Fairy Godmother struck her as almost cruel.

Mother awoke very late in the morning. When Cinderella brought up her breakfast tray, she lingered in the bed chamber, hanging mother's ball gown with care and brushing dirt from her slippers. She knew better than to ask questions. The only way she'd hear about the ball was to let Mother give details in her own way and time.

Mother was having a hard time waking up. The light from the window made her squint in pain; without being asked, Cinderella drew the curtains. Mother didn't offer thanks, but she did say, "Would you like to hear about the ball?"

"Very much … if you don't mind telling me."

While Mother recounted the evening's events, Cinderella kept busy about the room. She heaped coal onto the fire and swept ashes from the hearth. She wiped dust from the window sill, polished wood on the armoire, dropped to her knees and picked lint from the rug. She didn't want to look at her mother but she listened.

At first, she thought Mother had mis-remembered certain details because she got so many of them wrong – the number of guests, the size of the orchestra, the dimensions of the ballroom. With a growing discomfort, she eventually realized the exaggeration was intentional. Though her mother seemed to be describing the events of last night to an impersonal room, to no one in particular, she intended Cinderella to feel envious, filled with painful admiration, left out and unimportant. Mother wanted her to feel small.

"And the dancing!" she exclaimed. "Such beauty and elegance of movement! You can't imagine! I myself had a partner for almost every dance."

Liar. Mother hadn't danced a single time. She'd spent the evening guzzling free champagne.

"And Prince Charming must surely be the most accomplished dancer the world has ever known!"

"Did *you* dance with him?" Cinderella asked.

She could feel Mother struggling. Of course she wanted to say *yes* but must've decided she couldn't make the lie sound credible.

"I thought it best to leave time for the younger women."

"Like Griselda, you mean. *She* danced with the Prince."

"She was greatly admired, of course, but … well, with so many girls, there simply wasn't time." The evasive, pettish tone in Mother's voice filled Cinderella with shame but she couldn't stop herself.

"Did he dance with anyone in particular? Was there any young lady he seemed to prefer?" She wanted badly to look at Mother's face; she kept her gaze on the floor, studiously picking out the lint.

"There was one." Mother sounded resentful. "One of those clever beauties skilled in the arts of bewitchment."

"Anyone we know?"

"A complete stranger, as far as I could tell. Nobody seemed to know her."

"And she was very beautiful, you say?"

"Yes, very. Quite remarkable, really – you couldn't take your eyes off of her."

It didn't make Cinderella as happy as she'd expected, to hear that Mother found her beautiful, that Mother couldn't look away. It wasn't her daughter she found so very lovely. It was a woman named Isabella Saunders.

"It's the strangest thing, though," Mother added. She sounded puzzled but without worry. "I'm absolutely certain she was uncommonly beautiful, but for the life of me, I can't remember what she actually looked like."

* * *

The next time Mother sent her on errands, Cinderella spotted a crowd gathering in front of the church as soon as she entered town. A man in palace livery was nailing a large sheet of parchment to the massive wooden door; townspeople jostled for position in order to read it. As she eased into the crowd, she could feel the tense energy in the bodies around her. A woman with a hairy mole and drooping left eye shot her a nasty look when Cinderella tried to push in.

"Wait your turn!" the woman snapped.

Cinderella apologized and pulled back. She suddenly doubted whether she really wanted to find out what the parchment said. These proclamations from the palace usually meant bad news – a rise in taxes, the announcement of an epidemic. Strange inklings made her feel implicated, as if the bad news this time might be more personal. Maybe she should turn away now and get on with her errands. She felt she had to know.

After the crowd had thinned, she found a space before the door and placed herself in front of the proclamation.

> *Commencing at once, agents of the palace will be conducting a house-to-house search for the Prince's future bride, the young lady who lost one of her shoes at his birthday ball.*

At the words house-to-house search, Cinderella lost her concentration. Agents scouring the kingdom for a missing person sounded like the hunt for an escaped criminal. It was she, Cinderella, whom they hunted – the imposter-guest who'd stamped on the Prince's foot. She envisioned a scaffold and hanging rope, erected for her benefit before the royal stables.

> *Eligibility for marriage will be determined through size trials involving said shoe. In the case of lingering doubts about a precise fit, the prospective bride may be asked to present the shoe's match. All young ladies of every household will make themselves available for testing.*

It gradually sank in that the Prince didn't want her dead … he wanted to *marry* her. The idea seemed so improbable, she had a hard time taking it in and believing it. How could he want to marry her when they'd spent two or three hours, no more, dancing together? The procedure he'd selected to uncover her identity seemed odd, so outlandish that she wondered if it had been devised by the King, Charming's father, an old man grown simple with age. Why couldn't the Prince just look at her face to identify her?

As if Cinderella had spoken the question aloud, a red-haired girl standing nearby seemed to answer it. Gripping the edges of her apron, the girl excitedly flapped the fabric while she talked to her friend, a plump brunette about the same age wearing a gingham cap.

"They say he can't remember what she looks like," said the redhead. "Not a bit."

The plump girl laughed. "He danced with her half the night and he can't remember her face? Lord, he must be dim!"

The red-haired girl looked briefly askance at Cinderella and lowered her voice. "It's not that," she whispered to her friend. "It's all a part of the spell she cast. Bewitching him with her beauty so he'd fall in love, then wiping her face from his memory."

"Don't be daft!" the friend snorted. "That makes no sense at all."

"How else do you explain it, then? From what I hear, nobody who went to the ball can remember what she looked like. They can see the dress and the hair, but not ..."

"And why'd she leave the shoe behind, then? Is that all part of her wicked plot?"

"It's so he won't be able to forget her," the red-haired girl said, shaking her apron with excited emphasis. "She wants him to spend the rest of his life constantly reminded by the glass shoe, hopelessly looking for his lost love."

The plump girl threw her head back and laughed, a deep jovial laugh that shook her body. "I wouldn't go repeating that too often, Emily, or people will begin to think that you're the one who's dim."

Cinderella moved away from the girls, walking further into town without really seeing any of the people around her on the cobblestones, moving in and out of shops, chattering. It came back to her, what Mother had said that morning after the ball –

how she couldn't remember what Isabella Saunders had looked like. There must be magic involved. She felt cheated somehow, to have made such an impression upon a prince and then for him forget what she looked like. To have attracted the admiration and envy of everyone at the ball but for her face to be forgotten.

It seems I have more and more to thank you for, Fairy Godmother.

And yet the Prince was coming to look for her. Was that part of Fairy Godmother's magic plan? Did she intend for Cinderella and Charming to wed? "I never wished for that," Cinderella whispered. A memory came back to her – that wild look in Fairy Godmother's eyes as she spun the wand above her head, just before she made Cinderella's ball gown take shape. What if Fairy Godmother had some lunatic plan for her future, one that wouldn't suit Cinderella at all?

In the role of Isabella Saunders, under a spell of enchantment, she might have captured the heart of a prince, but once he saw her for who she truly was, a filthy servant girl … Proclaiming his intention to marry didn't necessarily mean he had to follow through on it. A prince could always change his mind. On a whim, he might decide to have her killed for masquerading as a lady of court. He could decide that breaking his toe was a capital offense.

Prince Charming couldn't possibly love her for herself. Nobody had every loved her. And when she searched her own heart to see how she felt about him, she found herself remembering that painted-on beauty mark and his strangely motionless hair. A prince who ordered another man put down for selling him a lame horse might be difficult to live with. No doubt Charming was used to having everything his own way. On the other hand, after Griselda, anyone else would be easy to live with.

That night on her pallet, Cinderella wished hard for Fairy Godmother to come. There were so many questions she wanted to ask her. With her eyes closed, she imagined the kitchen corner beginning to glow. She imagined that smiling face gathering detail within the light. Every time she opened her eyes, she found herself alone.

* * *

She didn't say a word about the proclamation to her mother or sister, but within a couple of days, the way Griselda kept glaring at Cinderella's feet made clear she'd heard about it. The size difference had always galled Griselda but now, an agonizing envy seemed to gnaw at her from within. Sometimes she'd pass uncomfortably close to Cinderella, pausing briefly with their feet in parallel, snarling at the comparison. Twice Griselda ran up and tried to stamp down hard on her sister's toes but Cinderella elbowed her out of the way. Once she carried a brick in from the courtyard but she was too obvious, too easily evaded.

One night at dinner, while Cinderella was ladling soup from the tureen, Griselda threw her head back and howled like an animal.

"I hate my feet!" she cried. "I hate them, I hate them, I hate them!" She burst into tears, burying her head in her arms.

"Are you all right, Griselda dear?" Mother didn't seem terribly worried. "Shall I send for the doctor? You know how I hate the expense, but if you're really not feeling well …"

"Can he give me new feet?" she sobbed.

"Give you new feet?" Now Mother looked alarmed, as if she wondered if Griselda were losing her mind. "Whatever can you mean?"

Cinderella knew what she meant. For the first time in their lives, she pitied her sister. She understood the agony of Griselda's longing, the desperate wish to be someone else. Smaller feet was but a part of it.

In the morning, Griselda tore her bed linens into long strips and wrapped them tightly around her feet. When Cinderella delivered her breakfast tray, she found Griselda seated in a chair with her bound feet on a footstool, tears on her cheeks. Cinderella had once heard that girls in some far-off country bound their feet to stunt their growth. Didn't Griselda realize it was too late, that once her feet had grown so large she couldn't ever shrink them? Poor thing. She looked so miserable, weeping in her chair with those big clumps of fabric at the end of her legs.

"I made your tea strong this morning," Cinderella said, "just the way you like."

Griselda turned away.

Later that afternoon, while polishing the leather shoes in Mother's closet, there came a shriek of pain from down the hall – high-pitched and fearsome to hear. She went running and met Mother at the threshold of Griselda's room.

On the floor inside, Griselda sat amidst a pool of blood, a kitchen knife in her hand and a hunk of nearly-severed flesh hanging from her right foot. She'd tried to hack a half-inch or so from its plumpest side.

"What in heaven's name?!" Mother cried. "Have you lost your mind?"

Despite her obvious pain, Griselda looked as if she were about to go to work on the other foot. Cinderella rushed forward and snatched the blade from her hand.

"Stop, sister dear! You mustn't hurt yourself. It won't help." Cinderella understood the power of blood, how watching it bubble up from a cut could bring you comfort, but that's not what Griselda was after.

"Give it back! Give it back or I'll kill you!" Griselda gnashed her teeth and looked wild. She really did seem to have lost her mind.

Mother came forward and took the knife from Cinderella's hand. "Run for the doctor, quickly!" She felt a bitter twinge, knowing that Mother would never look so terrified if her other daughter's life were the one at risk. "Take one of the ponies. And don't return without him!"

As she hurried away, Cinderella heard Griselda's crazed voice lashing into Mother. "These feet are all your fault. I hate you!"

The doctor cauterized the wound with a red hot poker. Griselda shrieked and fainted away. When she regained consciousness, he gave her a sleeping draught, bandaged her foot and put her to bed.

"Keep a sharp eye," he told Mother, without conscious irony. "She might try it again."

At dinner, when Cinderella placed a lonely plate before her, Mother left her food untouched. She closed her eyes, brought hands to cheeks and slowly shook her head from side to side. "What's to become of me?" she moaned. She kept repeating it. "The fortune spent, no husband, and now this. I'll wind up in the poor house, I just know it. Life is so unfair!"

Cinderella blamed herself. If she hadn't wished to go to the ball, Mother wouldn't be crying now. Griselda would have two uninjured (although undoubtedly large) feet.

"Can I get you anything else, Mother dear? A glass of brandy? It might settle your nerves."

"Bring me the whole bottle," Mother snapped, "and then go away. I want you out of my sight!"

That night on her pallet, shivering in the darkness, Cinderella made up her mind. She didn't love Charming, might never be able to love him as a wife ought to do, but she'd marry him if she had the chance. If she could save them all from the poorhouse, maybe that would earn Mother's love.

* * *

For the next two days while tending to her sister – bathing the wound, changing bandages on her foot, bringing more tea – Cinderella listened for the sound of wheels in the courtyard, or hooves crunching into gravel. Those agents of the palace would eventually show up with the shoe. Griselda was listening, too. The slightest sound made her jump and she'd ask excitedly, with a wild look in her eyes, "Did you hear that? Have they come?" Ten, twenty times a day she'd ask the question.

"It's only the wind." Even if Cinderella had heard nothing, she'd invent an explanation. "I think it was a woodpecker." No matter what she answered, it seemed to calm Griselda, if only for a few minutes.

Mother stayed away. She ordered up the carriage and went for long drives in the country. "The doctor recommended it for my poor nerves," she told Cinderella, as if she felt the need to justify herself. Apparently, the doctor had also recommended she consume large amounts of brandy because Cinderella found empty bottles on the rubbish heap. She wondered where Mother found the money until she realized the last of the family silver had disappeared.

The doctor returned each day and shook his head with rote concern as he emerged from Griselda's room. "Keep her quiet," he told Cinderella. "All we can do is hope for a return to her senses."

Griselda did seem to be deranged. Sometimes when Cinderella came into her room, she found her sister whispering to herself with a beatific smile. "He's coming for me. I know it will be soon. Then everything will be wonderful. I can feel them getting smaller by the minute!" She turned her scary smile on Cinderella. "You've been so very good to me. Don't worry – when the time comes, I'll make sure you're not turned out."

Mother would come back from one of her drives, looking bleary-eyed and rumpled. "Any better?" she'd ask then glare at Cinderella for telling her *no*.

On the third day, Griselda actually did seem calmer, more her usual self. After breakfast, she insisted on getting out of bed. Cinderella supported her arm as she limped across the bedroom floor, shifting her weight onto the heel of her injured foot and keeping her leg straight when she had to walk on it. After a few passages back and forth, she shook off Cinderella's grip. "I don't need your help," she snapped. "I'm not a cripple." She made Cinderella help her dress but wouldn't accept her assistance going downstairs. "Leave me alone! I'm sick of your hovering. Get away and keep out of my sight!"

No more than ten minutes later, Griselda rang for her. All day long, she'd send Cinderella away then call her back.

"More coffee!"

"I can't reach that book on the shelf – fetch it for me!"

"Where have you put my embroidery hoop, idiot girl? Find it at once!"

As the day wore on, Griselda seemed more and more herself.

That night, when Cinderella finally collapsed with exhaustion onto her pallet, sleep did not come to her directly. Shivering in the darkness, she felt consumed with worry – about Mother and the poorhouse, about Griselda's poor feet, about what Charming would do to her on their wedding night if they should actually marry. Perhaps those palace agents had over-looked this particular house; they might've found some other girl with feet small enough to fit and called off the search. Alone on the floor, she felt agitated, full of unbearable worry; the only thing that seemed to calm her was yanking hair from her scalp, several strands at the time, or scratching at her skin until it bled.

Where are you Fairy Godmother? What am I supposed to do?

She awoke late in the morning feeling much better, not so consumed by worry: Griselda was clearly on the mend, and once Mother could trust in this recovery, she might stop turning to the brandy bottle. If it might save them all, Cinderella would let Charming do what he liked with her. She stretched and rose up from her pallet, brushing straw from her old gray dress.

The kitchen door was locked. She couldn't remember having closed the door and besides, no one ever locked it. Why would they? For as long as she could remember, the key had remained untouched, dangling on its hook outside the door. Cinderella stood there, jiggling the handle as if this might coax the lock to release itself. She felt exceedingly puzzled. How had the door come to be locked and who had locked it? The idea came to her that Fairy Godmother might have done it. Punishment, for some crime she didn't yet understand. She couldn't imagine why Fairy Godmother should have turned against her.

She heard the distant blare of trumpets, a muted brassy sound filtering through the walls. The palace agents had come. In a moment, she knew what had happened, who had locked her in and why. Griselda. Of course. Everything inside her came to a sudden halt – her thoughts, her breathing … even her blood seemed to stop coursing through her veins. The world around her held briefly still.

Then her whole body caught fire. The inferno within spewed heat into the kitchen. With both hands, she yanked at the door handle, throwing her whole body into it. Again and again, she tried to wrest it open with all the strength she possessed. She growled and gritted her teeth, as if she could break the lock with the sheer force of her will. It wouldn't budge.

She felt as if she could kill her sister. Or herself. It could go either way. If Griselda were there at that moment, she would strangle her. Or better yet, gouge out her eyes with the fire poker. The way Griselda had gouged open the armoire to get at the hated dress. Cinderella lunged for the poker near the grate and began flailing at the door. She saw Griselda's face, her eyes and lips there in the knotty wood.

Over and over, she lunged at the lock. Its metal began to show dents and scars. She gouged out big chunks of wood around it, disappointed when blood didn't spurt from the wounds. She badly wanted the blood. She kept hacking at the lock and dryly wept. The fire within had seared her, with no water left to make tears.

One well-aimed plunge with the poker, straight into the keyhole, and the lock sprang open. The door came ajar. For one terrifying moment, the overwhelming thrill of success made her fear she would come apart, literally go to pieces. She stifled a sob, pulled herself together and threw the door fully open.

She was halfway up the stairs when she remembered the glass slipper. She hurried back, dug it from the rag pile and flew up the steps like a wild woman, possessed by some immense black power. As she came round the corner onto the landing, Griselda blocked her way to the front door. Weeping, the agony of disappointment on her face. Gaining speed, Cinderella hurtled into her sister and knocked her down. Griselda screamed in pain as she fell to the floor – Cinderella's foot had landed precisely where she'd aimed it on the wound. She shot out the front door into the courtyard, stumbling onto her knees. She winced at the pain.

Three palace agents were riding away, two mounted on chestnut-colored horses, the other on a small pony between them – the funny fat man who'd brought the invitation.

"Wait!" she cried. "Don't go! Don't go yet!" She stifled a sob and rose to her feet, running after them. "It's me, Isabella Saunders! I have the shoe!"

The three riders reined in their horses and looked back at her. "Listen to me," she cried, "I have the missing shoe and it fits me!"

A fourth rider, one who must've gone ahead, came back now into the courtyard. The Prince! She hadn't expected him to come. The sight of Charming, sitting proudly on his immense black horse, filled her with happiness and dread. He trotted toward her, posting in his saddle, up and down, up and down, until he came to a stop before her.

She took a deep shuddery breath. "It's me, Charming – Isabella." She reached down and slipped her bare foot into the glass slipper. "See? A perfect fit. Don't you recognize me?"

His bland handsome face tightened up; he squinted at her, as if she might appear differently that way. Then he opened his eyes wide.

"I can't be sure," he said.

"I can prove it to you! That night, we talked about the horse trader you had put down, remember? The one who sold you the lame horse." Panic thrummed in her chest. What if he didn't remember her?

"What else?" His voice was full of suspicion. He peered down at her from atop his black stallion.

"We talked about Guinevere, your cat, and how morbidly afraid you are of dragons. Surely you remember."

Charming looked as if he didn't like the reminder. He still appeared doubtful. "How do I know that shoe you're wearing is a match?"

She searched frantically and spotted the other glass slipper in the fat man's lap, perched upon a pillow.

"Bring it here!" she cried. "Let me try it on!"

Looking resentful, the fat man slid carefully from his pony, holding tight to the slipper. As he carried it toward Cinderella, he pulled a handkerchief from his waistcoat and pressed it to his nose. Onto how many smelly feet had he already tried to fit that shoe? Cinderella felt a small twinge of shame, that her own foot would stink.

The fat man knelt onto one knee. He extended the glass slipper toward her. Cinderella slipped her foot inside and felt its smooth glass encase her.

At that moment, the skin all over her body began to tingle; one by one, the threads of her dress had started to separate and reweave themselves. She could feel her hair lifting and coiling about her head. Suffused by a sudden warm light from within, a glow that felt like love though she couldn't actually see Fairy Godmother, she looked up at Prince Charming. The memory of her face had returned to him. He smiled.

"I forgive you for stepping on my foot," he told her, his voice warm with affection. "Once we're married, I promise never to reproach you for it."

THREE

Worried that she might once again run away from him, Charming insisted she move into the palace that very day. He tried to hoist Cinderella onto his horse but apparently over-estimated his strength because the fat man had to give her a leg up. Charming settled her onto the saddle in front of him.

"We'll send someone later to collect your things," he said, urging his horse forward.

"I have no things."

As they cantered out of the courtyard, Cinderella waved goodbye to Mother, who stood on the threshold looking baffled and bleary, no doubt from too much cognac, and to poor Grisel-da, weeping tears of misery.

I'm leaving home.

Cinderella had no idea how she felt about it.

The horse soon tired of carrying them both at canter gait and Charming brought him back to a walk. Cinderella felt awkward and uncomfortable, seated in the saddle before him. He kept an arm around her waist, which made her feel trapped, as if she'd never escape his grip. He chattered on as they walked, explaining how they'd live happily ever after once they were married.

"I know we'll be an uncommonly happy couple," he said. "You do love me, don't you, Isabella?"

"Yes, I do, Charming. Very much."

She didn't hesitate to lie. Charming was saving her from a life of tyranny and injustice; she owed him an enormous debt of gratitude. She made up her mind then and there to do everything within her power to please him. She'd dedicate her life to it.

When they arrived at the palace, Charming told his mother the Queen to find quarters befitting his future bride; Cinderella soon found herself in a chamber high up in one of the turrets – a large circular room with narrow windows that looked across the moat and croquet lawn toward the stables. Charming immediately sent for the royal dressmaker to begin work on her trousseau and wedding dress. Charming also assigned her a maid, a skinny girl named Lydia with the tiniest wrists Cinderella had ever seen. Lydia spoke in a high, pained voice and wore spectacles.

When Charming learned that Mother had employed Cinderella as a servant girl, he seemed less indignant than alarmed she might be deficient in the knowledge a future princess ought to possess. On her very first day, he arranged for instruction from members of his staff and retinue: etiquette lessons about forms of address and which fork to use for shellfish; an overview of the political landscape, the allies and enemies of the royal family; a list of the world's greatest books, with brief summaries of the most important ones provided by Charming's own boyhood tutor.

"At least you don't need dancing lessons," Charming told her with an adoring smile. "I'll never forget the feel of you in my arms – you dance divinely." Cinderella hoped the glass slippers had not forgotten how to dance. It was a good thing that slippers in glass matched just about any formal gown, even a wedding dress.

Charming had some doubts about her general carriage, so he arranged for deportment lessons, too. When she told him she didn't ride, he found her a mount and sent her to the Stable Master. It surprised her, just how many masters there were, with such varying areas of expertise. To think you could earn your livelihood by teaching people how to play croquet!

Charming picked out all her clothes, of course. She didn't mind because he had much better taste than she did. He brought her emeralds and rubies – the "lesser family jewels," he said, apologetically – and explained the correct outfit and occasion for each. He asked her if she'd mind changing her hair, and before she could answer brought in the hairdresser to trim her locks. Charming explained to Lydia how she ought to do Cinderella's hair and the maid took umbrage at his instruction. They had a tense exchange across Cinderella's head, almost as if she weren't there.

In those first days, Charming kept her so busy with lessons that she didn't see too much of him during the daytime. Now and then he'd look in, check on her progress then go fox-hunting with his friends or take one of his mounts through the steeple-chase course. Charming was passionate about his horses. When they were alone together, he tended to ramble on about his daily rides, referring to *half-halts*, *leg-aids* and a great many other terms she was only beginning to understand from equitation class.

"Are you happy, darling?" he often asked her. Charming needed a great deal of reassurance on that score.

"Delirious!" she told him. "I never dreamed I could be so happy."

Most of the time, she felt numb. When she thought about their wedding night, what he'd want to do to her, she felt queasy and tense.

Each night, he picked out a dress for her to wear and escorted her down to dinner. When they came to the grand marble staircase with its stone balustrade, Charming offered Cinderella his arm with great show, as if they were making an entrance into the immense reception hall below, as if the empty suits of armor lining its walls could actually see them.

The family dined beneath a powdery blue ceiling, surrounded by portraits of dead royals from centuries past. The King and Queen sat at opposing ends of a long table, Charming and Cinderella opposite one another at the center point. Charming's father ate little, said even less and paid a great deal of attention to his wine glass. His mother took tiny bites and hung on her son's every word. It was obvious she adored him, perhaps to excess. Sometimes Cinderella caught the Queen peering at her with an expression that made her think of Griselda – the way she used to glare at her feet.

She did not miss her sister. She did not miss her mother, not exactly, but she often thought of them at dinner time … how those disapproving lines in Mother's face would relax when Cinderella managed not to overcook the joint. Griselda's impersonation of the fat curate – cheeks puffed out, eyes bulging – and how she could make Mother laugh. Not all of her memories were unhappy ones. After the wedding, she'd see what she could do to help them. For the time being, she put Charming at the center of her universe.

At dinner, she'd listen as if enraptured by his talk of candlesticks he'd seen in a picture book, or the new stud he'd purchased for his stables. When he pointed out that she had once again used the wrong fork for the quail, or reminded her to keep her elbows off the table, she made her voice sound meek and answered, "Yes, Charming." The King and Queen seemed helpless, almost like children. He might be their son, a prince only and not yet the monarch, but Charming seemed to be the one in charge.

"Don't stare at the servants, dear," he once told her. "Just pretend they're pieces of furniture and pay them no heed."

"Yes, Charming." After that, she watched the liveried men furtively, from the corner of her eye. She tried very hard not to peer at the bulge below their waists. Sometimes she believed she could discern a shape beneath the fabric, the outline of it, tending to one side or the other. From what she could gather, Charming was alarmingly large in size.

After dinner, the family retired to one of the many sitting rooms, rotating between them. She had a hard time telling them apart. The massive dark furniture and brocade fabrics blended together in memory. Each night, the King promptly fell asleep in his chair and the Queen went to work with her tatting shuttle. Charming kept talking. He strode about the room, hands clasped at his back, and discussed his plans for their wedding. He made daily additions to and subtractions from the list of airs he wanted the orchestra to play; he couldn't decide between irises or lilies for the floral theme; the banquet menu went through countless iterations.

Sometimes, Cinderella felt a nostalgic twinge when she thought of her old pallet, the solitude of the kitchen, the sound of mouse claws against stone.

Most of the palace sitting rooms had a pianoforte and Charming seemed a little disappointed that she didn't play.

"Would you like me to learn?" she asked. "I'll try if you want me to."

"You're so sweet to offer," he said. "But there's no point in getting started now. Once we have children, you'll be too busy to play. I might be out of step with the times, but I believe that married women with children should give up such frivolous pleasures as music and dancing." He glanced over at his mother, tranquilly tatting her lace. "Within the privacy of the family, certain genteel preoccupations are of course acceptable."

Be grateful. You must always remember to be grateful.

She couldn't look at Charming just then. The way he was picking at his teeth made her want to slap him.

Whenever he felt sleepy, he'd announce that it was time for them all to retire, escorting Cinderella to her bed chamber. Outside her door, he'd bestow one chaste kiss upon her cheek, as if it were some ritual form that must be observed, then force her up against the wall and kiss her more urgently. He put his hands on her body, pressing himself against her. At those moments, when it seemed she had no choice, that he was coercing her against her will, she felt her numb flesh come to life.

After a few minutes, he'd pull back, give her another chaste kiss and whisper, "It won't be long now, my darling. Soon, it will be our wedding day!"

* * *

Cinderella had some doubts about inviting Mother and Griselda to the wedding, but Charming felt they had no choice but to ask her family. "How would it look, if no one from your side attended? Besides, don't you want them to see how happy we are?"

The question of which shoes she ought to wear had been the subject of their only argument, if you could call it that. For "something blue," Charming bought her a tiara with sapphires; for "something borrowed," he sent Lady Kilmartin a gift of pearls and followed up with a note asking a "special favor" – that she lend the necklace to his bride for their wedding. "Something new" was easy. Everything Cinderella owned was new.

"I'd like to wear my glass slippers," she said when the matter of "something old" came up.

"No," he said. "That's not how I envision your feet. I've already bought you the shoes I like."

Cinderella couldn't bear the thought of even more lessons. She doubted she could master so many dance patterns in the brief time remaining before their nuptials.

"Permit me to have my own way, Charming – just this once. I won't ask again." He grudgingly gave in.

On the day of their wedding, Cinderella awoke with a dry mouth and dread knotting her belly. Charming held that on the actual day, a bridegroom mustn't see his bride prior to the actual ceremony, but he kept sending Lydia to her with notes.

Don't forget – it's "My Lord" and not "Your Grace" – he's only a Bishop.

I've changed my mind again. The first dance will be a waltz.

I know we've been over this before, darling, but please reconsider the matter of your shoes. The satin slippers I bought will do much better.

When Lydia carried in the fourth note of the morning, she looked cross. She sniffed as she handed it to Cinderella, seated at her dressing table. The note, like all the others, was sealed with red wax bearing the initials *PC*.

"More urgent tidings from the Prince," Lydia announced, with heavy emphasis on the word urgent. "He didn't like the look of the sealing wax on this one, so he made me stand there waiting while he wrote the note all over again."

* * *

The ceremony went off without mishap; the only disappointment of the banquet concerned the chicken breasts in aspic, their decorative edible flowers encased within clear gelatin. With an adoring smile on his face, as if he had eyes only for his bride, Charming said, "They were supposed to be *violets*." Though she had no urge to touch him, Cinderella patted his hand.

"All the same," she said, "they're delicious. Each and every dish has been delicious. You have to agree that everything has come off remarkably well, Charming. Ours is a wedding no one will forget, not for years to come." He gazed out upon the banquet tables, all the guests in their finery, and looked very happy.

"You truly think so?"

"Yes, I do. You've done a remarkable job, down to the smallest detail." When she leaned over to give him a kiss, strands of his stiff hair grazed her skin in a way she found irritating. What *did* he use to keep every lock so firmly in place?

Mother and Griselda were seated at the far end of the family table, too remote for Cinderella to speak to them. Mother appeared to be enjoying her meal. Griselda was chattering to the man at her right, Charming's Uncle Edward, who looked bored.

"Don't stare that way down the table," Charming whispered, placing his hand over hers. "I need your complete and undivided attention."

"Yes, Charming."

After the banquet, there was dancing, of course. Charming escorted her onto the floor – the newlyweds alone for their first dance together as man and wife. Beneath the enormous crystal chandelier as orchestral strings played the opening notes of a waltz, Charming took her in his arms, placing a hand at her waist. Cinderella released the tension in her body, surrendering to the glass slippers ... and her feet didn't move.

She nearly stumbled as Charming threw his body into the dance; he caught and steadied her. She followed his lead as best she could, faking the steps, trying to feel her way into the music's rhythm. After a few interminable seconds, the magic in the glass slippers took hold. Falling into perfect harmony with Charming's motion, they guided her feet through the waltz steps.

"What was that all about?" he hissed. "Do you realize we almost fell down ... on our very first dance!" He never stopped smiling.

"Just nerves," she answered. "Sorry. I'm all right now."

As they glided across the floor, she kept her gaze upon his face, arranging her features in the way she knew he wanted. Only toward the end of the dance did he fully recover his composure.

"We make such a lovely couple," he said. "Don't you think?"

* * *

Charming's careful arrangements for the evening didn't end with the banquet: when she reached her "bridal bower," as he called it – a paneled dressing room off the bed chamber they were to share – she found a sheer new nightgown draped over a dress form, with a note in his familiar handwriting pinned to it. *Wear this and the blue satin slippers. No jewelry. Tie your hair back with the ribbon. I'll leave the choice of perfume to you, though I'm partial to gardenia.*

When she stepped from her bower into a room aglow with a hundred candles, she almost laughed at the sight of him. He'd taken up a pose near the fireplace and was staring with a look of rapt expectation toward her. It wasn't his expression that made her want to laugh so much as his costume. He wore a gauzy white shirt unbuttoned halfway down his chest, skin glistening in the firelight, hair perfectly in place. White tights and shoes with gold tassels.

Like a hero from some fairy tale, that's how he saw himself. She imagined him before his dressing room mirror earlier, trying to decide exactly how far down to unbutton the shirt. The sight of his manly chest stirred feeble desire that quickly died away.

As she was about to speak, he put his lips to his fingers and reached out to her. He took her hand, drew her close and kissed her gently. The urge to laugh disappeared at the feel of his body, the hardness of his presence. She began to pant in tight little breaths and Charming must have believed her to be excited. He pulled her closer, wrapped his arms more tightly around her; she stifled a scream.

She lifted out of her body then; all of a sudden, she seemed to be watching them both from a distance. She watched his little pantomime of romantic seduction, carefully slipping the nightgown over her head, stripping off his own shirt and placing it carefully onto a chair. He arranged her body across the bed linens, stepped back to admire the effect and approached her gently, still wearing his tights. He lowered his body onto hers; when she closed her eyes, he whispered, "No, look at me." He reached down, placed his hand between her legs and frowned. He'd clearly expected to find her wet.

Charming kissed her lips, then her neck, working his way down to her breasts. Again he felt her below and let out a small sigh of irritation. When he moved his mouth even lower, penetrating with his tongue, she came suddenly back inside her body and wanted to beat him with her fists. She forced herself to lie still but in her mind's eye, she bit him. She bit him hard enough to draw blood. In her imagination, he snarled at the pain and slapped her. She felt herself growing wet.

Imaginary Charming pinned her down with the force of his body and forced his way inside. His face kept shifting. First the peasant boy who'd touched her that day on the road, next the dressmaker with those large knuckles and tiny blood scars. Then a faceless man with large hands. He look her from behind.

After the third time that Charming (the real Charming) touched her between the legs, he peeled down his tights and pushed inside, moving against her. The *other* Charming, the angry one she envisioned on top, he pounded so hard that it seemed he wanted to kill her. The crude dressmaker pinched her nipples until she shrieked. The faceless man with the big hands – he held her from behind and forced his fingers inside of her, with such force that she felt as if he might rip her in half.

* * *

"Happy, darling?" he asked, after he'd finished making love to her. "Happy beyond your wildest dreams?"

"Yes, Charming."

He held her in his arms and told her how ecstatic she'd made him. He explained the other ways she could make him happy, too, especially with her mouth. He loved that form of pleasure "above all things." He also went on at great length about the different places and positions he'd like to try. With an embarrassed laugh, he confessed that he'd often imagined joining with her in the linen closet, while outside the door, an unknowing charwoman scrubbed the floor. He wanted her to remain open to different possibilities.

In the morning as they were dressing, she asked, "What am I to do with my time? That is, when we're not together or you're busy elsewhere. What should I do?"

"Why whatever you like," he laughed. "You're a princess now, free to indulge your smallest whim." Upon further thought, he added: "Within reason."

As far as she could tell, she had no whims to indulge. When confronted with an empty day ahead, she had no idea what to do with herself. After a lifetime as a servant, she had no talents or interests. In the end, the question of what she might like to do with her time became purely theoretical. Charming decided that her manner and talents wanted "rounding out," as he called it; the lessons continued. He even added some new ones.

A princess ought to speak French, of course, and so for two hours each morning, she sat at a small wooden desk in his old nursery, conjugating verbs with the Language Master, a pedantic old man who winced at her accent and slapped a ruler on the desk when she made mistakes. Charming was appalled at her complete ignorance of history, so in the afternoons, a tutor came to lecture. The subject matter seemed quite dry until the tutor began describing devices of torture used in the prior age. It turned out the two of them shared a deep interest in flaying and foot roasting.

Every night without fail, Charming wanted her in bed. Sometimes Cinderella incorporated images from those history lessons into her mental imagery. She submitted to her husband's wishes, shifting positions, doing whatever he told her to do, while before her mind's eye, he caused her pain and ravished her. Or somebody else did it. She could arouse herself that way, enough to satisfy Charming, though she never enjoyed what he *actually* did to her.

Daily riding lessons continued, as well. She made great progress – so much that she eventually realized Charming was but a middling rider. With heavy hands, he bullied his horses and used the crop as punishment rather than to give aids. One day when they were riding the steeplechase course together, Cinderella suggested he release the horse going into a jump rather than reining in. "I don't need advice from a beginner!" Charming snapped. The Riding Master made matters worse by praising her seat to Charming, who abruptly changed his mind and decided horseback riding was unladylike. In its place, he substituted tatting lessons.

Is this really what you intended for me, Fairy Godmother?

Whenever Charming invited his friends to come hunt or ride, he expected her to be in constant attendance once they returned from the fields. He expected her to dress with special care for dinner and reciprocate his adoring gazes across the table. He told her which of his now-familiar stories he wanted to tell, and how she might lead conversation around to that subject. He said she needed to smile more often, laugh louder at his jokes. In the presence of the other men, he gave her lavish compliments, following up with pointed sighs of contentment.

At times, she almost hated Fairy Godmother. Too late, she realized how the appearance of loving kindness could fool you.

In the aftermath of their physical congress, she found Charming pliable. During those drowsy moments before he drifted off, she could ask for a small favor and he'd usually grant it. Over the course of several months, she persuaded him to allow her a pet, a ginger cat, and to let her choose its name herself. *Pumpkin.* She asked for a small garden plot of her own where she might grow flowers. She asked if she might use her old room, the one in the turret where she had stayed before their marriage, as a place of retreat – during the afternoons only, of course, once she'd finished her lessons and made sure he didn't need her.

"Of course, my darling," he'd whisper. "You know I can deny you nothing." This vision of his immense generosity seemed to make him happy.

One morning not long after he'd agreed to her request for a turret sanctuary, he emerged from his dressing chamber, cheeks and chin white with lather, and said, "Isabella, where's my razor?" When frustrated, he had a way of blaming the nearest person. "I can't find it anywhere."

Charming insisted that this razor kept its edge better than any blade he'd ever owned; he prized it for its mother-of-pearl handle and the perfect heft of it in his hand.

"You know I don't go into your dressing room," Cinderella said. "You told me not to, remember? Maybe you placed it in the wrong drawer."

"I've looked everywhere. I guess I'll just have to order a new one. But what am I supposed to use in the meantime? – that's what I'd like to know. What a bother!"

"I'll ring for Mrs. Wallace. I'm sure she can find you a spare razor somewhere in the palace."

The idea of stealing the razor had come to Cinderella one day when seated at the library writing desk, taking her daily dictation. Under the Calligraphy Master's tutelage, her skills had improved so much that Charming decided to employ her as his secretary. Every morning at the same hour, she'd sharpen her quill pen, dip it into the inkwell and put words to paper. Charming's words, his never-ending stream of thank you notes, orders for his tailor, invitations to friends, advice on feed blends for the Stable Master. Charming never ran out of words. Cinderella scratched each and every one of them onto parchment.

After completing a note to his Uncle Edward – an invitation to come hunt grouse – she was sharpening her quill when the penknife slipped off and sliced into her thumb. Cinderella didn't mind the pain. When Charming saw blood welling from the cut, he grimaced and looked away. He handed her the monogrammed handkerchief he always kept in his tunic.

She didn't immediately wrap it round her finger but sat gaping at the blood, the way it seemed to jewel the crisp edges of the cut. Lovely.

"Don't let it drip on the note paper!" he cried. "You'll ruin it." The flare of anger she felt oozed away with her blood, sliding down the side of her hand.

She could have taken this very pen knife up to her turret room and nobody would've noticed, but as soon as the idea of cutting occurred to her, she thought of Charming's razor. The first time she used it – one afternoon in her sanctuary following another of Charming's endless lectures on personal grooming,

Pumpkin purring in her lap – the razor brought immediately relief. As long as she had this razor, she could bear anything.

She made sure to cut herself in places nobody would notice, not even Charming who saw her naked most nights. The back of her calves was a favorite place. She could rest the ankle of one leg on the knee of another, draw the razor across her skin and watch blood drip into the basin she'd placed below it. Sometimes she began with the ping of droplets onto metal; eventually, she'd fill the basin with water and watch wisps of red disperse into clear liquid. The memory of Charming's voice would grow faint as the water turned pink. The pinker the water, the less pain she felt. She could count on it.

She'd heard stories about doctors of old, deliberately causing their patients to bleed so as to release the evil spirits inside. Nobody these days believed blood-letting had any salutary effect, but more and more, Cinderella felt the good of it.

Often while bleeding, she'd pet her cat and ponder the magic that had brought her to this turret. Cinderella couldn't make her ideas about Fairy Godmother hold still. Only rarely did she think her truly malicious. Sometimes she believed that Fairy Godmother had used her wand with the best of intentions but simply wasn't very good at her work. Sometimes she told herself that Fairy Godmother's job was only to grant wishes, not to decide whether they were worth granting in the first place. Then the bitterness would rise up and she'd have to say it aloud: "All I wanted was to go to the ball!" In the end, Cinderella usually decided that what had come to pass must be her own fault, all of it. The blood flow brought greater acceptance.

Be grateful. Try to be good.

When she'd had enough, she could always stanch the wound. She knew how to make it stop, with pressure mostly, or sometimes with the help of a strip of cloth tied higher up. She never worried that she might go on bleeding forever, until there was no blood left inside, but now and then, she thought it might be pleasant. The water in the basin would turn very red, so deeply red that she'd never again feel pain.

Before climbing back down the turret stairs, Cinderella emptied her basin via the window so neither Lydia nor any of the chamber maids would find it. While walking the grounds and glancing up at her window, she sometimes imagined a pinkish stain beneath it, exactly where the bloody water would have landed – a long scar in the ancient stonework. Perhaps she only imagined it there, but from below, it sometimes appeared as if the palace itself were bleeding.

Her monthly flow, though she ached and cramped from it, had never brought the relief of blood-letting, where one kind of pain erased another. She usually anticipated that time of month with mild dread, but after a few months of marriage when the blood stopped coming, she felt a deeper premonitory gloom. A foreign life form had taken root inside and would gradually dominate her body. Charming outside, the baby within. Soon there'd be no room left for her.

Charming clapped his hands together with delight when she told him. "I'm going to be a father!" he cried. Then he frowned. "I hope it won't ruin your figure, at least not permanently. No one looks better in a ball gown than you do. I'd hate to lose that."

* * *

Cinderella hadn't seen her mother or sister since the wedding, but not long after the ceremony, letters from home began to arrive. Mother's notes showed up like clockwork, one per week, detailed accounts of goings-on in the neighborhood with a not-so-subtle bid for financial assistance. "Please don't worry about us," she'd conclude. "We'll manage to get by somehow. As a new bride, you must have so many more important things to attend to." Griselda wrote sporadically, long rambling letters about how guilty she felt for the way she'd treated Cinderella. Could her one and only sister ever find forgiveness in her heart?

Cinderella ignored Griselda's letters but dutifully answered each and every one that Mother wrote. Charming gave her no pocket money, so she couldn't provide the assistance that Mother wanted. When she finally broached the subject, Charming took a disapproving tone.

"Those who spend beyond their means must suffer the consequences of their own imprudent ways. It's not my fault your family can't manage their finances. I'll consider it an act of disobedience if you ask me again."

Sometimes when he talked to her that way, Cinderella lowered her gaze in submission and imagined cutting out his tongue.

"Yes, Charming."

As the weeks wore on, Griselda's letters grew longer and more blatantly self-pitying ("I suppose this miserable life is no more than I deserve!") and Mother's less self-effacing. "I have to say I'm surprised by your continuing neglect. Looking back, I admit I wasn't perfect, but I am nonetheless your mother. The gift of life alone puts you under a significant obligation."

Hadn't she married Charming, in part, to help her mother? What good had come of her marriage if she must endure his petty tyrannies, his pedantic lectures, his subjugation of her body and yet wield no power to help her family? Late one night after he'd taken her, just as he was drifting off, she worked up the courage to try Charming once again.

Would he do her the immense favor of letting Mother and Griselda move into one of the vacant houses on the palace grounds? It wouldn't be an inconvenience as nobody was using them at present. It would cost him nothing, and this act of kindness would mean a great deal to her.

"At a time like this," she explained, "a girl needs her mother."

"Why?" he sleepily asked. "Why do you need your mother?"

"Mothers know about babies."

"What about *my* mother? She knows about babies, too."

"Of course she does. But she's your mother not mine. A girl needs her own mother."

Charming seems to wake up a little. He opened his eyes and peered at her with mistrust. "I don't know. Are you planning to have them in the palace all the time?"

"Of course not. They could only come when we invited them – and rarely. I wouldn't do anything without your permission."

"I don't know," he repeated.

"Please, Charming," she whispered. She placed her head on his chest and fondled him below. He often liked it more than once a night.

"Oh, all right," he finally sighed. She felt him begin to swell. "Would you do that bit with your tongue I like?"

The prospect of Mother and Griselda living at hand, just across the palace grounds, aroused a peculiar longing for her former life – for that familiar moue of distaste on Mother's face when they used to pass one another in the hallway, for Griselda's pouty expression on those rare occasions when she didn't get her way. The sound of her own name, what she felt to be her true name, on familiar lips. *Cinderella.* As the baby grew inside of her, a powerful nostalgia took hold, for a time gone by when life had felt less awful to her than it did today. She blamed all this new emotion on that creature inside, the changes he had already begun to wreak upon her body.

Of course it would have to be a boy. That's what Charming expected her to deliver. A tiny replica of himself, clamoring for her breast, demanding that she come running whenever he screamed for her, another tyrant. She felt relieved, almost grateful when Charming told her they'd of course have a wet nurse. He didn't want the baby to ruin her breasts.

Both Mother and Griselda sent effusively grateful notes when Cinderella wrote to tell them of her plans. With Charming's grudging consent, she dispatched several wagons and a half-dozen servants to help on the day of their removal to their new abode, a two-story thatched cottage at the edge of the forest. According to family lore, Charming's great-grandfather had called it his "hunting lodge" even though he never used it for hunting. Cinderella gathered that he went there to escape his wife, Charming's great-grandmother, whom he feared and hated. The old king had decorated throughout with antlers, stuffed heads and cross-bows. So it had remained ever since, the animal parts gathering dust, the paneled walls yellowing with age.

The day after their arrival, Cinderella walked across the palace grounds to visit. From the moment Mother embraced her, gushing with gratitude, Cinderella could feel how entirely things had changed. *I'm the favorite now.* It didn't seem like love, at least not the kind she'd always longed for. The look in Mother's eyes didn't make her feel any less ugly or dirty, with the taste of Charming still in her mouth. Griselda, at least, seemed familiar. The patter of admiration – *Such a gorgeous dress! What brilliant jewels! I love the way you've done your hair!* – felt like pure hatred. Cinderella asked them to the palace for dinner on Tuesday week – a date remote enough to make clear such invitations would not be frequent.

As she watched Mother and Griselda fawn upon Charming, that first time they came for dinner, Cinderella felt her nostrils twitch, her lips curl as if she smelled something foul. With two more place settings at table, at least she didn't have to face Charming. She didn't have to look at him, stifling the urge to plunge her fork into his face because of the self-satisfied way he chewed. She sat alongside him instead, across from Mother, who praised the palace chef and Charming's menu choices, each course more exquisite, more subtle than the one before.

Griselda seemed awestruck, sitting in silence throughout the meal. When the Queen asked whether she found their new accommodations satisfactory, Griselda swallowed hard and nodded vigorously, eyes wide with terror. Now and then during the meal, the King would say, "Who are these people?" to no one in particular. As usual, Charming did most of the talking.

When the dessert course finally came, though she knew better, Cinderella couldn't stop herself. "Not floating island again," she said. A tight little shiver of excitement ran up her spine, along the nape of her neck. The image of it came to her – Charming's open palm, striking her face. She could feel the stinging heat.

His handsome bland face looked confused, as if he didn't know what to make of her comment. "But … but it's my favorite. You know that."

"Yes, I'm well aware it's your favorite. Not mine, I'm afraid. It grows tiresome."

Griselda gasped. Mother looked alarmed, her eyelids fluttering in distress. "I'm sure my daughter means no disrespect, your Highness."

"I absolutely adore floating island," Griselda managed to say.

"Try eating it three days a week, month after month," Cinderella told her. "See if you still adore it then."

"I would! I know I would!"

Cinderella felt Charming's glare of disapproval. She refused to be cowed by it and looked up. The steadfast way she stared back seemed to baffle him.

"Women with child often find their appetites altered," he finally decided. "So I've been told."

"Very true, your Highness," said Mother, a little too quickly. "Why, when I was carrying Cin … I mean, Isabella, I had the most intense longing for salad greens, all variety of lettuce. Can you imagine?" Anxiety cut her laugh short. "It makes no sense, a woman craving salad."

Mother's distress filled Cinderella with shame and regret. There were blessings to count, weren't there? Charming had a few irritating qualities, of course – maybe more than a few – but that didn't give her cause to provoke him. She ought to feel *grateful*. After all, he'd granted her wish, allowing Mother and Griselda to move into the old hunting lodge.

Why couldn't she be good, if not for her own sake then for benefit of others?

* * *

In the mornings, she began to feel nauseated. The thought of food repulsed her; when Charming wanted the use of her mouth, she couldn't bring herself to comply. At first, she forced herself to try but soon hurried over to the basin to disgorge the sour contents of her belly.

"I'm sorry, Charming," she said, bursting into tears.

"Of course you're sorry, but what about me? What am I supposed to do now? Wipe your mouth again, you've missed some of your sick. Ugh."

As her belly grew larger, he wanted her less often. "Women with child really are quite unattractive," he told her. "I'm sure you're as eager for this period to end as I am." By the sixth month, he left her entirely alone. The nausea finally passed but she didn't tell him. She let him believe it continued without reprieve and prevented her from doing for him what he loved "above all things."

Her growing physical discomfort made Cinderella toss and turn at night, unable to find a comfortable position. Charming finally suggested she move back into the room where she'd slept before their marriage.

"Only for a few months," he told her, "just so that I can get a good night's sleep. You have no idea how exhausted I am these days."

As much as she tried to be mild, too often when she began to speak, her words or tone of voice took an unexpected turn. She felt like that princess in the fairy tale who spewed nothing but toads every time she opened her mouth.

"However did you learn the best way to juice berries, Charming? Sometimes it seems that you know everything!"

"You're very wise to send the Walcotts packing, even if they do have so many small children. You wouldn't want to give the other tenants the impression you're soft-hearted."

"No, I wouldn't say you look ridiculous with your hair combed that way. I would never actually say such a thing."

Now and then when he listened to her speak, Charming narrowed his eyes and focused hard, as if trying to work out the solution to a difficult mathematics problem. "From your tone of voice," he said, "it sometimes seems like … well, that you mean the very opposite of what you say."

His manner toward her gradually cooled. Sometimes when she spat out a very large and ugly toad, even if he didn't fully understand it, he looked as if he loathed her.

"I don't see why you insist upon making yourself so unattractive."

When guests came for dinner or they hosted a ball, she kept herself tightly reined in. She played along with his charade of perfect marital bliss, the proud soon-to-be-parents overcome with joy. Cinderella knew better than to make him look bad in public: he could be quite vengeful if provoked. Lady Kellynch once laughed at him when he hadn't actually made a joke, during a banquet when all the other guests could hear, and he subsequently barred her from the palace. He poisoned all the other noble families against her, as well; she now lived in complete isolation. It would be more complicated to exact revenge upon his own wife but Cinderella had no doubt he could find a way.

At smaller dinners when only Mother and Griselda joined the family, Cinderella relaxed and often found herself interrupting him.

"Yes, we're well aware of how you think on the subject, Charming. Let someone else have a chance to speak."

On those occasions, Charming withdrew into silence; he pulled himself up and appeared to look down upon them all. Griselda would usually hurry to his defense. "I think exactly the same way!" she'd cry. "I'm sure what you say is absolutely the right way to think about it."

At the end of one such evening, Mother said to her, "I don't mean to interfere, but you really oughtn't to quarrel with him. You'll only make life more difficult for yourself—and for me and your sister as well, I might add."

"I'm sure you have nothing but my welfare at heart," Cinderella said. The sudden longing for Fairy Godmother, the very good one, nearly overwhelmed her. Later that night when she cut herself, watching blood drops fan out into water, she waited in vain for the special light to come.

Cinderella's back ached, she couldn't sleep for more than a few minutes at a time, and her body felt hideously bloated. She reminded herself of the rat in Fairy Godmother's transformation, just before he filled out his human body. Cinderella felt as if she, too, were changing shape, transforming into a different creature, one lower down in the animal kingdom. Breeding stock, like one of the heifers. She longed for the return of her own body and feared she was lost to herself forever. Every time the little prince kicked inside of her, she longed to smite her belly. Sometimes she actually did it.

During these final days before the baby was to come, her only relief was to work in the garden, her own small garden plot that Charming had granted her. She told Lydia to find her a smock of the type worn by scullery maids and donned it each morning after she'd made sure Charming had departed for the stables. She found some chunky old boots in one of the cellars and borrowed a pair of heavy gloves from the head gardener. Lydia smirked as she helped her mistress get dressed.

Down on her knees, turning soil and tending her flowers, she felt almost happy. Her life seemed to have a purpose. One day, she carried buckets of ash from the kitchen fireplace and spread them carefully beneath her azaleas. Then she gave them water to drink. Tomorrow or the next day, if the ground had dried out, she'd water them again. Beyond that, she couldn't think.

She toiled on her knees throughout the morning. The sun rose high into the sky, beating down upon her. She felt pain in her knees and hands but strangely enough, her back didn't ache in this position. The baby stirred but little. The sweat ran down her neck, onto her face; when she wiped it away, she could feel that she left streaks of mud and ash on her face. In the intense midday sun, her bloated body grew wet all over; the dirt seemed to have infiltrated her clothes. A fat sow, rooting in her wallow – that's how she saw herself.

Content. Unreflecting. No yesterday and no tomorrow, nothing but the feel of fecund warm soil beneath her.

"What in heaven's name are you doing?!"

So deeply had she settled into the mud, she needed long seconds to pull back, to recognize her husband's voice. She slowly craned her head around and took in the look of shock upon his face. Though he'd just come from his morning ride, he looked immaculate in his white britches and glossy high boots; he slapped his riding crop against his open palm. She fought down the urge to make herself still uglier, to distort her mouth, hunch her nose and snort at him. Perhaps he'd beat her with that crop. The sting of it against her back.

"I'm gardening," she said. At least she hadn't completely lost the faculty of speech.

Charming's face twisted up in disgust. "Do you have any idea what you look like? Your appearance … it's absolutely revolting. Get up at once and go make yourself clean! No wait – you can't let the servants see you that way. Go change at your mother's house. I'll send over fresh clothes."

With a look of near-horror on his face, he watched as she struggled to stand up. First one foot on the ground, then awkwardly pushing upward with both hands on her knee. The extra weight of her belly put her off balance. She nearly toppled over but Charming didn't offer to help.

"Who would ever have dreamed a wife of mine could sink this low. I quite literally cannot bear the sight of you." And he hurried away toward the palace steps.

She did as her husband commanded, plodding across the grounds toward the hunting lodge. She seemed to have no will of her own. Though he'd gone into the palace, she imagined Charming behind her like a drover, snapping his whip. Mother recoiled at the sight of her, averting her gaze with that familiar moue of distaste. It had been so very long since Mother had allowed herself to react that way.

"Charming told me to clean up. He's sending over fresh clothes." Short declarative sentences, that's all she could manage.

Mother insisted she bathe downstairs in the kitchen; she made the one servant girl douse Cinderella with buckets of water while from outside the door, she scolded.

"I'm not sure what you think you're doing. Do you want to have us turned out? If you make him unhappy, that's what he'll do. We live here at his sufferance – never forget that. You know how far he can go if you displease him – only think of poor Lady Kellynch. You have but one responsibility in life, Cinderella, and that's to keep your husband happy. For my sake, I think you might try a little harder."

Cinderella. The sound of her real name on Mother's lips brought tears to her eyes.

"I *will* try harder, I promise." She'd give up her garden, if that's what they all wanted. She'd sit quietly at dinner and let him speak. Once the baby came out, she'd regain her shape. Charming would again find her useful. She envisioned herself down on all fours while Charming took her from behind.

When she thought of Fairy Godmother, all she could find was a black empty space where the memory ought to be, a darkness at her very center that consumed all light.

The change of clothing arrived and the servant girl helped her dress. Cinderella trudged across the palace grounds, upright on both feet though she knew she ought to be crawling. Up in her turret sanctuary, she rang for Lydia and wondered whether to cut soon, directly after tea, or if she should wait until Charming released her following dinner. She'd have more time if she waited but she wasn't sure she could withstand the bloodlust that long.

As soon as Lydia came in, Cinderella could see her maid had been crying. Against her pale complexion, the redness of Lydia's eyes and nose looked garish.

"Yes, my Lady?" She sounded accusatory; she obviously wanted to be drawn out so she could state her grievance. Cinderella couldn't bring herself to care.

"I'd like my tea now," she said. "Bring it directly." Charming would have approved. He frequently found her too solicitous toward the feelings of their servants.

Lydia looked offended but bowed her head. "As you wish." At the doorway, she turned back, unable to hold her tongue. "It's not my responsibility how you dress and comport yourself. The Prince has no right to dock my wages." She glared at her mistress, trembling with rage. The injustice of it.

Cinderella sighed. She understood exactly how Lydia must feel. The blood-letting would have to wait. And it might do her some good, to help a defenseless maid even if she could no nothing for herself.

"You're absolutely right – it's not your fault. Let me speak to my husband. I'll go to him directly."

Lydia looked surprised – she hadn't expected her mistress to defend her. "Thank you, my Lady." She didn't sound grateful.

Cinderella knew exactly where to find Charming at that hour. After his ride, he would've bathed; now he'd be in his dressing room, puzzling over what to wear for dinner. Choosing an outfit usually took a great deal of time, and dressing even longer. She made her way downstairs and into their bed chamber, the one they formerly shared before she swelled and bloated to hideous size. From within the large dressing room that adjoined the chamber (twice as large as her own "bridal bower"), she made out his noises.

When Cinderella opened the door, though she physically startled, she wasn't surprised by what she saw there. Not really. She felt the baby kick inside of her. It had always seemed as if her story must end this way.

Charming stood with his back to the door, white riding britches pulled low about his ankles. Griselda kneeled in front of him, her eyes closed in blatant pleasure, doing for her brother-in-law what he loved above all things. When she opened her eyes and saw Cinderella, she smiled in triumph then went back to pleasuring him.

That night when she cut, Cinderella chose a new vein, this one in her arm, so close to the surface it traced a distinct blue line directly beneath her skin. Charming's blade sliced her open and the blood gushed out. She gasped at the speed of it. The candlelight on blood was as lustrous as rubies. Fluid pooled on her wrist, catching the flame's glow; then it slipped off her arm and pinged loudly into the metal basin below. Blood light and blood music, filling up her senses. She felt that she hated no one. The baby inside was still.

The candles seemed to burn brighter and brighter. It seemed as if their wicks had multiplied. She felt the light of a thousand candles flooding the room. At last, she realized it must be coming from behind her – not from candles but from the farthest edges of the room. Though her turret sanctuary was round, she felt light coming to her as if from the corners. In the old kitchen back in Mother's house, the good light always sprang to life in the corners. She felt the familiar warmth of it now at her back, intensifying, moving closer, so radiant and accepting you had to believe it meant love.

And then, all at once, the light snuffed out.

THE END

Snow White at the Dwarf Colony

PART I
THE HUNTSMAN

Jam Gereth, the Huntsman. At Queen Madlen's behest, I led Snow White into the forest but spared her life; instead, I carried her to the abode of the dwarfs and left her there. Do not judge me until you have heard all my story. Each one of us is a mixture of good and evil; in the end, you may find even Madlen deserving of your pity.

I have known Madlen all her life. My father served as Huntsman to the old Duke and I passed my youth on the estate until she married King Alec. From the time she was four, Madlen took an interest in her father's horses, and because the stables were near to the kennel where I lived and assisted my father, I saw her almost every day. Whilst I would be exercising the hounds, little Madlen would hang on the railings and watch for hours as trainers put the Duke's horses through their paces. Despite the distance, I could feel her fascination, how much she longed for connection with their strength and beauty. Though I was ten and she but four, I felt a special bond between us. It might have been our shared early loss that bound us together: each of our mothers had died not long after giving birth to us.

Or perhaps it was because we were both monsters in our own way, though I did not know it then.

Whenever some unexpected sound or movement agitated the horses and set them running, I sensed her excitement. Across the paddocks, tiny motions in her body spoke to me – the lift of her shoulders, head of raven hair tilting slightly back, the way she leaned forward as if to join with those powerful beasts. Though the horses were her father's possessions, and by extension hers as well, she wanted to own them in some deeper way, to make their magnificence a part of herself. This I could feel.

At home for the midday meal, I kept her in my sights. Our cottage was attached to the kennels, a lean-to with two small rooms, and from its single window I could spy the paddocks at a distance. It had always irked me that Madlen's grandfather, the Miser Duke who'd built the cottage, had set it so close to the kennels. We could never escape the stink of the hounds, their wet fur and excrement. It also brought the smell of urine-soaked hay, mucked from the stalls and piled upwind from us.

Now and then, Father caught me in my trance as I watched Madlen from the window, as still as a statue, and struck me on the ear, sometimes hard enough to make me bleed. For most of my life, I've been partially deaf on the right side.

"What're you glaring at, you idiot fool?" A single epithet never sufficed for my father. "Get to work or I'll give you what for!"

Giving me "what for" meant a hiding in the kennel feed room, trousers down around my ankles, his vicious crop leaving bloody welts across my buttocks. Though he never said so, I believe he blamed my birth for his wife's death, the one leading to the other.

Madlen was an unnaturally beautiful child. With skin the color of fresh cream, lips red as roses and hair black as midnight, she gathered more loveliness into one body than seemed just. Watching her from the enclosure, or from the cottage window, I sometimes wondered how it would feel to be little Madlen, living in the elegant manor house, a daughter of privilege and surely destined for a great marriage. What was it like, to know with certainty that you could have whatever you desired? I believe she knew it even then, at such an early age. Madlen was as shrewd as she was beautiful.

I might have been born Madlen rather than Gereth.

I had always considered myself beneath her notice. That gangly boy with protruding ears and a nose too large for his face, the one always watching from the kennels – he simply did not merit her attention.

She took me by surprise, then, when she one day dropped down from the paddock rails, snapped her head around (long raven hair flying out) and shouted at me. I was standing within the enclosure, attentive hounds awaiting my cue. Madlen wasn't much more than five years old.

"Why do you watch me so, boy?" She did not sound angry. I could see it surprised her that I wouldn't look away; I kept staring back as she strode toward me.

"Begging your pardon, Miss. Only keeping an eye out for you."

She stopped and planted her fists upon her hips, legs apart. It was a boyish pose that did not suit her. A distance of five yards, no more, lay between us.

"I don't need you watching out for me," she said, "and I don't like it. I command you to stop."

"Yes, Miss." I held my gaze steady. She didn't mean what she said, not exactly. She had no feeling for me, didn't even know my name, but admiring attention would always be welcome. It was the idea that she needed protection, from me or from anyone else, that offended her.

"Don't let me catch you doing it again."

I stared at her back as she stepped away. I watched until she disappeared behind the tall hedge that bordered the manor house. All afternoon, whenever the memory would return to me, I smiled.

* * *

I received my first glimpse of Madlen's true nature on her sixth birthday. She had begged her father for a horse of her very own, but fearing for her safety, the old Duke had told her she must wait until she was older. He gave her a snowy white rabbit instead, in addition to all the other fine birthday gifts, and ordered that a special gilded cage be built for it. After she had opened all her presents that day, Madlen came down to the stables, clutching the rabbit tightly to her chest, her face hard with unhappiness. I watched from the enclosure as she strode back and forth outside the paddocks.

The rabbit wanted to break free. The more it squirmed, the closer she held it. Tiny as she was, Madlen seemed huge with rage. I could almost hear her thoughts, a rant at the injustice of it: how dare they not give her what she wanted! Trapped in those suffocating arms, the panicky little rabbit finally bit her.

Madlen did not scream or drop the animal, as most children would have done. She seemed barely to notice the pain, though it tapped into the rage she felt; for that moment, the bite and the blood it drew seemed to explain everything that had gone wrong in her world. She took the rabbit by the scruff of its neck, carried it over to the nearest trough and plunged it into the water. The terrified animal flailed for its life but Madlen held it firmly below the surface, tensing the muscles in her arm. She glared at the roiling water, barely blinking. I held my breath.

When the splashing finally stopped, Madlen hoisted the limp creature into the air by its neck, shook it roughly then tossed the lifeless body onto the soil. She turned and walked away toward the manor house. About ten steps on, she came to an abrupt halt and stood very still. I could feel her thinking. I had no idea what she had in mind, but I sensed her body thrilling with intention. She finally turned, came back to retrieve the dead white rabbit, and walked toward the manor house, cradling the corpse as if it were her baby.

That night, I heard from my sister Ellen – in service at the manor house – what had transpired upon Madlen's return. Apparently beside herself with grief, the girl told a story of accidental death, the rabbit slipping unnoticed from the pond dock, drowning before she could save it. Madlen wept with a grief beyond consolation, refusing to eat her supper. She cried out with despair when the Duke tried to bring her another rabbit. All afternoon, she shrieked and wailed until the Duke seemed afraid she might actually lose her mind. The memory of his wife's madness and the rope around her neck must have haunted him.

The next day, he bought her a horse.

* * *

From that day forward, Madlen spent the majority of her time with her *several* mounts – for the birthday gift did not meet her needs for long. Her first was a staid old mare, a beast that never shied or bucked, suitable only for the most placid of trail rides. Madlen wanted a horse that would gallop. She wanted a horse that could clear the hedges and stiles, for her goal was to ride to hounds with her father and her older brother Creven. It took care and scheming, but she eventually got her way.

Madlen possessed an innate understanding of the horse breed, their fears and passions, the instinct of the herd. Though still a small girl, she knew at once that she must quickly establish her dominance over a beast many times her size and power. The stable master said he'd never taught a more gifted pupil, though he despised her. She pestered him for instruction but bristled whenever he corrected her. I often watched her lessons from the edge of the ring, at one with Madlen as she sailed above the rails.

"You're on the wrong lead, Miss!" the stable master would cry. "Look ahead into the turn as you take the jump and your horse will pick up the correct one."

"You've told me that before!" Madlen snapped. "I'm not a fool."

"No one is above instruction," he said, "not even me. One day, you'll learn the value of a pair of eyes on the ground."

She did learn, in her own way. She resented each correction he gave and took in every word.

The Duke insisted she not go unaccompanied on her daily rides, and the role of companion often fell to me. She felt my presence as a kind of insult.

"I don't need you," she often told me. "Return at once to the stables."

I never answered her but followed wherever she led, keeping several strides behind, smiling in a way that would have infuriated her if she'd ever looked back. Her father's command gave me the power to defy her. As she grew more accomplished, Madlen sometimes tried to lose me, lulling me first with a slow gait then spurring her horse into a sudden gallop. I knew her devious ways and she never caught me off guard, not once. I could ride as well as she; I took the hedges and rails right behind her. Eventually, she came to accept my presence as inevitable. For the most part she ignored me, behaving as if I weren't there.

On the morning of her first hunt – she would have been nine years old by then – my father and I walked with the pack of excited hounds from their kennel while mounted gentry gathered in front of the manor house. In her crisp new riding togs, Madlen looked small atop her chestnut gelding. She clutched the crop between her arm and torso. Even before the hunt began, her face glowed as if in victory. I knew how Madlen must feel, that no other experience could match this intensity of life, every sense at the highest pitch. Yelping hounds, the snorting horses, a smell of freshly mown hay in the air. A low mist clung to the earth, seeping into ivy that covered the manor house walls. I knew precisely how each detail would affect her, how the mist caused her to shiver in that delicious way, up her spine and into the soft hairs along her fine white neck.

I did not ride with the hunt that day. My father, though he had taught me everything he knew about hounds and hunting, rarely let me make full use of that knowledge. The more I understood and the taller I grew, the more he seemed to resent me. Though he knew it to be an inevitable part of the natural order for a growing son one day to take the father's place, I believe he hated me for it. By that time, he'd given over the beatings and found other ways to humiliate me.

"You boy," he called out, climbing onto his mount as the bugle sounded. "Don't stand there like an idiot with your mouth agape. Go see to your chores!"

I'm sure none of the gentry paid my father any heed, but the heat raced from my face to my crown until it seemed as if my hair might catch fire. As the bugles sounded, I watched Madlen urge her horse into motion. I felt the bite of her spur at the horse's flank. Would she return in triumph at the end of the hunt, her face alight with fierce joy, a long-cherished dream come true? She might also fall and break her neck.

All morning long as I mucked the kennels and gave exercise to those hounds that had not gone out, in my imagination I rode with Madlen across the fields. I forgot my father and what he'd said to me. Though I'd often counseled her on our rides to take more care, I knew her to be a fearless rider who balked at naught. She would not mind if someone else should claim the brush so long as she could lead the hunt. She would gallop over terrain where other, far more experienced riders might canter or even trot; she'd take the highest hedge at breakneck speed and laugh if another rider lost his mount. When the hounds ran the fox to ground, she would be there with the foremost riders. This I imagined.

When I met the hunting party upon their return, Madlen's name was on everyone's tongue. As servants carried trays from the house and handed each rider a steaming chalice, the gentry spoke of her daring. Some called her reckless and foolhardy, others praised her brave spirit. I had never seen Madlen look so exhilarated; the joy upon her face looked almost spiteful. I felt her exultation rising in my chest and at almost the same moment, we laughed.

* * *

Though worlds apart, we grew up together. We rode the trails together. As my father became frail, I took his place and shadowed her in the hunt. By the time Madlen turned 12, I was a full-grown man, tall and powerfully built. My sister Ellen said the other girls in service thought me handsome; she laughed and told me I could have my pick of the lot, but I did not believe her. How could I believe her when by that point, I knew myself to be a monster? I had slowly come to understand what I hungered for, knowing I could never have it. For the rest of my life, I'd have to keep my hideous nature hidden from view.

It was this need for disguise that deepened my bond with Madlen; it gave me a special understanding of her ways. Over the years as I watched, Madlen had learned to behave *as if* she possessed a feeling heart, *as if* she cared about the suffering of others. She studied the people around her and learned to simulate their humanity, just as I came to master the ways of other men – their gestures, their oaths, the ways they moved and the ways they laughed. As I came of age, I appeared to be a man like any other.

For her 16th birthday when Madlen entered womanhood, the Duke gave her a magical looking glass that had belonged to her mother, a family heirloom passed down through the ages from generation to generation. I believe such enchanted household items used to be quite common, though their magic has waned with time and they are now impossible to distinguish from the everyday and the ordinary. Madlen's glass would provide the answer to any question she put to it, as long she framed her query in a rhyming couplet, the first half of which must be stated as follows: *Looking-glass, Looking-glass on the wall ...* She could finish the couplet as she liked.

(I learned about the looking glass much later, from Madlen herself, during a time in her life when she came to rely upon me for a kind of solace, if not true friendship.)

For the most part, Madlen used the looking-glass to make mischief, to uncover the secrets of her enemies, the other young maidens at house parties or county balls, vying for the attention of eligible young men. *Looking-glass, Looking-glass on the wall, For whom does Gwyneth care most of all?* If *Euan* were the answer, Madlen would devote herself to that young man the next time they met, employing all her wiles to secure his affection. Of course she felt nothing for Euan, or for any other young man, but she could not bear that he should dote upon anyone but her.

She could have married any one of these young men, but Madlen wanted a title. And of course, it had to be the highest of titles. It would not do to be a mere lady or even a duchess; she had to be a queen, supreme above all others. So she told her father. And thus it transpired that an invitation was sent to Abergavenny and King Alec came courting.

I was there on the day he arrived in his gleaming coach, the family coat of arms emblazoned on its doors. His liveried servants wore blue linen and gold braid, more elegant than most of our local gentry. When he stepped from the coach, afternoon light caught his fair countenance and golden hair. If ever there were man on earth to match Madlen's beauty, Alec was he. My heart sank at the sight of him. The longing so overpowered me that I felt a weakness in my knees and I had to look away.

That night, I slept with the hounds in their kennel, not upon my pallet in the cottage. I spread fresh hay in a corner and lay myself upon it, welcoming the heat and aroma of the animals that came to lie beside me. One of the hounds licked tears from my face. Here among unthinking beasts, beyond morality, the nature of my desire did not matter.

My early feeling for Madlen's brother Creven had first opened my eyes. It had come upon me slowly; I tried hard to fight it off and give it some other name. I told myself that I admired his manly virtues, nothing more; I took him as my model and tried to mimic his ways. Creven had a full-throated, superior way of laughing, head thrown back, that struck me as the embodiment of self-confident manhood. Alone with the hounds, when I tried to replicate the sound, I felt idiotic, an unconvincing counterfeit. The day Creven fell from his horse and wrenched his ankle, I was forced to carry him back to the manor house. His body in my arms at last revealed to me the truth of my corrupt nature.

From that day forward I lived in agony, longing for and dreading his appearance every hour of my life. Like Madlen, he came down to the stables most days. Having mastered the art of secret observation, I watched them both, my gaze apparently elsewhere. Sometimes I followed him at a careful distance, or hid in waiting where I knew he would appear. One fateful day, I spied upon Creven from the barn loft as he forced himself upon Elspeth, the kitchen maid. He shoved her down into the hay, used his hand to stifle her screams and lay upon her. In that moment, my own desire died out; forever after, I felt nothing for him but contempt.

I assumed the same would hold true for King Alec. In time, he would expose his inner ugliness, a selfish disregard for the feelings of others, and my desire would pass. As much as I wanted to hide, I forced myself to be present for his visits. At first, my opportunities for close observation were few – a glimpse as he alit from his coach, longer moments when Madlen brought him down to the stables. They rode out together on occasion and she shaped herself into a careful, somewhat timid rider. She allowed Alec to help her mount and followed his lead down trails she knew as well as the pale blue veins at the back of her hand.

She's not what you think. Don't marry her.

Then one day, Alec came down to the kennels alone. He caught me off-guard in the outdoor run; my chores completed, I was playing tug-of-war with Sian, my favorite – a sweet-tempered bitch with black markings across her back that looked almost like a saddle. I flinched and briefly closed my eyes to the sight of Alec coming through the gate; then I opened them wide and took him in – sun on his hair, golden threads glinting in his tunic. Sian settled onto her belly and cocked her head to one side, puzzled as to why I'd suddenly dropped the rope. When Alec smiled at me, I didn't know what to do with my face.

"I hope I'm not intruding," he said. "Please don't let me interrupt."

"Not at all, your Majesty. I was just ... *playing.*" Speaking the word, I felt like an imbecile. Grown men did not *play.* Sian gripped the fallen rope between her teeth and nudged it against my hand. With my leg, I roughly pushed her aside.

"You are known as Gereth, I believe."

He knew my name. "Y-yes," I stammered. "I am Gereth."

"We haven't actually met though I expect you know who I am." Again he smiled.

"You are King Alec," I said, "of Abergavenny." I took his hand and gave it a manly grip. I nodded my head as I had seen Creven do when he greeted a friend – sharply dipping his chin and briefly lowering his brows. I stepped back and set my feet apart.

When Sian tried to engage him with the rope, King Alec gave her head an awkward pat and looked about him. "So this is your kennel," he said.

"My father is Huntsman here," I told him. "I am his assistant." In truth, my father kept to his bed most days and I had taken full responsibility for the kennel.

"But you know all about dogs and training them for the hunt. Madlen told me so. She said you know all there is to know about hounds … and horses, too. She's said you're one of the finest riders in the duchy."

The idea that Madlen and King Alec had made me the subject of conversation, however briefly, left me speechless. She had actually praised me to her suitor – the very idea seemed outlandish, inexplicable. I clasped my hands behind my back and put my head to one side, as if to make light of my skills.

King Alec must've seen he'd made me uncomfortable; with an oddly graceful motion of his hand, he brushed the subject aside. I felt grateful that he didn't try to meet my gaze but seemed more intent on the dog runs and exercise pen.

"And what do you think of your father's kennel? Is it everything a kennel should be? Is there any way you would like to improve it?"

King Alec of Abergavenny, one of the wealthiest men in the land and suitor to my Duke's daughter, was asking for my opinion. No one – not my father, not my sister, certainly not the Duke himself or even Madlen – had ever asked my opinion about anything.

"It is the only kennel I have ever known, your Majesty."

"Yes, of course. But you must have some views on ways to make things better." Once again he gave me that generous smile – so inclusive, almost as if we were friends. "No son wants to do things exactly as his father has done before him. I most certainly did not."

My chest grew tight. I was afraid that I might start crying. Could such beauty outside be matched by beauty within? I did not trust myself to speak.

"Give it some thought," he said, turning to face me. "We can talk it over another day."

As he was heading through the gate, I finally called out to him. "I'd set the cottage apart from the kennels, away from the smell."

I couldn't tell if he was amused or merely surprised. He certainly hadn't expected this particular bit of advice.

"I'll keep that in mind."

Once he'd gone, I dropped to my knees, called to Sian and wrapped her in my arms. I held her close, digging my fingers into the muscles of her chest, thrusting my face into her fur.

A week or so later, the engagement was announced. Not long after, I learned that, as part of the marriage settlement, it had been stipulated that King Alec would build a kennel at Abergavenny and that I was to be Huntsman there. This I learned from my father who'd been called to the manor house and told by the Duke. When Father returned to our cottage and gave me the news, his face was red and his left eye twitching. His raspy voice was even harsher than usual.

When I finally took it all in, what my fate was to be, I said, "The honor should have been yours, Father."

"What a stupid idea!" he snarled. "I could never leave my Duke!" He hated me so much now that he'd be glad to have me out of his sight. "Do you think me such an ingrate?"

"You have so much more experience than I do. I only meant that if the King wanted a huntsman ..."

It was too much for Father – the idea that I would have a place superior to his own. He balled his massive fist and took aim for my ear.

My own fist caught him first in the belly, so hard it drove the wind from his lungs. He dropped to his knees then fell onto his side. I left him gasping for air on the kitchen floor.

From that night on, I slept in the kennel with the hounds. Months later when Madlen and Alec were finally wed, I travelled to Abergavenny with the wedding party.

* * *

As one of his many wedding gifts, Madlen's father gave the bride and groom three breeding pair, among the finest of his hounds, to seed the new kennel at Abergavenny. A few days before the wedding party set forth, the Duke had come down and chosen them himself, my father seething behind him as we walked through the runs, rotely intoning the words he had no choice but to say.

Yes, milord.

As you wish, milord.

The six hounds grew agitated upon our approach to Abergavenny, yapping as if in readiness for a hunt. Perhaps they sensed my own eagerness, the urgency in my gait as I strained for this first glimpse of my new home. It was early spring, the trees lush with pale green leaves. In the pastures, cows gorged on new grass. At long last, the wedding party rounded a bend and Castle Abergavenny came into view.

Though I hadn't known what to expect, the palace and its situation seemed to correspond with something already familiar to my mind, a deep-seated expectation or ideal I hadn't realized that I cherished. Not only larger in scale than the Duke's manor house but more graceful in its proportions, more in harmony with its site. High burnished turrets, plated in copper, raked the sky; a moat of glassy water reflected stately walls above. Though Madlen rode in the carriage ahead and I could not see her, I imagined a gleeful smile upon her face, a gust of triumph swelling her breast.

Queen Madlen now, first lady of the court, supreme above all others. From this day forward, she would abide in this lovely castle, preside with King Alec over banquets and balls, share his bed.

Again the unwanted image intruded.

Since the wedding night, the idea of their coupling had never been far from my thoughts, a kind of ongoing torment for me. His lips upon her mouth, hands on her flesh, the weight of his body against her. He would be a gentle lover, I knew, unlike Creven who had taken poor Elspeth by force. The urgent pictures in my mind excited and agonized me, an unfolding image-story that always ended the same way. Me in her place. In bed at night, my hand would unleash a wave of relief and pleasure that always, seconds later, brought self-loathing in its wake.

As we approached the castle, a groundskeeper came forth and guided me away from the wedding party toward the kennels, set on a newly cleared plot of land, with a view of distant turrets and battlements above the trees. The reddish-brown soil around the enclosures looked naked, almost raw; inside the kennel, I inhaled the scent of milled wood and fresh hay.

After releasing the hounds into the large pen, I brought water from the well (new masonry with a virgin bucket) and filled their trough. I saw to their feeding. As I was inspecting the storerooms and runs with approval, everything as it should, an old woman approached, wearing a white apron over bulky skirts, her hair bound up in a checkered kerchief. Wrinkles were etched deeply into her face but they spoke of age only and not bitterness.

Her name, she told me, was Brigid. "I'll take you now to the cottage."

Though Alec had never come back to finish that conversation, to ask me for more advice, he had obviously remembered what I'd told him. The cottage – *my* cottage – was set at a goodly distance from the kennels and separated from it by a barrier of dense evergreens. It, too, looked newly made, with yellow-blond thatch and shutters not yet weathered by the seasons. Inside, Brigid showed me the sitting room and bedchamber, the closet with fresh linens, the wood stove and washing basin.

"You can take your meals in the servants' hall," she said, "or I can bring them here instead if you like." I searched her face for signs of resentment – the extra work, carrying my supper pot down from the palace kitchens – but she didn't seem to care, one way or the other.

"Here, I think. For now."

I stood in the sitting room after she left and looked around me. One comfortable chair. A footstool. Tin coal scuttle by the fireplace. I fought back tears. A home of my own, yes, but the one chair only.

* * *

To fill out the King's pack, I scoured the countryside for suitable hounds, travelling from duchy to duchy on the excellent mount Alec had provided for me, dispensing gold coins from his purse. "Spare no expense," he had said, placing the leather pouch in my hands, his fingers grazing mine. I saw him rarely after that, once a fortnight or so when he visited the kennels to check on my progress. Eager to provide his bride with the hunting life she craved, he always asked the same question: "How much longer till the pack is ready?"

During those first few months, I saw Madlen only once – in the mid-distance, standing up in her stirrups at full gallop across the fields. I recognized Trevian, her favorite mount, a 17-hand gelding with a sorrel coat whose white mane caught the sunlight. In the dust behind her, Alec galloped in pursuit and was losing ground. On rides before their wedding, Madlen had always reined in and let Alec take the lead.

As summer waned and the hunting season approached, she and I began taking rides together. Madlen knew the hunt country back home as well as my father, better even than the Duke, but now she needed to map out Abergavenny. I'd already spent months getting to know the local foxes and their coverts, possible routes for the hunt, prevailing winds and how they might affect the scent hounds. Deference did not come naturally to Madlen but she allowed me to show it all to her. I pointed out the likely hazards, the stone walls and their stiles, a few steeply banked streams and ways to avoid them. After she'd learned all I had to teach her, she had no further use for me and I didn't see her for weeks.

Then in early November, two days before the first hunt, she came down to the kennels in her ordinary riding clothes and greeted me as if no time had passed since our last meeting. She didn't bother to use my name. She found me at feeding time, filling the troughs with raw meat.

"What about the whippers-in?" she asked, beginning in mid-conversation. "Do they understand what they're to do?" She watched with keen interest as the hounds jostled for position at the troughs and tore in. Despite her apparent calm, I sensed anxiety below the surface. Again and again she flexed the riding crop in her hands. It looked brittle, as if it might snap.

"I've done my best with the two stable boys," I told her, "but there's no substitute for experience. Young Hagan from your father's estate arrived last night – I assume you sent for him. He'll make a difference." I did not add: *You should have consulted me first.*

"And the hounds – how many couple will there be?"

"Seven and half, Your Majesty, no more." I emptied the last bucket of bloody flesh into the trough. "We'll have twice that many next year once we cub the pups, but they're too young and inexperienced now. They'll only cause trouble."

I cast a brief glance her way. She frowned with displeasure and said, more to herself than to me, "I suppose there's nothing I can do about it now."

When I returned with a full bucket of water from the well, she stood brooding in the same place. I caught her in profile. After so many years of observation, I had the lines and contours of her body by heart. There was an unfamiliar bulge at the belly, so slight that no one less familiar with her shape would have noticed.

Alec's child. I pictured it, the moment when he'd unleashed his seed inside her.

She turned and caught me staring at her waistline. I waited a few moments before slowly lifting my gaze to her face. I didn't need to say the words, *You are with child.* After a lifetime under my scrutiny, she took it for granted; she felt no surprise that I had noticed the change.

"Nature's nasty little trick," she said, scowling at the ground.

"In your condition, should you be riding to hounds? Is it safe?"

"You're not to speak of this to the other servants," she told me, ignoring my questions. "Do you understand?"

I am not one of the servants, I wanted to say. *I am the King's Huntsman.*

"As you wish, Your Majesty."

But surely the servants already knew. Madlen's chamber-maid must have seen that her monthly blood had stopped coming. The laundress would have read it in the unsullied sheets and underclothes.

"You've had your fitting, I presume," she said.

"Indeed I have." A tailor had come down to the cottage one day to take my measurements and returned a week later with clothes I was to wear as Master of the hunt. When I donned my scarlet coat and buff-colored breeches, tied the white stock around my neck and placed the black velvet cap on my head, I longed for a looking glass. Was mine a manly appearance, or did I seem like the imposter I'd always felt myself to be?

"You'll cut an imposing figure." She didn't mean it as a compliment. I was merely an asset, part of the impression she wanted to create.

I dropped my head to the side and said nothing.

"Do me proud," she added. It seemed an odd expression to use, one a mother might put to her child, but I knew what she meant. I could read it in her eyes, shining with a hungry sort of light.

Make them envy me.

* * *

I awarded Madlen the brush, of course. I didn't need to be told that she expected this particular honor. As Queen and sponsor of the hunt, she had a right to it, even without her bravado display of horsemanship, superior to every rider in the field (other than me). Spurring Trevian forward, she alone had followed me over the high wall beyond Ciaran Field. Most riders had taken a safer route, skirting the wall, and the few who'd braved it had lost their mounts. Madlen *deserved* the brush. Astride Trevian before the castle, she received the severed pads and tail from my hands with a smile of triumph.

Alec had held back for most of the hunt – I scarcely caught sight of him until we returned to the castle. Like most of the other men and even some of the women, he'd begun drinking early, well before the riders mounted and I winded the bugle. He kept his chalice fully charged right through the hunt breakfast, too, motioning for servants across the room whenever he'd emptied it. With a group of his friends, some in black coats and others wearing scarlet, he talked and laughed in a way that struck me as overly hearty.

It was my first time inside the castle's vast banquet hall, with its huge beams and long wooden tables, midday light streaming through high windows. I'd asked to be excused but

Madlen insisted that as Master, my attendance at the hunt breakfast was mandatory. I stayed for an hour or so, observing from my spot near a standing suit of armor, nearly as motionless as the hollow metallic form at my side. No one spoke to me. As I watched Alec drink and laugh, the impression that he was unhappy seeped into me. From time to time, he gazed across the room at his wife, thronged by men whose faces were lit up by wine and admiration.

Though I'd known and watched Madlen all her life, few opportunities had come my way to observe her behavior toward men other than her father and brother, or those of us lower in status and largely beneath her notice. I'd never seen her exert herself so forcefully to charm. She was but 17, in the full bloom of youthful beauty, and fully aware of it. She had singled out one of the men, a neighboring duke and close companion of the king, with red hair and a thrusting chin. Madlen's gaze did not waver from his face; she held her torso forward, fingers grazing his arm, listening as if rapt when he spoke, with one slender hand resting at the base of her long white neck. From time to time, she laughed in a musical way, seemingly charmed by his wit.

If I were that man, standing in his place, I would have believed that she was offering herself to me.

Across the room, Alec sometimes gazed toward his wife with a fixed, lifeless smile on his face. Then he would look away. As I watched him, my right hand began to rise, almost with a mind of its own, and settled high on my chest.

If Trevian's hooves had only clipped the wall at Ciaran Field, Madlen could easily have fallen and broken her neck. She might be dead now.

I met Brigid on my way back home after I finally broke free. As I travelled down the path toward my cottage, she came along in the opposite direction with a basket of linens propped on her hip. The soiled sheets from my bed. Laundry day.

"I hear your lady mazed the gentry with her wild riding." Brigid's voice, normally low and languid, sliced the air with high notes.

"The Queen does ride exceptionally well," I said, hesitating. I'd be be unwise to let my true feelings show; on the other hand, I could not have Brigid thinking of Madlen as *my* lady, scorning us together when she gossiped in the servants' hall. "Though sometimes she does seem more foolhardy than brave, it has to be said. I've often had to caution her."

My response seemed to satisfy Brigid. "As well you should, from what I hear. But the King will soon put a stop to such nonsense, I expect. Especially now."

So she already knew, and therefore all the other servants must know, of Madlen's condition. A possible heir to the kingdom was growing in her womb. The King and Queen couldn't keep such a secret for long, of course – not with servant-hands on their clothes and bed linens, ears pressed against locked doors, eyes inspecting the chamber pots before the contents were tossed out.

How much could one glean from my own bed sheets, there in the basket on Brigid's hip? Surely I didn't rise to that level of interest.

* * *

I began taking more of my meals in the servants' hall where my quiet ways provoked gentle teasing and my neutral response to their observations on the queen's behavior soon prompted the cooks, maids, and housemen to speak freely. To a one, they hated her. Feeling that she had nothing to gain from their favor, Madlen treated her servants with undisguised contempt, as barely sentient beings far far beneath her. She erred in judgment there. A devoted lady's maid may keep your secrets while an unhappy one will make sure your husband's valet knows all.

Alec soon learned of her secret assignations, the men who bedded her, and how quickly she tired of them. Not even the growing child within her womb could stop Madlen. Scarcely a year into their marriage, Alec had taken the full measure of her character and fallen into despair. With fascination and outrage, we discussed it in the servants' hall – how he'd given up his favorite old pursuits, riding and shooting, and replaced them with wine; how he'd taken on pounds and begun to lose his shape. No one blamed Alec for his debauched condition. Madlen was the canker in the wood, the source of a vicious rot that was spreading.

I saw her often during the hunt season, and well afterward, too, for she regularly required my company on horseback. Contrary to Brigid's prediction, Alec had not put a stop to her riding, though surely he had tried. She and I spoke little as we rode together side-by-side; I knew she did not care for me in the least. I was merely a fixture of her past, something to remind her of a childhood for which she did not pine, not precisely, but which preoccupied her all the same. An easier, less complicated time when endless gratification lay ahead in the unwritten future. Having a husband, even when he was a king, had turned out to be a bore. Blatant enmity from the ladies of court, though she had seduced their husbands and made them look like fools, was proving to be a bore. The burgeoning life within her was turning out to be a tedious, and physically uncomfortable, bore. Nothing satisfied her.

One night late in spring as I sat yawning in my chair, feet warming on the footstool before a lively fire, Madlen entered the cottage without knocking. I hadn't been expecting her to come – why would she? – but oddly enough, I felt no surprise as she came forward, cast an incurious glance about her and said, "So this is where you live." A bloated belly pushed out her dress. The child inside would soon come forth.

I should have stood up. After all, she was my queen. I should have offered her my chair.

"Is there something you require?" My question seemed bald, my tone just shy of insolence. "Your Majesty," I added, to soften the effect.

She laughed. She might not care how and why I felt the way I did, but she had no trouble reading me.

"Merely the pleasure of your company." I felt the sting of her mockery, though she must want something of me, to come so late in the day to my cottage. She once again took the measure of my sitting room. "Have you only the one chair?"

No choice now but to rise and make way. With hands on the chair arms for support, she awkwardly lowered herself into my place. So late in her term, she should have withdrawn into confinement. Her gravid shape in my home offended me.

"Now this is quite cozy," she said, in the same mocking tone. She gathered her shawl more closely about her shoulders. "Far superior to that nasty little lean-to on my father's estate. I used to wonder how you bore the stench."

"We had no choice," I pointed out. With no place to sit, I leaned against the mantle and felt heat lance my shins.

"No, I suppose not. Well, I must say that my husband has done well by you, Gereth. Very well indeed. But then, he's such a thoughtful man." Her contempt for Alec shone clear. "Who looks after you?" she asked, without real interest, "the cooking and the cleaning?"

"One of the old retainers comes down to clean. I take most of my meals in the servants' hall."

"You ought to have a wife. How old are you now?"

"Twenty-five, come my next birthday."

"Yes, high time you had a wife. What about that pretty downstairs maid, the one with the freckles? I've forgotten her name. She'd suit you nicely. I'm sure Alec would be happy to oblige you with a second chair."

Years ago on the Duke's estate, one of the chambermaids (made pregnant by a footman) had died in childbirth. It was not uncommon for a birthing mother such as Madlen to die.

"What do you want?"

Her sneer of offense (how dare I use that tone!) lasted only a moment. She sighed and leaned back in the chair. My chair.

"They all hate me," she said. "Not that I care, but it does grow tiresome. I realize that you hate me too, of course, only …" She struggled to finish her thought. "You know me. You've always known me."

A faint, unwelcome twinge of fellow feeling took hold. Madlen might be profoundly indifferent to other people, she might not long for love or true friendship, but she could nonetheless feel lonely. As I stood there by the fire and studied her face, unbearably lovely despite the added weight, I felt the force of her loneliness. Different from mine and yet not entirely so. The elaborate game she played – inciting masculine desire and admiration, humiliating the ladies of court – might distract her for a time, the way strong drink can make you forget your sorrows. Triumphing over the entire field in the foxhunt was a more potent brew. But the intoxication never lasted. Over time, the pleasures of winning had grown dim.

No worlds left to conquer. Lonely (or perhaps *alone* might be the word), she looked forward to nothing. She was only 18.

We said little after that and she didn't stay much longer. A few days later, two men from the castle brought down a second chair and matching footstool – larger and more deeply cushioned, upholstered in brocade with gold threads shot through it. A chair fit for a queen.

But even before her chair was in place, she came down to my cottage once again, to tell me about her magical looking glass and what she'd seen there.

* * *

She was waiting as I returned from the kennel at dusk. I found her inside my cottage, wrapped in full-length furs against the cold, standing before the coal fire that Brigid and I kept burning throughout these short winter days. She cast a dissatisfied glance down at the meager flames.

"That old woman, the one who looks after you – she left you something there on the table."

"My trousers," I said, needlessly. The castle seamstress had repaired a rent in the left leg, occasioned by a nail obtruding from one of the pasture fences.

As I came forward to tend the fire, she stepped away. "I've been so cold here, waiting." It hadn't occurred to Madlen that she herself might heap more coal onto the fire. She was the queen.

"I'm very sorry, Majesty. You must have been so *uncomfortable*."

I had found my tone with her, a compromise between necessary caution and the loathing that spread daily poison in my breast. It felt to me as if the irony, which she chose to ignore, brought her down and lessened the distance between us. Kneeling at the hearth, I placed lumps of coal from the scuttle onto the fire.

Had she come to unburden herself once again, to sigh over the ennui of her life, to rail against the ladies who hated her?

Standing before the fire with my back to her, I warmed myself. The coal gave off a vaguely dirty but not unpleasant smell, something akin to tobacco. I knew I ought to step aside and make way but I held my ground. The longer the silence went on, the deeper grew my sense of risk.

"Did I never tell you of the looking glass my father gave to me upon my 16th birthday?"

The odd and abrupt question put me instantly on guard, made me pay attention more closely. Madlen seemed strangely eager, excited even. She'd come searching for me, a mere servant, and actually waited for my return.

"No, Majesty. I know nothing of it."

Without preamble, she began telling me about her 16th birthday and the looking glass that had once belonged to her mother, and to her mother's mother before her. Madlen explained its magic, how the looking glass would answer any question you might ask provided you framed it correctly: the rhyming couplet, the obligatory first line. The reflecting surface would grow cloudy as the looking glass opened a window onto the answer. A still image might take shape – like a painting only more life-like; sometimes the image moved as if its subject were in actual motion. The looking glass could even make sounds – voices, laughter, cries of pain or grief.

Looking glass, looking glass on the wall
What torments Tierney most of all?

With a spiteful laugh, she told me how she had made use of it to thwart her rivals, the other young ladies of the gentry, bewitching their beaux until she could she read the suffering in their eyes. It helped to alleviate the boredom, she explained.

At the basin, I lathered my hands and scrubbed away the coal dust. I had no idea where Madlen's story was tending though it made me uneasy. As she paced before the spirited fire, a reddish glow made her fur cloak glisten. Her eyes seemed alight, too: avid, predatory, like those of a glorious prowling cat from some fabled place.

"Eventually the looking glass grew tiresome," she said. "In the end, it can do no more than answer questions, and how often do I need to be told that I am the fairest in the land? One doesn't require magic to perceive the obvious."

What, I wondered, did the looking glass show her when she asked that question? By way of answer, did it continue reflecting back her face without altering? Was that a true answer?

"How can you be certain it is telling you the truth?"

She ignored the question, as if I hadn't spoken.

"Other people are disappointingly dreary, as it turns out, even in private. Duke Ogilvy likes to be spanked when having congress with his kitchen maid. The same way, night after night. She must tell him he has been a naughty boy." She laughed with disdain. "I really don't understand people. Why should a spanking increase one's pleasure?"

I dried my hands with the towel and studied Madlen's face. She seemed to be talking more to herself now than to me.

"Last night, I felt so utterly weary of life that I did not know what to do with myself. Now that the birth is nigh, we have no guests, no banquets, no music. Whoever thought that being a queen would turn out to be so tedious." Still she paced, her gaze focused in the distance. "I began to ask the looking glass questions in order to while away the time. *For whom doth Lady Tamwyn care most of all?* I knew the answer to that one even before I asked it. Down the list I went, one after the other, all the lords and ladies of the court. And then, when it seemed I had no one's secrets left to expose, I thought of you. Imagine how desperately bored I must have felt to take an interest in a lowly huntsman."

I grew instantly still, my gaze downcast, the blood-pulse of danger thrumming in my ears.

"'Looking-glass, looking glass on the wall, for whom doth Gereth care most of all?' I thought the glass might show you in the forcing pen with one of the sheep, the way Lord Arvil enjoys himself. You seem to care for no one … at least not other people. I used to think we were alike in that way."

I could not look up. A trembling had taken hold of me, my indignation at the insult overwhelmed by fear. What if I should lose control of my bowels, right there before her?

"To my amazement, an image of my husband's face took shape in the glass. Gereth cares most of all for his king!" She hung fire. I felt like a mouse between her paws, the talons sheathed in restraint. "I knew right away this was no innocent sort of caring, though it had never before occurred to me that nature might shape a man that way, to desire another man." I felt her staring at me for long moments. When she finally continued, her tone of voice was factual, without scorn or loathing. "You are an abomination, Gareth. You understand that, do you not? An offense against the natural order of things. I thought nothing could ever surprise me so very much."

If I could believe her tone of voice, she did not feel about me the way I had always felt about myself. She sounded strangely, inexplicably pleased.

I mustered the courage to look at her. In Madlen's expression, I read my future. From this day forward, she could bend me to her will no matter what she asked. The risk of exposure would make me compliant. What took me longer to grasp was the relief she felt, to find another human being as deviant in his own way as she was from other people. It did not bring us any closer though in the end, each one of us felt less alone in the world.

The next day the new chair and footstool came down. Two chairs facing the fire, one abomination seated beside the other. Before she could make much use of it, the pains of labor took hold and the child at last was born.

* * *

To say that Madlen took no interest in motherhood would be to understate her indifference. Consigning little Elwyn to the care of wet nurse and nanny, she went back to her accustomed ways and never visited the nursery. Not once. Her lack of motherly feeling scandalized the court and deepened the contempt the servants felt for her. Over our evening meals, she was scorned as unnatural and even monstrous.

"Has your lady always been so unfeeling?" I was asked on more than one occasion. Madlen's new hold upon me made my answers even more cautious than before.

"Like many young ladies of her station, I believe, she was encouraged to think first of herself, to care little for the feelings of other people."

"But not to love your own child! An offense against nature, that's what she is!"

And so am I.

In the weeks after she gave birth, Madlen seemed bent on regaining her figure and resuming her daily rides. Within a month, she appeared as lithe and lovely as before. She had said it herself: one didn't need a magical looking glass to perceive that she was still the fairest of them all.

On occasion, we rode out together, mostly in silence though sometimes making desultory conversation about the hunt season, still months away. Once a fortnight, she came down to my cottage and unburdened herself. She sat in her chair before the fire, by turns angry and mirthful, recounting the idiocies of everyone she knew. No one escaped her scorn. She seemed to take special pleasure in mocking her husband – how he'd gone to seed, drank too much, cared for nothing now but cards.

"I suppose I shouldn't speak of him this way," she told me, more than once, with a malicious lilt in her voice. "Not to you, of all people. I keep forgetting."

"Your majesty is all kindness and consideration," I might say, or words to that effect, and she would laugh. My irony seemed to please her now. I no longer needed to disguise my true feelings.

As time went on, she took special exception to the way everyone – first the servants and then other members of the court – had begun referring to baby Elwyn as Snow White, as if she were some fairy tale princess rather than a real person. I never learned how the custom began though I assume it grew from observations upon her preternaturally beautiful skin, truly as pure as the driven snow. Never before had I seen such a flawless complexion, even more perfect than her mother's.

"She's a mewling puking brat like every other baby," Madlen insisted. "There's nothing special about her. Absolutely nothing. Even Alec has taken to calling her that ridiculous name." Though we never discussed it, I think she understood the contrast that was being drawn, white and black, as if all the goodness in the world had condensed in the shape of this innocent creature while all the evil resided in the queen. The more the world despised the mother, the more they adored the child.

When Snow White took her first steps and spoke her first words, courtiers and palace retainers alike discussed the events with keen interest. Her childish utterances never failed to charm. "Have you heard what she said the other day about the goslings?" they would ask, in the vast halls below and the cramped garrets above. "Adorable!" On Madlen's *plaint nights*, as I came to think of the hours she spent in my cottage, unburdening herself into my ear, she told me how tedious she found the endless repetitive conversations about her daughter.

"Why should a child's lisp make them laugh?" she once said. "What do these imbeciles find so amusing about a dwarf unable to speak clearly?"

"It is her innocence that charms them," I explained. "Her lack of guile. She is the embodiment of all that is pure and good."

She brooded upon the flames. "They do it to spite me. Everyone knows how it grates upon my nerves, to hear nothing but Snow-White-this and Snow-White-that, hour after tedious hour."

"Indeed, Majesty – they can have no other motive. Everything said and done has special reference to your nerves."

We laughed together in mutual dislike. On occasion, she could find brief humor in the way she made herself the sun, holding stars and planets in orbit around her. She also loathed me for my true vision.

"*You* should have been born her mother," Madlen sneered. "Motherhood would have suited you."

"No doubt. Much better than it suits you."

It was a wishful fancy I dare not indulge, for in that direction lay bitterness and despair. Envy, too. No matter the dragons a man might slay or countries he might conquer, he could not bring a child forth from his body and feed it with his breasts.

In truth, I doted upon Snow White, the true and natural heir to the man I loved, a man slowly climbing up from the depths of debauchery. As he grew into fatherhood, Alec was regaining his former self, though never again would he be as perfect and beautiful as before Madlen. He adored his daughter and this love was making him a better man. He gave up cards and drink. He spent less time on horseback and more hours in the nursery. With her tiny hand clasped in his own, he walked about the castle grounds, a beaming smile on his face and a kind word for everyone they met.

So little time did Snow White spend in her mother's company that for a long while, she believed herself to be Mrs. Duffy the nanny's child. So we were told in the servant's hall over many a meal when Mrs. Duffy came down to join us, unable to conceal her delight at the child's misapprehension.

"She called me 'mama' again today. Of course I corrected her but I don't think the wee thing comprehends."

After hearing the words "No, the *Queen* is your mother" a hundred times, Snow White must finally have understood. Before the coal fire in my cottage, fur-lined boots resting on the footstool, Madlen complained that her daughter had suddenly begun entering her bedchamber in the mornings and invading her privacy throughout the day.

"Why doesn't she confine herself to the nursery where she belongs?"

"You are her mother. She naturally craves your company."

Madlen scoffed at the idea. "I don't see why she wants a mother. I never had one."

As well as I knew the history – how the duchess Madlen's mother had succumbed to black despair following childbirth and hanged herself not long after – this knowledge always seemed to slip away. For reasons that eluded me, Madlen seemed entirely motherless, born of no one.

"Why does it irk you so?" I asked. "She's a sweet-tempered a child whose only aim is to please."

"That's precisely what I object to. I feel like she's making a study of me, trying to parse out what I want. And what I want most of all is to be left in peace."

While Snow White continued pursuing her mother, she must have understood well enough to stay silent when they were together. At banquets and affairs of state, she could be seen on the dais, seated at Madlen's feet, silent, nearly motionless, a smile of contentment upon her face. She looked like a tiny replica of the queen only more delicate, with hair an even deeper shade of raven, redder lips, and a complexion more pure. Madlen at last became inured to her presence.

* * *

At midsummer during his daughter's sixth year, Alec invited all the gentry for a feasting day, held out of doors on the greensward beyond the moat. Servants set up a long banquet table beneath a canopy, with linens and china carried out from the palace. There were games and races for the children and a servants' pavilion with food and drink for all. Jugglers and minstrels made for entertainment.

As part of the festivities, Alec had planned a surprise for his daughter – a cream-colored pony to be her very own. Before the feast itself commenced, as he and I had conspired, I led the pony forward on a rope, to the place where Snow White sat in contentment at her mother's feet. When she caught sight of it and understood that the pony was to be hers, she clapped her hands in delight.

"Now I'll be able to go out riding with my dearest mother!"

Madlen looked peevish.

Alec lifted Snow White onto the pony's back. She wept with joy, evoking gentle laughter from all the gentry. Turning her gaze toward me, she said, "And you Gereth must teach me to ride. I want no other master."

"I shall be honored," I choked out. She had granted my deepest wish.

I heard the portly Duke of Medullium, seated near the head of the table, say to his wife, "She'll grow to be a great beauty like her mother – there can be no doubt."

"Nay," answered the Duchess. "She'll surpass her in beauty – mark my words."

Madlen had heard, as the Duchess no doubt intended. A wince of malice flickered across her face. She gazed intently at Snow White, who was smiling brightly as Alec led her about on the pony. Then Madlen looked away, stretched her arms, and yawned.

* * *

It was on this feasting day that I also made the acquaintance of the dwarfs, for they too had been engaged to amuse us. Acrobats and tumblers had performed at Castle Abergavenny on prior occasions, eliciting cries of admiration from the audience with their nimble, quick-footed ways; these dwarfs (there were five of them, three men and two women) made mockery of such sport. Or perhaps it was their own deformity that they mocked. With stunted arms and legs, they assayed cartwheels that fell absurdly short of roundness. They tried to form a tower by clambering upon each other's shoulders only to collapse, again and again, stirring loud mirth from the spectators. As they ran about in confusion they continually collided one with the other, angrily shouting out reprimands and absurd childish names like Grumpy or Bashful, chiding each other for their clumsiness.

"You be a stupid oaf!" one said. "You be the idiot, not me!" said another. I wasn't sure whether their curious diction was part of the act or their normal speech pattern.

At the outset, I laughed along with the crowd but a vague discomfort soon began to gnaw at me. Freaks of nature – that's what they were, fit only to amuse those with more wholesome bodies. How, I wondered, could they endure such an existence? Perhaps they felt grateful merely to be alive: here in Abergavenny, with an enlightened king and a fairly tolerant populace, it was customary to drown an infant born with a deformity, or leave it in some remote place to be eaten by wild animals. The mothers of these dwarf acrobats must have spared their lives and made some provision for them.

That night when I visited them in their encampment within the forest, I learned that they lived together with other dwarfs in a remote colony, a cluster of cottages at the base of snow-capped mountains visible from Abergavenny on a clear day. From time to time, parents would abandon their misshapen babies outside the colony gates; the residents would adopt these children and rear them as their own, teaching them to mine for gold and other ore at the mountain roots and fashion it into metal wares for sale abroad. The population of the colony ebbed and flowed over time, increasing with a new arrival and diminishing when one of their number died.

In more challenging periods when the veins produced little or the dwarfs could not sell their wares, this acrobatic quintet would venture forth in search of custom. So they told me as I sat beside them round the encampment fire. They did not seem infected with bitterness, as I had expected. They had one another.

It seemed unimaginable, that there could be others like me elsewhere in the wide world. I envied these dwarfs, despite their deformity.

We sat cross-legged together round the fire as they devoured the evening meal – remnants from the king's feast held earlier that day beneath the white canopy. Each one of them, male and female alike, wore the same rough leather tunic and leggings, with a broad belt secured by a buckle of intricately worked silver. They all wore jewels, too – around their wrists, in their ears, on their fingers. I was aware of a faint unpleasant aroma from their bodies, both acrid and moldering, as if they had not bathed for long days.

The dwarfs did not especially welcome my company but they did not appear to resent it either. They answered my questions with terse replies and mostly ate in silence, plucking chunks of meat from their supper pots and shoving them into their mouths. The male dwarfs sported beards that glistened with grease in the firelight. As they ate, they used their strangely long tongues to lap up meat sauce from their fingers. I struggled to hide the disgust I felt and not let it show upon my face.

There did not seem to be a leader among them. The one they had called Sneezy during the earlier amusements, though reticent by Abergavenny standards, seemed the more talkative. He looked older, too, with a longer, whiter beard and sagging skin at the jowls. While entertaining the gentry earlier that day, he had again and again erupted in big comical sneezes that leveled his companions like a ball toppling lawn skittles, but around the fire that night, I never once heard him sneeze.

"Is that your true name?" I eventually asked him, another in my long list of questions.

"Nay," he said, his mouth over-charged with meat. "'Tis but a part of our performance." Unlike the other dwarfs, he didn't use the word "be" in every sentence.

"How then should I address you?"

"You may call me 'Milord,' if it please you," he said, and the other dwarfs broke into laughter, spewing bits of food into the fire. One wet chunk landed on my arm and I quickly brushed it away.

"Caleb," he finally said. "My name is Caleb."

"And are there any dwarf children?" I asked. Perhaps it was rude to go on interrogating them so directly, but in truth, I felt exceedingly curious.

"Nay, Master Huntsman. We are born fully formed, beards and all."

Again the dwarfs laughed. Though I felt ridiculed and excluded, I kept on.

"You've already said that many of you were abandoned there at the colony by your mothers, but are there no dwarf children born to you? Do you not … marry?" An image came unbidden to mind: copulating dwarf bodies, with arms so short they could not fully embrace one another. I fought down the urge to laugh.

"But rarely," Caleb said. As if he knew what had passed before my mind's eye, he glared at me now above his supper pot, across his sticky moist fingers. "Children are sometimes born to us, it is true. The ones shaped like us we keep and the ones like you we chop up and feed to our livestock." The others did not laugh.

My face burned hot with indignation, but as the seconds passed, the heat took on a different complexion. "I must beg your pardon," I said. "I have been impertinent." We sat in charged silence as the fire flickered and snapped.

"Because we are curiosities of nature," Caleb finally said, "small and powerless, we have no choice but to submit when a big person like you puts such questions to us." His anger had relented but little. The others had ceased eating. "But before sating your curiosity further, Master Huntsman, place yourself in our boots and imagine yourself an object of fascinated disgust. Do not protest – you can hide how you feel no better than others of your kind. Imagine yourself as Caleb the ridiculous dwarf then. Ugly. Misshapen. So absurd as to be scarcely human. Can you see it before your mind's eye? Now imagine big people staring at you with no regard for your privacy. Imagine them asking questions they would never put to one of their own kind." He glared at me and I have never felt so hated. "How might you feel were others to probe your most personal secrets, to force you to say what you do not want to say and to feel they have a right?"

I hung my head and said nothing.

"With no disrespect for your superior size and shape," he said, "I most humbly suggest that the time has come for you take your leave of us."

I spoke no further words, rose to my feet and left them. I had no way of knowing it then, but this would not be the last time that Caleb and I were to meet.

* * *

During my years on this earth, I have observed that there is a sameness to our daily routines that numbs us to the inevitability of change. Day after repetitive day, we rise from our beds, toil for long hours, eat and then sleep until the morning when we begin anew. We come to believe that our lives will always be thus, until something unexpected occurs and everything changes. At one time, I believed I would always suffer at my father's hand; then I learned I was to be Huntsman at Abergavenny.

Within the space of a few short weeks during my 39th year, my entire world collapsed. It began with an ache in my hands I had not before experienced. I awoke one morning to throbbing knuckles and a conviction that such pain would be a feature of my life to some degree from that day forward. All of a sudden it seemed – though time had been passing in its usual way, week after to week, month after month – I was no longer a young man.

A few days later, Alec succumbed to a vicious fever and passed away. One moment he was alive and healthy, riding out on horseback with his daughter, and the next he was gone. Like his other subjects, I visibly grieved during the day and spoke of his many virtues in the servants' hall at night. Alone in bed, I sobbed into my pillow and railed against life's injustice. My feelings for him had never changed. I had accepted that I must love him at a certain distance and that my desires could never be fulfilled. I had made peace with my existence: it would be enough to be near him. But then he died.

I might have grown inured even to this loss and settled back into my daily routines, utterly joyless now due to Alec's complete absence from them, but a change even more disruptive to my accustomed world was underway. I did not realize it at first, for even knowing Madlen as well as I did – better, surely, than any other living creature – my estimate of her ruthless nature fell short.

One afternoon while on a long walk through the woods, giving solitary voice to my grief, I espied a distant figure coming along the trail toward me. Hastily wiping away my tears,

I gathered myself together and prepared for the encounter. It was Snow White. I recognized her from afar, her size and shape as familiar to me as her mother's, though something about her seemed vaguely different. Gaze downcast, she hadn't yet noticed me. She was but 14 years old at the time, on the verge of womanhood.

As she came closer, I at last took in the change that had been wrought upon her. When she heard my footfall and looked up, only a few yards away, the shock must have been evident upon my features.

"Dearest child!" I cried. "What has happened to your beautiful hair?" It had been cropped short like a boy's, only more ragged. White spots showed through where whole clumps of hair had been uprooted. Long scratches marred her perfect skin, and on her arms were purple bruises in a pattern that could only have been written by angry fingertips digging in.

"I have behaved very badly." She, too, had been crying as she walked along the trail. I heard tear-remnants in her trembling voice. "I have been punished."

"But you are incapable of anything base or wicked! What can you have done to deserve such harsh treatment?" I wanted to put my arms around Snow White, to offer her comfort, but I feared she would not welcome it. "You must tell me."

She peered forlornly at my feet. "I do not know, but a child must have done something terribly wrong for a mother ..." Her chest heaved with a quivery breath. Tears sprouted at the corners of her eyes and spilled down her cheeks.

A sudden trembling took hold of me. "Your mother the queen did this to you? But why?"

"I begged her to tell me but she would not answer. I know it must have been something unforgivable for her to treat me this way. But I have searched my recollections in vain and can think of nothing."

"Dear girl, you cannot have done anything wrong. I am certain of it."

"But I *must* have done. There *has* to be a reason." She grew pensive for a moment, still peering at my feet. Then she looked up. "As I think about it now, I believe you are right. It is nothing I have done." She paused and looked unbearably sad. "It is *who I am* that offends her. This I have long felt but not wanted to acknowledge, not even to myself. That is the reason, the only possible explanation. I am very bad by nature, unworthy of a mother's love."

"What you say is false. You are goodness itself!"

She gave me a wan smile. "I am grateful to you for saying so though we both know it cannot be true."

"Your mother is an evil woman with an unfeeling heart."

"You must not say such things," she told me, her face contracting in a sudden frown. "It pains me more than you can imagine. I will leave you now." She moved away along the trail. Rage mingled with pity as I watched her fade into the distance.

* * *

Madlen paid a visit to my cottage that night, her first since Alec's death. I would have barred her entry, but as ever, she opened the door without knocking and walked directly in. Taking her accustomed chair before the fire, she raised her boots onto the footstool. In my own chair beside her, I glared at the flames. I was determined not to break the silence. Turning my thoughts inward, I imagined myself to be still alone.

I could not sustain the pretense. As a magnet attracts iron, so she drew my attention in despite of myself. It seemed I had no choice but to study her face, to admire her perfect features, to feel again how gladly I would have exchanged places with her though I knew her to be a monster.

Blinded by my hatred, it took me long moments to recognize that Madlen was deeply unhappy. She did not mourn for Alec, I knew; genuine grief for any other being was beyond her. But the longer I looked, the more miserable she seemed: skin bunched between her brows, mouth turned downward as she squinted at the fire. For the first time, I noticed a lacery of fine lines at the edges of her eyes. Madlen had always struck me as ageless, forever young, though of course it could not be so.

The glee swelling my heart would not be contained. It burst forth in laughter as all at once I understood why Madlen had savaged her own daughter. The looking glass had at last changed its answer.

"You are no longer the fairest of them all!" I cried in delight.

She did not acknowledge my joy and addressed herself to the fact only. "Even now, with hair despoiled and scratches on her face, it shows her as she appeared before, every time, no matter how I frame the question. Sometimes I think I must shatter the glass but that would be an even worse torment, not to know."

"We've both grown older," I said. The pain in my hands, the onset of middle age, and the approach of death all seemed more bearable with the knowledge that I would be taking Madlen with me to the grave.

"'Tis unfair! I will not accept it!" So enraged did she feel that she could not remain seated. Balling her fists and stamping, she seemed beset by some terrible demon. She began pacing about the room, talking more to herself than to me. "What cruel trick of the universe makes it so, that our bodies must give birth to those who will one day surpass us in beauty? They steal our youth and usurp our rightful place. How can it be thus? It shall not be so!"

Few moments in my life have given me such pleasure, to bear witness as Madlen railed against the passage of time. "I am afraid, Majesty, that you have but little choice in the matter."

"No!" she shrieked. "I will not have it!"

Again I laughed. "Rage as you might, it makes no alteration. Time will have its way."

She ceased pacing and grew still. She peered into the distance, as if concocting some desperate scheme to stem the flow of sands through her private hourglass. Then she turned her gaze upon me.

"You must slay her. Nothing less will answer."

"Now you have taken leave of your senses," I said. My mirth was turning scornful.

"I command you to slay her. It matters not how you do it. And it won't prove too difficult. She's simple. She cares for you. Take her riding into the forest and slit her throat."

I gazed at her in disgust. Never was there woman so monstrous, so entirely unnatural.

"You would sacrifice your daughter so that you could once again be the fairest of them all?"

"Or I shall go mad!"

"Even were I to do something so unthinkable, it could not last. You must know that. You will, you *must* grow old and ugly."

"Today alone matters." As I studied her now, she seemed truly crazed. "You must do it at once. Tomorrow and no later. Or I shall go mad," she repeated.

"You are already mad. Of course I will not do your bidding.

"You will," she insisted, hanging fire for one moment. "Or I will tell."

She did not need to explain. If I did not agree to slay Snow White, Madlen would gather the gentry round her looking glass, the servants too, and ask her favorite question. *For whom doth Gereth care most of all?*

"He's dead," I said in weak protest.

"Did your love die along with him?" she asked. "The mirror still answers in the same way." My scornful mirth was on the wane and hers growing. Still seated in my chair, I felt her menace. She seemed to be absorbing the fire's heat and expanding in size.

"I could say I loved my king." In my own ears, I sounded weak.

"Perhaps. They might even believe you. But I have thought of a much better question." She smiled down at me in triumph. "Looking glass, looking glass, on the wall, what doth Gereth crave most of all?" She laughed. "I've already asked it. I've seen the answer." I felt myself wither beneath her smirk of contempt.

That degrading position, so exciting in the darkness of my bed, with Alec coming at me from behind. The gathered gentry and all the servants watching.

"They might hang you. Or draw and quarter you. Perhaps they would stone you to death or burn you like a faggot of wood."

I could not shake the image, ghostly Alec possessing me while the eyes of the kingdom looked on aghast. I would not survive, even if they chose not to kill me.

"You cannot escape this choice. Which is it to be, your life or hers?"

A third option came to mind. I could unleash my hands and let them do what they so desperately longed to do – close around her throat and choke the life from her body.

Or I could run. I could vanish from Abergavenny during the middle of the night, never to return. It might be a solution for me, but I knew Madlen would soon find someone else to do her bidding. In her desperation, she might even undertake the chore herself.

At that moment, with firelight glinting in her eyes, tall and slender and strong, she looked capable of anything.

What other choice did I have?

Memory is so very curious a thing, bringing forth the past unbidden at the most unlikely moments. Why should I have re-called, in my agony of distress, the image of short bodies cop-ulating that had taken shape within my mind, years ago during my interrogation of Caleb the dwarf? Perhaps it was the idea of spectators intruding on one's most private moments that brought us together, the dwarf and me.

The plan unfolded all at once. I would appear to do the Queen's bidding and take Snow White with me into the forest.

We would fly to the colony at the base of those distant mountains and there take shelter. Beyond that, I could not see.

PART II
THE DWARF

*F*or precise reasons now lost in the forgotten history of the dwarfs, the leader of our colony has always been referred to as "Mother," regardless of his or her anatomical gender. Given how most of us came to live here – abandoned by parents who couldn't quite face drowning us, as was and I believe still is common practice when dwarf babies are born – it's not so hard to imagine those reasons. Everyone needs a mother.

Though Mother I have been for nearly a decade, I am a male dwarf, 47 years of age, formerly known as Giddeus prior to my elevation. I cannot say what name my birth mother gave to me, or if indeed she bothered to supply me with one. She left me outside the colony gates when I was weeks old, wrapped in a thin blanket to which she had pinned a long rambling note that justified her actions. Throughout the note, she referred to me merely as "it."

Snow White and the huntsman came to our colony in the sixth year of my tenure and as it happened, I was present when they arrived at the iron gates, the sole point of entry within the perimeter wall that protects us. Every day after visiting my private herb garden, I make an inspection tour of the colony grounds – around the two long dormitory buildings, past the dining hall, and terminating at those gates in time for their closing. I prefer to supervise this procedure, as I do not trust the sentries to apply the secondary chains and locks I have seen fit to introduce.

On that particular day (chill and cloudy as I recall, though four years have since passed), I approached the gatehouse where Edmyg was standing watch and found him in conversation with two strangers on horseback – Big People, as we call them – a middle-aged man and young girl, both arrayed in gray cloaks stained and dusty from their travels. Beyond them massed the thick dark trees of Lagavulin Wood.

On his feet beneath them, Edmyg looked very small in comparison. No doubt he had once again fallen asleep during his watch for he had that blear-eyed look of the recently awakened. The side straps on his leather jerkin were unbuckled and the laces on his boots untied. If his belt had been cinched any looser, his trousers would have fallen around his ankles. All this I took in with my usual acuity of observation, feeling the sting of shame, that he should appear thus to these strangers, that their first impression of dwarfdom should arise from such a slovenly specimen.

At my approach, Edmyg stopped in mid-sentence and gestured toward me with his thumb. "This here be Mother," he told the strangers. "You be needing to ask his permission."

I deemed it the wrong time to correct Edmyg's grammar and made a mental note to do so later. Since my elevation to Motherhood, I have taken it upon myself to improve how the common dwarf speaks and in particular to eradicate this non-conjugation of verbs and other oddities of diction that no doubt make us quaint to outsiders. I sadly admit that I have had but little success.

I detected a glint of mirth in the man's eye, no doubt because Edmyg had called me Mother.

"We have journeyed a very long way," the man said, looking down upon me from astride his horse. "Night is at hand and we've asked your guard here if you might give us lodging. We don't have much gold but we will gladly pay for your hospitality."

My instinct was to turn them away. I did not like the look of the man, who initially struck me as crafty, quite possibly dangerous, and not merely because of his size. The extremely pretty girl seemed harmless enough but something in her air offended me. I did not like the way Edmyg stared up at her as if bewitched.

"Please, Mother," she said with an ingratiating smile. We've traveled a great distance since morning and we're very tired. We'd be forever grateful if you'd give us shelter." Though she had adopted the correct form of address, calling me by my title, I did not trust her. No doubt she was merely attempting to curry favor.

"Might I know your names?" I asked.

"I am Gereth," the man told me, "and my companion here is named Elwyn, though more often, those who know her well call her Snow White."

It seemed uncanny, that of all the Big People in the wide world, one whose name I had actually heard before should have arrived at our gates. Snow White is not a name one easily forgets.

"You may enter," I said, with as much gravity as I could muster. I did not stammer, as I sometimes do in emotionally fraught moments. "We will share our evening meal with you but beyond that, I cannot promise."

"We thank you most gratefully," said the man. They urged their horses forward; after they had passed through, Edmyg closed and barred the gates behind them. I had to remind him for the millionth time about the additional locks and chains.

* * *

Years earlier during a lean period, Caleb and the four other acrobats had ventured forth from our colony, returning with badly needed coin as well as tales of Abergavenny, of an overly inquisitive visitor to their encampment, and a princess whose complexion was as pure as virgin snow. At the time, I did not lend much credence to Caleb's description of Snow White as he has an unfortunate tendency to exaggerate about which I have had to caution him on many occasions.

As for Caleb's description of Snow White, however, I must acknowledge that in this rare instance, he did not err. Having spent my entire life here at the colony, I have encountered few

Big People and even fewer who strike me as physically attractive, but one does not need vast experience to recognize profound beauty when one sees it. The more time I spent in Snow White's company, the more diminished I felt, as if her physical perfection made me less the man I have always felt myself to be. From nearly the first moment, I disliked her.

The night of their arrival, we all gathered in the large hall at the center of our colony where we take our meals. Constructed to suit dwarf proportions, the ceiling proved too low for the huntsman, and even for Snow White, who struck me as uncommonly tall for her age. Because they could not stand fully upright or sit comfortably at the benches flanking the two long tables, Gereth and Snow White sat on the floor near the hearth where an immense fire was blazing, he cross-legged and she with her legs demurely drawn up beneath her.

I could not help but wonder whether the fire seemed large by dwarf standards only, and might leave our visitors unimpressed. Body smells I took for granted, a background part of what I considered home, now made my nose twitch. Would the Big People find it stale or salty? What did they make of the modest meal we served them, roast fowl and plain boiled potatoes, brought out as always in gleaming bowls wrought by our metal smiths? Even a Big Person would have to acknowledge the superiority of our craftwork – of this I am certain, for we have sold many pieces abroad, to lords and dukes and even to kings.

In my carved wooden chair at the head of one table, with the other dwarfs seated on benches, I listened as Gereth relayed his account of Snow White's unnatural mother, a beautiful queen who had ordered that she be put to death. As might have been expected, a story featuring a woman bent on murdering her own child held special power for an audience that might easily have suffered the same fate, though not of course as a result of maternal envy. For most of the dwarfs, Snow White at once became a romantic figure from a storybook tale. I am immune to this kind of simplistic and sentimental appeal, of course. The misfortune of having suffered at the hands of an envious mother does not, in and of itself, qualify one as a heroine.

Snow White's captivating effect on the dwarfs was all too clear. The men and women alike kept glancing her way, each one eager for her attention, so solicitous of her needs they paid little heed to their own.

"Please, Snow White – take my portion. It be the most tender breast meat."

"I be not hungry, Snow White – would you care for my potatoes?"

"Your flagon be empty, Snow White – let me run fill it for you."

Their fawning behavior sickened me. They struck me as too utterly simple, under the spell of a pretty face and so smitten they could not think for themselves or attend closely to the man's tale. By nature credulous and openhearted, the common dwarf is easily deceived, but as Gareth continued, I felt my own misgivings grow sharper by the minute.

"Why not simply refuse?" I finally asked. "Though she was your queen and able to command you, surely she could not force you to commit such a heinous crime."

Along the table, the other dwarfs seemed startled by my question, as if skepticism were alien to their nature. We were 39 in number during this period – 22 females and 17 males, including myself.

"Indeed she could," said Gereth. "I have known her all my life. Had I remained in Abergavenny and refused her, I would soon have been a dead man." He had averted his eyes and was peering intently into the flames. My intuition into hidden motives and emotions, honed over the years of my leadership, told me that here was a man with a secret.

"You have said less than you might on this subject," I told him. "I invite you to unburden your heart and be candid with us."

The man shook his head. "I beg you not to press me further on this question. She had it within her power to coerce me. There was no alternative but to take flight."

"Though you might have gone alone," I pointed out. A few of the less dull-witted dwarfs had followed my train of thought and were nodding along the table. The others looked muddled.

"I knew the queen would only have found someone else to do her bidding."

"But why should you have taken such a dangerous course of action, disobeying your queen and taking flight with her daughter? I cannot understand your reasons."

His visage clouded; he shot a quick glance in Snow White's direction. "Do I need to speak them? She is but a child."

"Yes, but not *your* child."

Gereth lowered his gaze and once again I perceived his guilt. "Perhaps not," he said, "but I have always felt a special attachment to her, almost … almost as if she were my own."

I felt the presence of some unspoken truth behind his words. Perhaps he had designs of an unwholesome nature. Snow White was indeed a child but would remain so for only a few months longer. Already a spark of vitality seemed alight within her, ready to burst forth into the flames of womanhood. I studied her face to ascertain what she made of this huntsman who had saved her. How did she feel, knowing that her mother the queen wished her dead? My own mother, though she had abandoned me, had at least hoped I would survive.

Snow White gazed upon Gereth with an adoring light in her eyes. To the credulous, she no doubt appeared entirely convincing: a lovely young girl filled with gratitude for the man who had saved her.

Caleb, who seemed to take a proprietary interest in Snow White simply because he had met her years before I did, suddenly spoke up. "The child is fairly fainting with exhaustion," he said. "Are we so ungenerous that we welcome these weary travelers into our abode only to interrogate them as if they were criminals? Can't these questions wait for morning?"

While I felt his words as a challenge to my authority, I could not help but notice how well he expressed himself. The other dwarfs made noises of agreement and I had to silence them with my customary glare of disapproval. For my part, I could detect no special signs of fatigue in the girl.

"Are we to house them, then?" I replied. "What d-do we truly know of these strangers, and why should we make ourselves vulnerable by opening our doors? We m-m-might make an enemy of this d-dangerous queen." I felt my face go hot with shame though by no other sign did I acknowledge awareness of my stammer.

"Please give us shelter, I beg of you," Gereth said, reaching out for Snow White's hand. "We will take our leave tomorrow if we must but tonight we can go no further."

I felt the other dwarfs awaiting my decree. I focused all my energy on suppressing my stammer, briefly closing my eyes and attempting to release the tightness in my jaws and throat.

"Never in our long history have we invited a Big Person to remain with us overnight," I told them, though strictly speaking – as I had read in the Colony Annals – this was untrue. "Are we to break with tradition now for these people, complete strangers, however affecting their tale?"

"Ay!" came a chorus of voices.

The women seemed especially moved by Gereth's account. To my knowledge, all female dwarfs are barren, but they nonetheless possess strong maternal instincts, and so their hearts went out to Snow White. Over the years, I have learned to recognize when an irrational force is at work that not even my native authority can overcome. I bowed to the inevitable, at least for the moment, though my intuition told me I was making a mistake.

"S-so be it," I proclaimed. "We will meet again and d-discuss this further over the morning meal. The girl will sleep in the women's d-dormitory and I will make a bed for Gereth in my own quarters."

And so it was that Snow White came to abide with us, and the huntsman, too, though he for a much shorter period of time.

* * *

Since coming to reside at the Mother's Cottage upon my elevation, I have taken great pride in its high ceiling and generous size, in the views of wood and mountain from its windows. In truth, my lifelong desire to live there had fueled the vigorous campaign I waged against Caleb during the Choosing, after our last had Mother died, and in the end I was forced to make some unorthodox promises in order to win over the undecided voters.

It is a lovely home, superior to all other structures within the colony, but Gereth's presence there made the one large room seem small and cramped. He was just able to stand without stooping. I had no bed to offer him, as a generous host should have done. Gathering a few cushions normally stacked near the hearth, I assembled a makeshift pallet and offered him blankets too short to cover the full length of his body. As it was entirely too small and thin to be of use, I did not offer him the blanket in which my birth mother had wrapped me. It remained within the ornate silver box atop the mantle where I have always kept it.

Normally I would have changed into my nightshirt before retiring, but to display my nakedness before him was unthinkable. Like Gereth, I slept in my unsanitary undergarments. Neither of us fell quickly asleep. In the waning light of the fire, I could see him tossing and turning on his pallet, continually adjusting the blankets to cover his exceptionally large feet.

"You are awake, dwarf?" he finally said.

For some reason, I did not take umbrage at his rude form of address. To this Big Person, "Mother" I could not be, of course. "My name is Giddeus," I told him.

"Then Giddeus, I will acknowledge now what you so clearly perceived – there is more to my story than I have allowed. If sleep eludes you as well, I will tell it in full if you like. It is a long tale but it may help us to pass this tedious time."

I invited him to proceed and thereby learned how he had grown up alongside the Queen, moving with her to Abergavenny when she married, to take charge of new kennels there and to supervise the hunting of foxes. I believe my continual interruptions may have irritated him, for I had never before heard of foxhunting as a sport and probed deeply into this subject. I thereby learned the meaning of many new words such as *covert* and *cubbing*. I have always taken a special pleasure in the enlargement of my vocabulary.

I derived a curious comfort from hearing this Big Person's tale. Wrapped in my blankets, I felt entirely safe, which is not my usual experience of darkness during the small hours. I am an indifferent sleeper and often troubled by childish visions of dangerous animals prowling at the colony perimeter. I felt sure that with this Big Person at hand, no predator would manage to break into my cottage and devour me. I found his deep tone of voice quite soothing.

Gereth also told me of a magical looking glass in the queen's possession. He conveyed his deepest fear, that she would use it to determine their location and send riders after them – that a life of continual exile, forever in flight, was to be his fate. I imagined him pursued like one of the foxes in the hunts he had described, driven "to ground," as he put it and eventually torn to pieces by the dogs. Some deeper sense of fear and alienation, as if he had always felt himself to be a hated outsider, lay on the underside of his words though I didn't understand it.

At the end of his tale, Gereth asked for my advice. "Where can I go?" he pleaded. The fire had died out and I could barely discern his shape in the darkness. "Where is a man like me to find shelter?" I noted that he spoke in the singular and not the plural.

I had no idea what to tell him. Searching my memory for the tales I had heard from Caleb and other dwarfs who carried our wares to market, I spoke of the amazing diversity to be found abroad. Men took to ships upon the ocean, I had heard tell, and perhaps he could find passage to a distant, safer land. Or he might take refuge within a leper's colony, where no one would willingly pursue him.

I felt the poverty of my guidance but it seemed important that he respect my wisdom. Wracking my brain, I even mentioned a fabled city – Sudom or Shadom or some such, rumored to lie near the southern deserts – where the sexes copulated each with their own kind. Unable to conceal my disgust at the thought, I said, "Surely no one would follow you there."

We both fell asleep not long after, though before slipping away I thought I could hear Gereth weeping. In the morning, he was gone.

* * *

The note he left behind on my small desk was folded, one crease along the middle, and though he had written "For Elwyn" on the outside, I felt no scruple in reading it. After all, he had made use of my paper and quill pen without asking leave. In any event, it contained nothing especially private or personal. *Forgive me* was all he wrote, in a remarkably fine hand. He had signed it with a single *G*.

When we gathered in the dining hall for our morning meal, I gave the note to Snow White straight away. "He has abandoned you," I told her, thinking it best not to soften the blow. It couldn't have taken more than a second to read those two words, but she kept her gaze fixed upon the paper. Her lower lip began to tremble and her eyes filled with tears. Then she refolded the note and slipped it into the pocket her apron.

"I hope now he will find his heart's desire," she said. "He has been suffering for a very long time."

All around her, my credulous dwarfs murmured with pity and admiration, moved by her show of forgiveness.

Gereth's departure must have wounded Snow White but she gave little sign of it during the next few days. She seemed remarkably cheerful as she settled in and adapted to our routines, serving as scullery maid in the kitchen, weeding in the vegetable garden, plying her needle to mend tears in our worn clothes. If her behavior were an accurate guide to her feelings, she wanted nothing more than to be of use to others. Experience has taught me that no one is truly selfless, however.

Without further discussion after that first night, the question of whether to shelter Snow White had been answered. Taking pity on her friendless plight, my fellow dwarfs embraced her, and I knew better than to argue my own preferred course of action. While I may recognize that Big and Little People have virtually nothing in common and do not belong together, the others did not see it. How could I suggest we shut her out and leave her exposed to the elements, which would of course have made her easy prey for the predators at large in Lagavulin Wood?

On the third or fourth day of her stay, as I was passing through the kitchens, I stopped at the work table to correct Trevina, who was chopping off the darker green stems from spring onions and setting them apart from the whites. Trevina normally wore a sour look when on her feet before the chopping board, the corners of her mouth downturned in a way that seemed to exaggerate the hook in her nose. Today, she looked surprisingly eager, almost happy. She was actually whistling a light-hearted tune.

"You know we make use of the *entire* onion in our cooking," I told her. "We mustn't waste the greens."

"We be not wasting them," Trevina said. "Snow White say add them to our broth to make it more full of flavor. She say that be done by the cooks in her father's castle."

I stifled my irritation and moved away.

From that point on, it seemed I heard nothing but "Snow White be saying this" and "Snow White be saying that," irritating for both the bad grammar and the fatuous tone in which the words were spoken. My fellow dwarfs took childish delight in her ways and words; no matter what she said, they found it worth repeating. Due to my depth of knowledge concerning native herbs and plants, they had formerly consulted me about the healing of their wounds; now, they turned to Snow White for even the smallest of cuts. I believe some of them even injured themselves on purpose in order to receive her ministrations.

I watched her once while she tended to a scrape on Caleb's elbow. As she washed the bloody spot clean, she cooed and soothed him in an overly solicitous tone of voice, just the opposite of what Caleb truly needed. Due to my superior age and wisdom, I know that such softness tends only to encourage self-pity. Under my guidance, an injured dwarf would immediately go back to work, rather than taking rest as Snow White advised.

As time wore on, her presence at the Colony became increasingly irksome to me. Her influence upon the other dwarfs was rapidly transforming them into a bunch of indolent children, eager to dance and tell stories after the evening meal instead of returning to their dormitories for needed sleep. Because Snow White possessed a singing voice of surpassing beauty – I freely acknowledge it – they would listen to her as if transfixed, begging for one song after another until she grew tired. I of course did not enter into such entertainments but instead retired to my cottage at an early hour as was my wont.

Unlike the others, I recognized that her behavior was calculating, though I could not see to what end it tended. Even Caleb, normally more astute than the others, was taken in. Snow White badly wanted our admiration, this much I understood, and she had an uncanny knack for knowing just what to say or do in order to evoke it. No doubt she would one day use her influence in order to get something she wanted from us – precious stones from the mines or aid of one kind or another against her mother the Queen. She might simply have enjoyed the exercise of her power, an all too common vice among Big People, as I have heard.

Her presence at the colony at last became intolerable when she tried to work her influence upon *me*. One day while I was kneeling in my private herb garden, pulling weeds and lost in thought, I grew conscious of her glossy black boots in the dirt beside me. Though showing their wear, the boots were handsomely made, of finely tooled leather. The boots of a princess.

I felt quite certain I had closed the gate behind me when I entered; how had Snow White managed to open it without my hearing the rusty plaint of its hinges?

"Is there something you want?" I asked, standing up and brushing the soil from my trouser knees.

"Only to ask you a question," she said. "If it's not too much trouble."

"What is it then?"

Her delicate pale features were carefully arranged to convey meek submission. I could not bear to look at her face for more than a few seconds: arching my neck to gaze upward ignited the joint and back pain that had long plagued me.

"Caleb insisted that you were the one to ask. I was wondering if you could tell me about these mushrooms I found in the woods, whether it be safe to eat them."

She reached into the front pocket of her apron and, as if in offering, extended her cupped hands toward me. Several whitecapped mushrooms with long stems lay across her palms. I felt suddenly aware of my own hands, my short stubby fingers, filthy from the soil in which I had been working.

"Do you recognize them? Caleb said your knowledge of plant lore runs deep. I'm hoping you can tell me about them."

While I may be prone to a certain degree of vanity where my intellect and store of knowledge are concerned, I am not susceptible to flattery, especially when it is so plainly calculating. The thought briefly crossed my mind – *lie to her*. After all, the death cap mushroom closely resembles several edible varieties. Once she was dead, I could have told the others I'd made an honest mistake.

But would they believe me?

"They are highly lethal," I said. "If consumed, even one of those mushrooms would be enough to kill you."

With a sudden look of horror, she cast them away and jumped back.

I laughed at her. "You're at no serious risk ... though I advise you to wash your hands before eating."

I turned away, indicating that the conversation had drawn to a close. I dropped to the ground and began tending once again to the plants. My back and knees ached badly. I remembered the tincture I'd made from last year's belladonna crop; I would use it later that night to ease my pain.

No sounds of her retreat came to me. I focused with special intensity on the leaves, pulling off and discarding the yellowed ones. No doubt I appeared deeply absorbed in tending those plants.

"I don't understand what you want from me," she finally said.

"Want from you? Why should I want anything from you?"

"What can I do to earn your trust? The others here, they all accept me. They like me to do for them."

"And I do not. Pray save yourself the trouble and leave me in peace." Still I remained focused on my plants. I wished her a thousand miles away.

"Why do you hate me?" The baldness of the question set me back, made me catch my breath. I could simply ignore her. Or then again, perhaps the time had come to be more forthright.

"You don't belong here. We were better off before you came."

"How were you better off?" she asked. "I don't understand what harm I do."

I rested my hands upon my knees and collected my thoughts before speaking. When I finally looked up at Snow White, she appeared to be trembling, with fear or rage I could not say.

"You have unsettled our habits and routines. We were happy before. Now the others are discontented with our former life."

"They were not happy – you only say that because you want to believe it. They have talked to me about what it was like before I came, the heartless way you treated them. All those rules!"

This was more than I could bear – the thought that my own dwarfs had confided in a Big Person, possibly spoken ill of me to an outsider. I deeply regretted telling her the truth about those mushrooms.

What *had* the others said to her about me?

"I am their M-mother," I stammered out. "I know what is best for them. B-b-better than you."

I could not look at her now. I felt her tall shape looming over me.

She made a soft sound like laughter. Was she mocking me?

"I can't help it if they prefer me to you. It is not my fault."

And then she was gone, the rusty hinges of the gate squealing as it slammed shut.

* * *

That evening as I was making my customary tour of the grounds, turning over various schemes in my mind for disposing of Snow White, I came upon Edmyg and an old hag at the gatehouse – a hunch-backed Big Person with knotty gray hair. In tattered rags, she leaned upon a walking stick with one hand and clutched a large shiny apple in the other. As I drew closer, however, I could see that the hair upon her head was false, not truly her own. Though she had smeared it with dirt, her skin was youthful still, without wrinkle or blemish.

Edmyg, simpleton that he was, did not detect the subterfuge. "It be a gift for Snow White," he told me as I came up. "So kind! She be wanting to give it to her directly."

The pretend old woman kept her head bowed, peering up at me through the scraggly strands of her hair. Though I had never seen her before, I instantly gleaned the woman's true identity. I understood how the apple figured into her plan.

"I'll deal with this myself, Edmyg," I told him. "You may go now – I'll see to the locking up. And cinch your belt before you trip and fall on your trousers! How many times must I tell you?"

After he had gone, I decided to speak plainly though I felt the danger.

"Your d-daughter will recognize you at once, y-y-your highness. If you wish to p-poison her, you'll need more cunning."

For a few moments, the Queen remained hunched over, her gaze averted. She let out a hiss of frustration, then abruptly stood up and glared at me with eyes opened wide. The muscles in her right cheek twitched in a way that made her seem deranged.

"You have a name, I suppose," she said.

I could not help but admire her tone of distilled contempt, the sense of superiority it conveyed. If I were to tell her my honorary name, no doubt she would have mocked me with a sneer or even laughed at me.

"I am called G-Giddeus. I am the head of this colony and at your s-s-service."

She looked me up and down. "You are very small, G-G-Gideous. Ugly, too."

"And you are exceedingly beautiful," I said. "More beautiful even than Snow White, no matter what the looking glass may tell you."

She dragged the wig from her head and thrust angry fingers into her actual hair, black and lustrous.

"How is it that you know about my looking glass?"

"Gereth your huntsman told me when they first arrived. He brought Snow White here."

She pounded her walking stick into the ground. "Where is he now? I'll have his head!"

"He d-did not stay with us long. He fled in the dark of night for parts unknown. S-several weeks ago."

"I will find him," she said in a calmer tone. "I will hunt him down wherever he has gone." For long moments, she gazed off into the distance. "But first …" she finally whispered. She had forgotten all about me.

"But first we must deal with your daughter."

My words penetrated very slowly. Eventually, she rotated her long neck and peered down at me, less disdainful than before but fully regal, utterly and admirably superior.

"We?"

An eager trembling took hold of my body. "I may be able to help. Tell me – what poison did you use?"

She hesitated then gave me her answer.

"I have a better one," I said.

* * *

Beautiful the Queen might be, but strategic planning was clearly beyond her. She had devised this absurd scheme – an easy-to-penetrate disguise and the offer of a poisoned apple – without perceiving how likely it was to fail. Snow White obviously knew that her mother wished her dead and would therefore view any gift from a stranger with suspicion. If our plot were to succeed, we'd first have to place her off guard.

As the Queen and I paced together beyond the gates, I unfolded a new and superior plan. I doubt she fully understood me, but through the force of my intellect, I at last gained her trust. She agreed to come back a week later with another present, this one a comb for Snow White's hair, to be laced with a different poison I would conceal outside the gates for her.

After the Queen took her leave, I traced Snow White to the kitchen where she was helping Trevina and the others prepare our evening meal. Edmyg had no doubt told her about the hag at the gates, her generous offer of an apple, and my intercession before he could accept it. From the expression on Snow White's face as she looked up from the cutting board, a small paring knife in her hand, I could see she had been expecting me. She and the others must have been talking about this unusual piece of news just before I entered.

"It was your mother, the Queen," I told her. Trevina gasped and dropped the bunch of carrots she was holding onto the stone floor. "No!" cried another of the dwarfs.

"She wore a wig and old clothes," I said, "but she could not conceal her beauty."

Snow White had indeed guessed – I read it in her gaze. "And the apple?" she asked. "What have you done with it?"

"I cast it far away into the forest. Surely it was poisoned."

"Surely," she agreed. A look of far-away sadness came over her. "As a treat, my father used to bring me apples when he … before he died. Mother knows how dearly I love the fruit. A clever choice indeed." An edge of cynicism gave her voice an unaccustomed harshness.

That night when we gathered for the evening meal, I sat in my stately chair and adopted my most solemn manner. I glanced from one to another, reading the apprehension on their fire-lit faces. I sensed how much they needed the reassurance of a firm hand.

"From now on, we must all be on our guard. We can expect the Queen to make another attempt on Snow White's life, and the next time might be more difficult to penetrate. I am to be notified at once of all arrivals at the gate. Any unexpected deliveries will be reported to me. Is that understood?"

"Ay!" came a chorus of voices.

"We will allow no harm to befall our guest," I said.

At the far end of the table, kneeling near the fire, Snow White looked at me with doubt clouding her expression. She could not have forgotten our conversation that morning in the herb garden. In retrospect, I saw that I had spoken too plainly and now regretted my candor.

Before she retired for the evening, I took her aside for a quiet word. Standing near the doorway, she looked deeply tired, her face taut with distress. No doubt she was haunted by thoughts of her mother the Queen and what she intended to.

"Earlier today I was unkind to you," I told her. "I am truly sorry."

Snow White's expression remained unchanged as she looked down upon me. "You only spoke your mind. To be honest, I knew you felt that way before you told me."

As if abashed, I shook my head and lowered my gaze. "But when I think of your evil mother, the grave danger that awaits you beyond our gates ..."

I left the thought unfinished, assuming she would complete it as I intended, endowing me with feelings of shame and concern.

"Don't give it another thought," she said. As I peered down at her shoes, I saw them pivot and move away from me. "Perhaps Mother will prevail as she usually does and I'll no longer be a burden to *anyone.*"

I could not read her tone of voice. Though she didn't sound full of self-pity, I felt somehow blamed, as if behind her words, a finger was pointing at me.

* * *

Late in the day on which I was expecting the Queen's next visit, I heard the alarm bells ring out from the gatehouse. Around the colony, dwarfs dropped their tools and we all went running toward the sound. As we converged on the gates, several dozen of us, I espied a hunched-over shape beyond, her hands gripping the iron pickets. Nowhere to be seen, Edmyg was probably cowering inside the gatehouse. As planned, Snow White had remained behind in the women's dormitory.

The Queen wore a different wig this time, even more tangled and knottier than before, in a dress of coarse gray wool rather than black. She kept her gaze downcast and shuffled her feet. The other dwarfs held back as I stepped forward to greet her.

"What brings you to our gates, old woman?" I deepened my voice so that it would carry to my audience behind me.

The Queen reached into her pocket, pulled out an object wrapped in shiny cloth, and thrust it forward between the pickets. "I bear a present for the young woman who dwells within," she said, adding a tremolo to her voice to make it sound old. The feigned palsy in her hand struck me as an effective touch, albeit overplayed. "Word of her great beauty has spread throughout the land. Perhaps she would care for this comb to adorn her hair. I wore it as a younger woman myself, in happier days."

"I will accept it on her behalf." I could sense how we held the spectators in our thrall, the Queen and I.

"But might I not place it into her hands myself? I would dearly love to behold such beauty."

"Nay, she lies in bed with fever. But I will give it to her directly, I promise you."

I stepped forward and took the gift from her hand, careful not to let the comb within the cloth touch my skin. As the Queen shuffled off and disappeared down the road, I felt the crowd behind me relax. I avoided Caleb's gaze: I sensed him watching me closely as I carried the comb toward the poultry yard.

Snow White emerged from the dormitory and met us near the chickens. While the others looked on, I let myself into the fenced enclosure and selected a speckled fowl from the flock (an older hen that I knew had stopped laying) and clutched her by the throat. Gripping the edge of the ebony comb between folds of cloth, I stroked it along the hen's feathers. I turned the comb so its tines would penetrate into her flesh, then I placed her back onto the ground and stepped away to watch along with the others.

There were gasps of horror and dismay as the hen began to twitch. Soon she fell onto her side, flopping about in the dust, her talons scratching wildly in the air. It was over quickly. Soon the hen lay dead and the crowd was struck dumb by the horror of it – to think Snow White might have been lying there instead! I felt pleased that events had unfolded so perfectly according to plan, though my pleasure was sullied somewhat by Caleb's scrutiny. He never left off watching me. He might have harbored some doubts but the others were completely taken in.

Several of the dwarfs had drawn close to Snow White, to comfort her or to receive comfort themselves. Trevina took hold of one pale hand and held it to her own face. Snow White began to weep in silence though her expression remained inscrutable. I had no idea how to interpret those tears. As I watched, she made eye contact with Caleb and a look of understanding seemed to pass between them.

As I glanced back down at the lifeless hen, dust encrusting her feathers, a sudden foreboding chilled my back. As a rule, I am not prone to morbid thoughts, but all at once I felt the inevitability of death, how it comes to each of us in the end, whether by violence or disease. One day, another dwarf would become the next Mother, to serve in my place after I had passed on.

* * *

Upon her third visit, the Queen and I repeated our mock confrontation at the gates and I accepted her new gift, an embroidered girdle with poisoned stays. We lost another hen that day when I removed one of those stays and poked her with it. By this point, the other dwarfs were all convinced that the Queen would never relent until she had killed her daughter, and a state of constant dread took hold of the colony. I need only bide my time and be prepared.

I'd had some prior experience with the poison I intended to employ. A few years earlier, I brewed it myself from special herbs I'd grown and then used it upon Macklin, a young dwarf who'd voted for me in the Choosing. When he began to bridle under the reforms I instituted upon my elevation, he threatened to tell the others about the gift I'd given to secure his vote. It would have called the election results into question, of course.

So I slipped the poison into his drink one night. Not long after, he went to sleep as usual and settled into a coma from which he never awoke. I did not take the prospect of Macklin's death lightly, of course, and as concerned leader, I naturally had my reservations about what I had done. Before he finally passed away, I did consider administering the antidote, also brewed from herbs in my garden, but the threat he posed to my stewardship of the colony remained insuperable. Sometimes a leader must undertake unsavory acts to do what is best for his people. I have no regrets.

With everyone in the colony now on guard, it would be far more difficult to deliver my poison to Snow White. Nothing she consumed could come directly from my hands, for I had to make certain no suspicion would fall upon me. I waited and watched and began to despair of ever finding the right method. Then Edmyg showed me the way.

During the incident of the poisoned apple, everyone had learned that Snow White considered the fruit a special treat; in particular, she preferred a sweet and somewhat rare variety known to us as Maiden Blush, pale yellow in color with a crimson flush. Because my beguiled dwarfs wanted to give Snow White pleasure, they began searching for her favorite fruit in the wild; but while many apple trees grow within an easy distance of the colony, this particular variety is quite difficult to find. At the time, no one informed me of this ongoing search or I would naturally have forbidden it. In retrospect, I am glad I did not know.

To his great delight, Edmyg discovered a Maiden Blush tree within a mile or two of the colony gates. One day he returned from his search with a shiny apple – plucked by his own hands, he said – and refused to disclose the tree's location. With a smug and triumphant look upon his face, he placed the apple in Snow White's hands; he clearly wanted the exclusive power to give her such pleasure. I asked him how he had managed to reach so high, up into the boughs of the tree; he only shrugged and said, "I be knowing and you be guessing."

Bearing an apple to Snow White became a part of Edmyg's daily routine. Sometimes he brought more than one and shared them with the others. It irked me at first, that the girl should receive such lavish attention. I felt disgusted at the sight of my dwarfs cramming their mouths with apple slices, the juice dripping onto their chins and beards, the pulp encrusting their teeth. Then I saw how I could turn the situation to my advantage.

One day when nobody was watching closely, I pocketed one of the extra apples and dripped poison into it that night through a thin reed. The tiny hole I'd made near the stem was almost imperceptible. The following afternoon, I waited near the gates for Edmyg to return, the poisoned fruit concealed within the pocket of my cloak. As expected, he came back from his daily trip with a happy grin on his face and a shiny apple in his hand.

"Another one!" I cried upon meeting him. "It looks to be a great beauty this time. May I see?"

Hapless Edmyg placed the apple in my hand. "What's that?" I suddenly cried, glancing with alarm over his shoulder.

When he turned to look, I made the switch.

"What?" he said, turning back. "What be the matter?"

"I guess it's nothing," I said. "I'm just so jumpy these days. We all are."

I placed my poisoned apple in his hand. The idiot was so unobservant that he didn't notice the difference in size.

Later that evening after consuming her apple, Snow White complained of headache and retired to her bed in the women's dormitory. That night, I drifted off easily and slept well for the first time in weeks. At last my troubles were over! So soundly did I sleep that I only awakened when there came a pounding on the door of Mother's Cottage late in the morning. Groggy and a bit unsteady on my feet, I shuffled to the door and found Trevina on the doorstep, barefoot and dressed in her nightshirt. With tears on her cheeks and frantic wide eyes, she looked deeply distraught. Her hair was a tangled mess.

"What is it?" I asked, rubbing my brow. Of course I knew why she had come but I feigned ignorance.

"It be Snow White," Trevina cried. A sob made her voice tremble. "We be not able to waken her."

I noted with satisfaction that in her moment of fear and distress, Trevina had come directly to me, her Mother. Already life at the colony was returning to normal.

Or so I thought.

My dwarfs' attachment to Snow White did not relent when she fell into a coma. In fact, it seemed only to intensify. In rotating shifts, they kept vigil at her side, the men and women alike, now and then chafing her hands in a vain attempt to revive her. They took constant hope from the rise and fall of her chest: perhaps she would yet awaken! So stricken were they by grief that they lost all interest in daily life and their usual routines. Nobody cared to tend the fowl or till the soil. In the end, I had to be quite stern with them and issue direct commands. Otherwise, we might have starved.

Macklin had died within days of entering a coma but Snow White lingered for weeks. In retrospect, I saw that I should have administered a more potent dose, given her larger portion. When I finally tired of arguing against hope and decreed that we must bury her, the outcry was tremendous.

They seemed terrified by the thought of her sentient body trapped underground, as if she might awaken one day and find herself caged within darkness. Facing the inevitable, I realized I had no choice but to relent. She could not remain forever in state upon her bed, however.

In the end, wasting labor and precious resources, we constructed a glass coffin and placed it on a raised platform as a kind of monument. Every day, my grief-stricken dwarfs would pass by and pay tribute, standing on the narrow step and peering mournfully through the glass. I found their obsession most galling. Though I had believed myself rid of Snow White's pernicious influence, she continued to wield power over my people.

It seemed she would never die. And strangely enough, she didn't waste away as one might have expected, given that no food had passed her lips for many weeks. On the contrary, her body seemed to thrive and mature. The promise of impending womanhood I had glimpsed upon her arrival now blossomed forth. She seemed even more beautiful than before, her bosom fuller, her lips more voluptuous. When I had told the Queen she was still the fairest in the land, I believed it; now I could see that Snow White had indeed surpassed her in beauty.

I tried to avoid passing by her coffin, but given its placement near the dining hall, at the intersection of paths between the dormitories and workshops, I found it almost impossible to do. Young and beautiful and maddeningly vital, she seemed to mock me from the very center of the colony. Sometimes I thought I might lose my mind in frustration.

Meanwhile, I was puzzled that we had seen nothing of the Queen during all this time. Once it became clear that Snow White would not die, I kept on the lookout for the Queen's return, but she never came. Perhaps she was satisfied at last. Or perhaps Snow White's comatose state made the magical looking glass change its answer. She might be dead as far as the glass was concerned. I really didn't know what to make of it.

* * *

Though their grief was heavy, my dwarfs eventually roused themselves and went back to their accustomed chores. The miners and metalworkers resumed work; the traders carried our wares to market; Caleb and the other acrobats once again went abroad. It would not have been surprising if the travelers unburdened themselves to the Big People they met, and I can think of no other way that the rumor should have started and spread throughout the land – of an undying princess in a glass coffin, lovely beyond compare, housed within the dwarf colony near the mountains.

Strangers began showing up at our gate, asking for permission to see her. I ordered the guards to turn them away at first, until it occurred to me that here might be another source of income. We began charging one gold coin for each viewing, and this helped to salve my resentment. If I could not permanently rid myself of Snow White, even if I had to walk by her coffin every day and witness the way she yet held my dwarfs in thrall, at least I could profit from her.

Whenever these pilgrims showed up, I usually withdrew to the Mother's Cottage and let one of the other dwarfs show them the coffin, for I found their gasps of amazement and tears of pity quite annoying. But on the day when a handsome coach showed up at our gates, emblazoned with a coat of arms and pulled by four glistening black steeds, I thought it better to stay close. Only a person of great wealth and importance would arrive in such an elegant equipage, attended by a groom and coachman in scarlet livery with gold braid at the epaulets.

The coach and four stopped just outside the gates. As I approached, the groom placed a small wooden step before the door and opened it; from within, a man attired in thick gray furs stepped carefully down onto the ground. For a Big Person, he was remarkably small – only six or so inches taller than myself. He struck me as quite ugly, too, with sallow skin, protruding teeth, and a jagged scar along his cheekbone. I bowed low and made him welcome. When Edmyg emerged from the guard-house bearing the coin box, I waved him aside. Of course we would not charge admission to royalty.

For royalty he was, one Prince Liam of Catterick, come from afar to see the beauty in the box. I personally escorted him to Snow White's altar and waited at a respectful distance while he climbed onto the platform for his viewing. He didn't weep or remark upon her beauty though he did seem riveted in place. His steady gaze never faltered. After long minutes, he briefly glanced back at me and inclined his head toward the coffin, indicating that I should join him. Though I mounted the platform and stood beside him, I refused to look at Snow White, instead fixing my gaze upon his face. I tried hard not to focus too closely on the scar.

"She is Princess Elwyn of Abergavenny," he said, "better known as Snow White. Yes?"

"You are correct, your highness."

"Rumors of her great beauty fall short of the truth. She is loveliness itself."

I held my tongue.

"How long has she been this way?" he asked.

"Several months now. We've tried everything we can to revive her."

"And how did it come about?"

"We believe her mother the Queen somehow slipped poison into her food, despite all our efforts to protect her."

"It would not surprise me. That woman was capable of anything."

"You know her?" I asked.

"*Knew* her. She is dead now."

At last I understood her absence. "I am sorry."

"Don't be," he said, never moving his eyes from the coffin. "She was a selfish and vindictive shrew. She never cared about anyone or anything other than the satisfaction of her own desires. After her husband's death and Snow White's disappearance, the court finally rose up against her. The story going round is that they placed her bare feet in red-hot iron shoes and forced her to dance until she died from pain and exhaustion. Sounds a bit fantastical to me. In any event, she is dead."

My whole body winced in sympathy and I shut my eyes tight. A mental image came unbidden – the lovely Queen frantically dancing in glowing red boots, shrieking in agony. When I opened my eyes again, Prince Liam was still fixated upon Snow White. All at once, I noticed that his limbs fell short of normal size. I wondered if he might be akin to us, a near-dwarf whose life had been spared because of those extra few inches.

"And now," he continued, "a struggle over the succession is underway. King Alec had no child other than Snow White, and no surviving brothers or sisters, but there are distant cousins who have a claim to the thrown. Of course, the man who married Alec's daughter would have an uncontested claim and take precedence over all the contenders. 'Tis a pity you cannot wake her."

I had the uncomfortable sense that he knew more about what had happened to Snow White than he let on. Perhaps because we were so close in height, the Prince only half a foot taller, I felt we could speak man to man.

"I suppose she cannot be married without her verbal consent," I said.

"Of course not. And there would have to be witnesses."

"Even if she were to awaken, there's no guarantee she would agree to marry you."

Prince Liam gave out a short bitter laugh. "Indeed. I am not the type of tall handsome prince maidens usually dream about." He paused. "But she might be amenable to persuasion."

He gave me a penetrating look. The jagged scar along his cheekbone seemed to lengthen. Something in his air said he knew how to make people do what he wanted, perhaps by resorting to pain when both kindness and argument could not persuade them.

"Only if she were to awaken, of course," I said.

"Of course," he repeated. He didn't glance away.

In the end, without many more words, we understood each other. I provided him with the antidote for later use and we informed the dwarfs that Prince Liam believed conjurers in his court could use their powerful magic to awaken her. He offered a bag of gold to compensate me for lost viewing revenues. Later that very day, we loaded her coffin onto a horse-drawn wagon the Prince had concealed within the woods nearby. I normally assign such duties to lesser dwarfs, but in this case, I chose to help lift the coffin myself onto the wagon. I groaned and strained and pushed with all my might.

Wailing with exaggerated grief outside the gates, the dwarfs watched the handsome coach depart, followed by the wagon. After a few moments, I retired to the Mother's Cottage, but the rest of them wept and carried on until the wagon had completely disappeared from view. Only then did they come back inside the gates and resume, at long last, our former way of life.

* * *

Pealing alarm bells awakened me from deep sleep in the morning. As terror made my heart race, my first thought was that Prince Liam had returned to reclaim the bag of gold he'd given me. He might want to plunder our wares, or to punish us for some undefined crime he believed we had committed. I thrust my feet into my boots and went running toward the gatehouse, still clad in my nightshirt. It was early yet, the sky clinging to darkness.

With a pain in my chest and breathing heavily, I approached the gates. The entire colony had turned out, most of them in their nightshirts like me. But Caleb was fully clothed and shouldered a pack, as if prepared for a journey. He had a walking stick in hand and stood apart from the others. All eyes turned toward me as I came to a stop. Though I didn't understand what was happening, I instantly felt at a disadvantage – vulnerable in my nightshirt, hair disheveled, my beard uncombed. I struggled to catch my breath.

"What is this about? Why has the alarm been sounded?" I looked directly at Caleb, sensing the threat he posed to me. I had always felt him to be a threat.

"I rang the bells myself," he said in a commanding voice that carried. "I've decided to depart because I can no longer accept you as leader of this colony. I will go forth and find a new home. I've called the entire colony together to say my farewell but also to speak truth to you, Giddeus, before I go."

I felt the diminishment – my name and not my title. The early morning air felt cold upon my genitals.

"You might have waited for a more reasonable hour," I sneered. I wanted my voice to convey pure contempt in the way the Queen's voice had done. "Why drag everyone from their warm beds just so you can have your say?"

Ignoring me, Caleb glanced around him at the three dozen or so dwarfs assembled there at the gates. They were all looking at him and not at me.

"I speak of what I myself believe but cannot prove," he said. "You must decide for yourselves what to think. But I say this to you now: Giddeus is no Mother to his people. Giddeus is unworthy to hold that title and in choosing to depart, I reject him utterly."

I felt it best to stare back in defiance rather than to speak. Let him make a fool of himself. I would maintain a dignified silence.

Now Caleb turned back to face me. "These are the charges I bring against you, Giddeus. As I say, I have no proof, only the conviction that comes from knowing you these many years." He paused, as if for dramatic effect. "First, that in the Choosing, you offered gifts in exchange for support, knowing I would have prevailed otherwise."

A low murmur ran through the crowd, whether of agreement or dissent, I could not say.

"Second, that Macklin was among those you influenced, and that you played some part in his untimely death when he threatened to expose you."

Several of the women cried out in dismay. Trevina put her hands to her face and rocked her head from side to side. I thought I heard one of the men whisper, "It be truth."

"Third, that you conspired with the Queen, Snow White's mother, to dispatch her with poison. I believe it to have been in that last apple Edmyg brought. And finally, that you sold her to Prince Liam, for what nefarious purpose I cannot say."

A shocked "No!" came from three or more voices in the crowd. No doubt they found these claims as offensive as I did. I locked eyes with Caleb and glared back.

"How do you answer, Giddeus? What do you say to these charges?"

"N-nothing," I said. Due to the cold, I could not stop my body from trembling. "As M-mother, I n-need make no answer."

Caleb continued staring accusation. I would not be cowed. At last, he looked away, shaking his head. "So be it," he said. "My mind will be at ease now, knowing I have spoken truth."

"*Your* truth," I sneered. With these words, it seemed I had brought this ridiculous scene to a close and Caleb would now take his leave of us.

Then a voice from the back called out, "I be coming with you, Caleb!" It sounded like one of the young dwarfs who'd been with us for only a few years, a gullible lad without a brain in his head. "Wait for me – I be only five minutes." I heard the thudding sound of footsteps as the defector hurried off to the dormitory.

"Me, too!" a woman's voice cried. Young and credulous, she, too, had been persuaded by Caleb's rhetoric. Whatever else I might think of him, the man did have a way with words.

I declined to take further part in this outrageous spectacle and returned to the Mother's Cottage. Only later did I hear the tally: By the time Caleb finally set off, 15 traitorous dwarfs had decided to join him. Although I mourned the loss of my people, I took comfort that more of them had decided to remain behind than to leave. 24 for me, 14 for Caleb. It was a second vote that validated my original election to the Motherhood.

* * *

More than three years have passed since that day and life here in the colony truly has returned to normal. We may be fewer in number but we are more harmonious now, more settled in our routines and accepting of them. I find the common dwarf to be almost in awe of me, and even more obedient than before. Perhaps it is the awareness that poison might be the price of open defiance that makes them so docile.

Rumor reached us that Caleb and the others have established their own colony in distant Dulcium. We hear that they are thriving. I am disinclined to believe this tale, however, for as articulate and perceptive as he might occasionally be, Caleb is not a natural leader. Under his lax guidance, common dwarfs would no doubt fall back into the sloth from which I rescued them. They would neglect their work and give themselves over to self-indulgence. Indeed I do not envy the ones who departed.

Of Snow White, I have heard that she recovered from her coma, married Prince Liam, and ascended to the throne. I hear she bore him a child. Whether she be happy in her new life, I cannot say. She no longer concerns me.

Trevina died last year of natural causes, and Edmyg the year before her. Several others are currently ailing and will soon depart. Because there have been no new arrivals, and no dwarf babies left at the gates, our number has dwindled. Sometimes I wonder if this era will mark the end of our colony. Most of us are advanced in dwarf years, for we do not often live past the age of 60. Perhaps the others will die off, one by one, until I am left alone. The prospect does not frighten me, though as Mother, it saddens me to think of the colony unpeopled, gradually falling into decay.

In the end, we all die alone, of course, no matter how many of our kin surround us – dwarfs and Big People alike. I am not afraid of death. And sometimes when the pain in my joints is severe on cold winter nights, when the wind howls in the trees and I envision hungry predators outside the perimeter wall, ready to break through, I even feel that I am ready for it.

THE END

Rapunzelmother

PART ONE

*e*ven here behind my high garden walls, the chill wind cuts through me. Nature's hostile little jest, to send such cold this late in spring. My poor old joints ache so. And this shawl doesn't keep me warm enough, not nearly.

It would be so very pleasant inside by the fire. But I mustn't. The rampion plants need tending. If I don't thin them soon, the leaves might start to grow bitter. The crowded roots won't thicken properly, or develop their full power.

That noise … what do I hear?

Nothing. Only an old woman's fancy, misled by the wind in the trees. No one comes to visit me. No one from the village ever travels this way, not since I quarreled with the carpenter's wife from across the lane and they disappeared.

I'll stay outside and thin the plants, then reward myself with two rampion pickles. I'm a little worried about running out, but I should have enough in my pantry to last until this new crop matures. Two pickled rampion roots, a cup of herb tea, and the pain in my joints will vanish. Perhaps these budding plants will prove even more uplifting than the ones from last season. My spells seem to grow stronger with every passing year.

There it is again!

Not my imagination, but the certain rumble of wheels along the road. The hollow clip-clop of hooves. The landlord may have finally found replacement tenants for the carpenter and his wife. I would be the last to know, of course. Nobody in the village ever tells me anything. Nobody talks to me.

161

My eye at the wall chink, I can barely see through dense ivy on the other side. A dray. One horse in harness. Two shapes seated in front … a man and a woman? If I poke one of these plant stakes through the wall chink, it might just … there! Now I have a better view.

The dray pulls to a stop in front of the small cottage, and the man looks up at the roof shingles, scratching his neck. Crates and a few sticks of furniture fill the back of the wagon. A bed frame and mattress. Not much … they must be very poor.

The woman seems to study the shuttered windows, the twin chimneys, plaster in need of repair. I can't see her face. She has flaxen hair, I think, tucked into a checkered blue kerchief. Not fat like me. Not ugly like me. Her coarse woolen skirts spread around her on the bench.

Later when I'm sure they're asleep, I'll slip out and trim back the ivy.

* * *

A wisp of blue smoke is rising from one of their chimneys now. It disperses in the wind above my garden wall. She must be in the kitchen, tending to their supper. A bubbling pot suspended in the fireplace. I could bring her a jar of something from my pantry.

No, not yet. You're always too hasty. Wait a few days until they've settled in. A jar of pickled rutabaga might be just the thing.

But not the rampion pickles. I've never shared my rampion.

One more look through the wall chink. The man has already emptied the dray and unharnessed the horse. He's leading it toward the small barn behind the cottage. Brown woolen breeches and a white linen shirt. Tall and well built, although he has lost most of his hair. As he removes his cap and drags a sleeve across his brow, his pate glistens.

He's a long time inside the barn. When he comes out, he closes the twin doors behind him, dropping the crossbar into place. He looks up at the sky where dark clouds are shutting out the sun. A storm is coming – he sees it.

Better hurry if you're going to finish thinning the rampion plants before the rain begins. Not much more to do now, only one row. The sprouts that I have culled, lying there in my basket – they'll make a nice salad. Not potent like the fully-grown root but pleasant enough. Rampion salad always makes me feel drowsy and warm, like a cat curled up in a patch of sunlight.

All finished now, at long last. My toes and fingers ache from the cold. And I'm so hungry! Some cold mutton with the rampion pickles might be nice, and a slice of pumpernickel with butter. I'll save the sprout salad for tomorrow.

Does she set his dinner plate on the table and hover over him like a serving wench? I always hated the way the carpenter treated his wife. He deserved what came to him.

* * *

They've opened the curtains in their sitting room window. My old neighbors always used to keep them closed. They knew I could look down upon them from up here in my bedroom, though I always took care not to be obvious about it. Tonight I've left my candle unlit and I'm concealed now within the darkness. The rain has passed and the breeze from the window feels wholesome.

The new tenants have placed two wooden chairs close to the fireplace. Otherwise the room is bare, and dark but for the firelight. The wife extends her hands toward the heat. I'm almost certain now her hair is flaxen in color. She has removed the kerchief and loosened her tresses so they trail down her back. Very long, almost to her waist.

I hate my own hair! Coarse and gray, fit only to be tied back in this bun.

163

The husband seems to be smoking a pipe. The wife drops to her knees before him and places her head in his lap. Too far away and not enough light … I can't tell if she's crying. He strokes her long hair. A kind man, not like the carpenter. She lifts her head to look up at him. He places his hand upon her cheek and even from this distance I can feel his gentle touch.

Maybe it's the lingering effects of rampion, but my heart suddenly swells with emotion. I could love these people. This kind man, this beautiful woman. I haven't yet seen her face, not in full light, but I'm certain she is beautiful.

Earlier, I saw him unload it from the cart – a single mattress, large enough for them both if they sleep close together, their bodies touching. I'm tired now. When he takes her hand and leads her upstairs, I'll put myself to bed, too.

But what about the ivy? The wall chink? I hate to bundle up and go back out into the cold but I have to do it. They can't see me now, concealed in darkness. I use my bare hands to tear away the leaves and stems. The rampion root hasn't fully worn off yet because I feel no pain, not even when a sharp-edged stem across my palm draws blood. Now when I peer out from behind the wall, I'll be able to see them clearly.

* * *

Morning in the garden and I'm weeding the vegetable patch. I hear more wheels along the road. Putting my eye to the wall chink, I see a large heavy wagon pulled by two draft horses coming down the lane. Three burly men seated on the bench. Behind them is some massive object, black and metallic. Closer and closer. It must be the largest iron stove I've ever seen.

Just as the wagon pulls to a stop, the husband opens the kitchen door and comes out. The wife follows a moment later. The morning sunlight hits her full face. Hair more the color of gold than flax. And what a beauty! Too beautiful for her drab skirt and chemise, all in gray. She looks excited.

She watches from the side as her husband and the other three men prepare to unload the stove. She wrings her hands with worry: What if the men should drop the stove? What if their strength gives way and it tumbles from the ramps? Though the planks appear to be thick, they could still snap under all that weight. I feel her anxiety so acutely I cannot bear to watch. From time to time, I come back to the wall chink and check on their progress.

The stove's front legs securely positioned on the twin planks that angle down from the wagon bed.

Now all four legs on the ramps and midway down.

Safely on the ground!

The wife laughs and claps her hands with relief. I don't see why anyone should care so much about a stove. It only means more drudgery for her, more cooking she'll have to do. And why do they need such a large one, two people alone? Four oven doors with brass handles.

Imbecile! Her husband is a baker, of course.

What luck! A baker and his wife right across the lane. Now I won't have to buy loaves from that baker in the village. I don't mind *him*, but I've always hated *her*, ever since she insisted the rye was freshly baked when I could see for myself it was day-old. She must've thought me a fool.

Not pickled rutabaga for *this* baker's wife. Some of my quince jam from last summer will do much better. Or strawberry. She'll slice into a loaf still warm from the oven. Seated at her kitchen table, we'll slather big slabs of rye or pumpernickel with creamy butter first, then with big dollops of jam. We'll sip tea and she'll tell me all about herself. She'll let me know why she buried her face in her husband's lap and what has made her so very sad.

* * *

Before the sun has fully risen, he's outside splitting logs from the woodpile. I can see him from the upstairs window. After a while, she comes out to help. Heavy woolen coat, gray like most of her other clothes, with a blue scarf and bonnet. She stacks the split logs outside the kitchen door. A baker must need a great deal of wood to keep his oven hot.

Their work looks tedious. Yesterday, they spent what seemed like hours unloading flour sacks from the miller's wagon.

Looking out my window later in the day – he has removed his shirt. The sun is high and warm. What a change from yesterday! He may have lost most of his hair but his body is taut and muscled. No sign of fat.

Does he sleep naked or wear a nightshirt?

Much later when I look – he has taken her into his arms and is kissing her. Outside, for all the world to see! My heart beats so fiercely that it hurts. I know what men and women do when they are alone together, his part into her part. Why should I be so frightened?

It's not only fear that I feel.

* * *

Early on the morning of their fourth day, he puts the horse in harness and loads the dray – loaves of freshly baked bread, of course, wrapped in cloth and stacked in baskets. Where is he taking them? Not to our own little village, surely. Probably to town. He'll set up shop on the square and sell bread from the back of his wagon. Other vendors alongside him … cheese and meats, mostly. Not many fruits or vegetables this early in the season. Unless he sells all his loaves in the first hour, the baker won't arrive back home until dark.

Funny how these sealed jars on my pantry shelf make me happy. They make me feel safe. Quince jam. Strawberry jam. Apricot jam. Such abundance! Which would she like best? The carpenter's wife didn't love my jams as much as she pretended. I found out later – she emptied the jars onto the compost heap whenever she found them on her doorstep.

The color of the fruit within this jar is still a vivid red. The seal remains intact. She'll break the wax with her little spoon and dip into the strawberry jam. Pleasure will erase the sadness on her face.

Ugh – that nasty pink scar on my hand where the molten wax scalded me last year.

Maybe she won't like me. The carpenter's wife didn't like me. I thought she did but she only pretended, the way she pretended to like my jam. Better not to expect too much this time. Consider it one neighbor welcoming another, nothing more. She has no one else but me along this narrow lane.

My heart beats faster as I cross the road. My palms sweat, too, and I have to wipe them on my apron. Imbecile! You should have changed it to a clean one before you came over. She might already have spotted me and would think it odd if I turned back now.

The kitchen door is ajar, just a few inches. A slice of her in the opening as she washes something in the sink. A pot? A plate? Over her gray dress, she has tied a checkered apron. Closer now and I can see the apron is no cleaner than my own. Clutching the jam jar to my breast, I rap my knuckles on the doorframe. She startles at the sound and turns toward me.

That wary look on her face, I know what it means. She's been into the village and people have been talking about me. What tales have they told? No doubt she's heard all about my feud with the carpenter and his wife. Of course everyone blames me for what happened. They've probably warned my new neighbor to be careful.

They have no idea what really happened. No idea what I can do when I make full user of my powers.

"I'm your neighbor," I say. "Just across the lane. I've brought you this gift from my pantry."

The baker's wife smiles and seems to relax. "How very kind of you!" She takes the jar from my hand and reads the label I attached before bringing it over. She'll see what an elegant hand I write. "Strawberry! My husband adores strawberry jam. However can I thank you?" Such an expression of goodness in her face. No guile, none at all.

"You're more than welcome."

The massive iron stove takes up one entire wall. Brass handles on the four doors glisten in the light. A plain farm table with two chairs and a half-eaten loaf of bread upon it.

She sees me taking it all in. "I'd offer you refreshment," she says, "but …"

"Please don't trouble yourself. I only wanted to drop this off and now I'll be on my way. Good day!"

I hope we'll become fast friends – I do not say it, though I badly want to. I feel very pleased with myself for my restraint.

* * *

Is it self-indulgent to eat so many rampion pickles? At least a few every day. Is that too many?

Long ago – that awful time I tried to stop, for a few days my life became a torment. Aches and pains. Sweating even in the coldest weather. After a week, my flesh felt so very hot I thought I might catch fire. Now I don't even try to resist.

And why should I? How can something that yields such joy be bad for you? I've had moments nigh on ecstasy. As far as I can tell, it does me no harm. Besides, an old woman alone has so few pleasures. I'm not hurting anyone.

I've doubled my planting this year, with more rampion where I used to raise leeks. I cannot bear the prospect of exhausting my stores next year before the new crop comes in.

Tonight I let myself have an extra pickle after supper. I nibble it slowly in the darkness while I watch them down in their sitting room. Day and night, they always leave the curtains open. She'll ruin her eyes if she continues doing needlework in such meager light, one candle only. He was smoking his pipe earlier but now I think he has fallen asleep in his chair. His legs are thrust out toward the fire and he hasn't stirred in long minutes.

They've been here two weeks now and already I know their routines. At bedtime, she'll nudge him gently awake. He'll pretend to resist. Reaching out, she'll take his hand and then, throwing all her weight into it, pull him upright from his chair. He'll play along, letting her believe she has the strength to do it.

Not every night, but most nights. I imagine them smiling together as they make their way into the bedroom.

Tonight after they snuff out the candle and turn in, I go to my own bed but cannot sleep. The night is warm and the sheets grow moist against my skin. The room feels stuffy. Side by side, their two bodies together must generate even more heat than mine alone. Perhaps they're awake too. They might whisper together in the darkness, though there is no one to hear them. He might reach out for her.

How does she feel when he goes inside? Does it feel like this, like a finger? Or more than one? What does it look like? Him on top of her. The weight of his body. Him behind. Or her on top. Many ways to imagine it. I want to see for myself.

This ... this is how they must feel once it's over.

Now I can sleep.

* * *

A knock at the door as I'm preparing my rampion salad. She stands on the stoop when I open up. An empty jar in her hand ... *my* jar, of course, empty and clean. She also has a loaf of bread tucked under her arm. The smile on my face feels too large and I try to make it smaller. Do I look now as if I'm wincing?

"I've brought back your jar," she says, extending it toward me. "The jam was delicious. Thank you again." She can't seem to settle her gaze in one place. "I also brought you this." The loaf ... rye from the look of it.

"You didn't have to do that," I say. But I take the loaf and thank her. He goes off to market most days now. She's probably alone.

169

"I was just about to have my salad," I say, the impulse of the moment. "Would you care to join me? We'll share the loaf, as well."

"No, the bread is for you. I only dropped it by to thank you. And I don't want to impose." She looks past me into my house, the eagerness on her face belying her words. She's lonely. It's not hard for me to convince her.

What does she make of my sitting room, with its high-backed chairs and the needlepoint settee? The copper pots in my kitchen, suspended from ceiling hooks, the ornate dining table, and all the other furnishings I've gathered over the years? To see your familiar old possessions through the eyes of a stranger makes them new again. Compared to her, I must seem like a wealthy woman.

"So many beautiful things!" she cries.

She might envy me.

Lifting rampion leaves from the wooden bowl onto her plate, I feel the sting of regret. I don't want to share. The bread, the butter cheese, the dandelion wine – those I gladly give to her, as much as she likes, but not the rampion. No matter how many pickle jars in the pantry, no matter how large a crop I plant each year, there is never enough. I know it's not true but it always feels that way.

I hope she appreciates the extent of my generosity.

After her first bite, she says, "Delicious! I never cared much for rampion before, not the leaves anyway, but yours tastes … different."

Another of my enhancement spells, but of course I cannot tell her.

When she chews, she keeps her mouth closed, not like the uncouth carpenter's wife who had no manners. The baker's wife swallows and wipes her mouth with the cloth napkin from her lap. The carpenter's wife used her sleeve.

The rye bread tastes sour and tangy, with a dense crumb superior to the town baker's bread. The butter cheese from my larder complements it perfectly. My guest the baker's wife doesn't seem interested in the bread or the cheese. She has emptied her goblet and her plate of salad before I'm halfway through my own.

"Would you care for some more?" I hope I don't sound resentful.

"Please!" she says. I'm glad that she likes my salad but I hope there will be enough left for me. Even though I'm not finished with my first, I'd better take my second helping now before she eats it all up.

Over the years, I've grown accustomed to the effects of my special rampion but it's a new sensation for the baker's wife. Her creamy complexion has flushed a lovely pink color and her limpid blue eyes have a faraway look. No doubt the two glasses of dandelion wine have heightened the rampion's influence. Strands of her flaxen hair have slipped out of the braids and fallen forward onto her face. The sad expression she normally wears has vanished and now she seems to feel elated. I know the feeling well.

Rampion bliss.

We mostly eat without talk. Because I spend my days alone, in silence, idle conversation does not come easily to me. I imagine we are alike that way. She seems intent upon her food. She asks about my garden and what I grow there; I give her brief answers and wonder if she's truly interested. I'd like to ask her a suitable question, one that will lift her attention away from the plate.

"Do you have no children?" I finally ask.

All at once, with a mouthful of salad, she bursts into tears. Bits of half-chewed rampion spew onto the table. Pity overcomes my feeling of disgust. For the most part. She lifts her napkin, covers her mouth, and sobs into it.

"Whatever is the matter, my dear? Here – take some water. Take a sip, go ahead."

She goes on sobbing, unable to speak, though after a while, she does manage to swallow her mouthful. What am I to say to her? The sound of her sorrow penetrates into me, fills me first with a matching sorrow and then with irritation when it begins to seem unbearable. I'd like to shake her. Instead I cover her trembling hand with my own.

"It will be all right," I say. I don't know exactly what's wrong but I have the beginnings of an idea. These seem the appropriate words.

At last she gains control of herself. "I'm so sorry," she says. "I don't know what's come over me. Too much wine, I expect. I'm not used to it. I hope you'll forgive me. I feel such a fool."

It's the rampion that has unleashed her emotions, not the wine. I know from experience how it takes hold of some feeling inside and makes it seem much bigger. But it can only work on what is already there.

"You've been sad about something for a while now. I've seen it on your face."

I wish I could take back the words because now I've given myself away, revealing to her that I watch. Rather than recoiling as I feared she might, she bursts anew into tears. Another few minutes pass before she can calm herself. While she's crying, I remove the plates and goblets from the table and carry them to the sink. I should never have given her that second portion of rampion salad. She's not used to it as I am. But how could I say "no" without explaining?

A cup of strong tea, that's what she needs. By the time I have it brewed and carry it to the table, her grief has subsided. Her breast shudders with quivery little breaths but the big sobs no longer wrack her body. Once again I take her hand and the story spills out.

"We've tried for years now," she says. I must not picture it, the act of trying. "In the beginning, I believed a child would be granted to us with time, but now I've given up all hope." With red-rimmed eyes and a stony expression on her face, she stares down at the table. "I must accept the truth: I am barren."

A potion that stops life from taking hold in a woman's womb, or just the opposite, one that makes her fertile – both are simple and not so difficult to prepare. I even know one that will cause a child to emerge stillborn from the womb. The carpenter's wife already had so many children, she didn't grieve for long.

Years from now when I finally tell her, my dear friend the baker's wife will feel such gratitude that the bond between us will grow even deeper. Once she knows the full extent of my extraordinary kindness, she'll feel forever indebted to me. Having the power to alter the course of a person's life, for better or worse, has rarely felt more gratifying.

Perhaps they will name me godmother to their first child. Or possibly the second. Of course I can't directly ask for such an honor. It would have to spring naturally from their hearts or it would mean nothing.

* * *

She comes back the next day with two more loaves of bread wrapped in a kitchen towel. Standing in my doorway, she holds them out to me. She keeps her gaze downcast.

"I'm so ashamed," she says. "I hope you'll forgive me for making such a fool of myself."

"Think nothing of it," I tell her, taking the gift from her hands. "To want and not to have a child is a terrible curse."

As I say the words, it occurs to me for the first time – did she offend some other witch and so bring the curse of barrenness upon herself? Not every woman unable to bear children is under such a curse but many of them are so without knowing it. The simplest way is to give them a potion. Most of the women in the village hate and fear me too much to touch anything that has passed my hands.

"Would you care to join me for a cup of tea?" I ask.

173

If some other witch is to blame for my dear friend's grief, I have no doubt that my own potion will prove stronger.

"No, I have much work to do." She begins to turn away. "But I wanted to thank you for your kindness."

"Whatever I can do," I say, "you need only ask." I watch her as she crosses the lane to her own cottage. At the stoop, she turns back and waves to me.

Eventually, perhaps one day soon, she will accept my invitation and join me for that cup of tea. By then, I'll have my potion ready. Slipping it into the teapot while I'm brewing it will be simple. The potion will have no effect upon me, of course. I'm long past my childbearing years, and there's only so much a witch's magic can do.

* * *

We've fallen into a pattern now. On days when her husband goes to market, she often drops by for tea and conversation or companionable silence. Sometimes she brings her knitting. I take out quill pens and paper to work on my set of plant illustrations. She thinks I'm terribly clever and I will admit to having some talent. I don't explain the magical properties of those plants, the myriad ways a witch can make use of them. One day I may have an apprentice and I will teach her everything I learned from my own teacher, but such knowledge is not for the baker's wife. She hasn't the gift.

She swallowed the potion weeks ago. I gave it to her more than once, just to be sure. Since then, I've been waiting for her to tell me good news. For some days past, the look of sadness seems to have lifted. Hope has returned, but even if her monthly blood has stopped coming, she is afraid to believe it.

When we do talk, we always talk about her. She knows practically nothing about me while I know her life story complete. The impoverished mother who died young. The drunken father who abandoned her. The aunt who had married well and took my friend in. The aunt who then disowned her for falling in love with a baker.

She has given me to understand that her aunt possessed nice furnishings like my own, nicer even, and a lovely large house in the best part of town. I really don't care to hear anything more about that wealthy the aunt.

Several times my friend has asked me, without looking up from her knitting, "Do you by chance have any more of that rampion salad? It was so very delicious."

"I'm afraid I've exhausted my stores," I tell her. "Let me offer you some shepherd's pie instead. We'll have it with that lovely pumpernickel you brought."

If she were to go into my garden, she would see the leafy rampion plants in long neat rows. Or spying upon me from outside my kitchen, she'd see me enjoying a large rampion salad alone at night. If she knew about the pickles, she might start craving them, too.

* * *

I am certain she has been with child for weeks now but she won't tell me. Does she plan to keep this secret to herself, to share it with her husband only? She doesn't know she owes it all to me, but I am still her closest friend. She ought to confide in me.

Today she has her knitting in hand while I'm putting detail on a sketch of the belladonna plant. Does she think I'm such an unobservant fool that I can't see the tiny size of the thing she's knitting? Does she think I can't perceive the slight alterations in her body? Fuller cheeks, a fresher color, a very slight enlargement in her waistline. Why won't she let me in on her secret?

Maybe she's waiting for me to ask. She might be the sort of person who needs to be coaxed before she can share something so sensitive.

I'm forming the question in my thoughts when all of a sudden, she gasps. One short intake of breath and she grows very

175

still. Her eyes have an inward look. She puts her hand to her belly.

"What is it?" I ask.

* * *

I am here. Now I exist.

* * *

"I felt it move!" she cries. Her eyes overflow with tears.

"You are with child! Why didn't you tell me?" I can't keep a slight tone of accusation from edging my words.

"I was afraid to tell you," she says. Tears are streaming down her cheeks. "I was afraid I might … I don't know, that it might be bad luck. Like a jinx, you know? I've been so worried that I might be wrong."

Silly little thing. She knows nothing of jinxes, or how they are actually brought about.

But I forgive her. I understand now – her foolish superstitions stopped her from confiding in her dearest friend in the world.

"We ought to celebrate!" I say. I am overjoyed and feeling especially generous, now that she has told me. "We'll have that rampion salad you've been asking for. A special treat."

"I thought you told me you had exhausted your stores."

I give her a wink, a special smile meant only for her. "I've been holding some back for a special occasion. I've had my suspicions that good news was on the way. You didn't think you had me completely fooled, did you? Not me, of all people in the world."

* * *

Rampion loosens her tongue. I don't like sharing my salad but I do enjoy her confidence. We have rampion salad most days now when her husband goes to market. She doesn't question where it comes from.

Our favorite topic of conversation is the baby, of course. She doesn't understand why I'm so confident it will be a girl because she has no way of knowing that my potion made it so. I have always wanted a daughter of my own and I'm sure her feelings are no different from mine.

We both love to think of possible names to call her. I keep a list of them all in the back of my sketchbook, even the ones she has already rejected. She might change her mind. Of course it's too much to expect that they will name her after me. My dear friend hasn't yet asked me to be godmother despite a few gentle hints I've given.

Sometimes when we're in the sitting room, me at my drawing table and she in one of the high-backed chairs, she puts down her knitting and sits with a faraway look in her eyes. I know her thoughts have turned inward to the baby, moving inside of her. What does it feel like, to have another being trapped within your body, so fully enclosed as to be a part of you?

* * *

I am not alone. Something else is there, all around me. Another.

* * *

I know to hold my tongue when the baker's wife turns inward, though I long to share in her experience. Sometimes, I even feel a little angry about it – that I cannot know exactly what she feels. But I can imagine it. I can close my eyes and bring us together so that her body is my body, her baby is my baby, and I feel it swimming around within me. Unborn babies live inside the mother's water, but they don't actually swim. Of course not. I push away the mental picture of a fetus with tiny fins.

I open my eyes and the baker's wife has returned to her knitting, a contented smile upon her face. As much love as I feel for my dearest friend, I can't help but hate her a little when she smiles that way. She looks almost smug.

"What does it feel like?" I've asked this question a few times before but the answer never satisfies. She usually puts me off by saying it's impossible to describe.

Today she makes more of an effort. "It feels a bit different lately," she says, "now that the baby is growing larger." She lays her knitting upon her lap and gazes through the window. "Sometimes when I can feel him moving, it's like … now don't laugh at me."

"I promise not to laugh."

"Well, if I close my eyes and try to imagine him inside of me …"

"*Her*," I say. Why can't she remember?

Does that tight look on her face mean I've annoyed her?

"If you insist. When I look inside to where I feel *her* to be, it's as if she is … *waiting* for me." Again she closes her eyes. "It's like she's a tiny spark of light and I have my own light and for one moment when our lights touch, we … we *feel* each other. I know she is there and aware that I am near to her." She opens her eyes and laughs. I feel almost certain she's laughing at herself and not at me. "It's probably just my imagination, what I *want* to be true, but that's what it's like. I've never felt so close, so fully connected to anyone else."

I want to say, "It's only the rampion at work. Sometimes it makes you imagine things that aren't true." But she knows nothing about the rampion, or any of my other enchantments. I've never told her. She has no idea what I'm capable of doing.

She should have guessed, though. Sometimes she strikes me as dim, too stupid to grasp what ought to be obvious.

Later when I'm alone and close my eyes, I cannot find my own light. Every time I envision a spark of life within my body, the light flickers for a moment and quickly dies out. It's probably not like that at all and she only put it that way to make me jealous. That smug look, as if she's better than me because she has a spark of life shining inside, deep within where I cannot reach.

Sometimes I almost regret giving her that potion.

* * *

I've sewn a second rampion crop because she has eaten so much of the first that soon there will be nothing left but roots, which means I'll have to pickle them early, before they've had a chance to grow large. She has no idea about rampion pickles, how superior they are in effect to the leaves, and I do not intend to tell her about them.

The time has come to thin the second crop and here I am, down on my knees, doing the work alone, as ever. She complains of backache but I doubt her pain is more severe than my own. And she's young – she doesn't yet have joint pain. She could at least offer to help, even if I would have felt obligated to decline her assistance. One ought to make allowances for a woman with child. I see her less these days than before. Too tired to move, she tells me. Sometimes I think she only visits me for the salad. I'm down on my knees in the dirt like an old beggar woman while she reclines on her feather bed.

The sound of wheels along the road.

I can distinguish every cart and wagon by now. The baker's dray. The miller's wagon that brings bags of flour. The neighboring farmer who drops by to visit (them but not me). This is a new and unfamiliar pair of wheels.

Through the wall chink: A closed carriage is coming down the road. Black lacquered finish, edged in gold around the doors and windows. Large wheels in back, smaller ones in front. A liveried coachman reins in a pair of dapple-gray horses and brings the carriage to a halt in front of the baker's cottage. The coachman has on white gloves and a top hat.

Not a local carriage, not even from town. It has no insignia, no coat of arms emblazoned on the sides, but this carriage clearly belongs to a wealthy person from some unknown city afar, a place I've never been before.

With surprising grace, the footman hops to the ground and opens the carriage door, flipping down a set of steps from inside. They are lined in red fabric. The baker's wife has made no mention of any visitor she expected.

A wiry little woman dressed all in black takes the footman's hand and comes gingerly down the steps. Black gloves, black hat and veil, black shawl. A widow's weeds. She lifts the veil and looks around her with obvious disdain.

This must be the wealthy aunt who reared the baker's wife and then disowned her. She obviously feels this squalid place is beneath her. Soon the baker and his wife emerge from the cottage. Despite that look of disdain on the aunt's face, there are sudden tears and a joyful embrace. Holding my friend's hands, the aunt takes a step backward and runs her gaze up and down her pregnant body. I strain to make out what they are saying. Only a word here and there.

She must have written to her aunt. She must have told her of the coming child and now there will be a healing of the rift. She never mentioned that letter to me, not even once. I hate people who keep secrets. They go inside the tiny cottage together and close the door behind them. I have my own pressing matters at hand – to finish the thinning of my rampion plants.

Down on my knees again, my hands in the soil. Perhaps she will send for me. She ought to send for me, or come over herself to bid me join them. After all, I am her dearest friend in the world, nearly as close to her as a family member. She will naturally want to introduce me, even if she doesn't know I gave her that child she so desperately wanted.

I had better make myself ready. In my current state, filthy from work in the garden, I am unfit to be seen. As soon as I finish this row, I will go inside to bathe and change my clothing.

* * *

I've been sitting here in the high-backed chair for over an hour now and still no word. My impatience grows. What can they be talking about? How can my friend forget me so completely? I'm beginning to question the depth of her regard.

I don't want to appear as if I've been waiting for her. She mustn't assume I have nothing better to do than sit hoping for a knock at the door. Even if I have no interest in my drawings just now, opening my sketchbook and setting out my pens this way will make it seem as if I've been busy.

What reason do I have for wearing my best dress, the one with lace at the collar and cuffs? What will I say if she asks?

* * *

They're in the sitting room now, all three of them, caught like figures in a painting by the afternoon light. The coachman has unharnessed the horses and led them into the barn. Surely this wealthy aunt doesn't intend to spend the night, not in this hovel. Perhaps she'll take a room at the local inn. Without darkness to conceal me, I mustn't stand too close to my bedroom window as I watch.

The baker's wife has made them tea. Or maybe coffee. And small sandwiches, too. She sits at her aunt's feet like a supplicant, cradling a mug between her hands. No fine china, not a delicate cup and saucer like the aunt no doubt uses at home. Perhaps my friend wants to curry favor. Didn't she tell me the aunt had no children of her own? My friend might be hoping for the inheritance.

She has never invited me over for tea, not once. I've never penetrated as far inside as their sitting room, only once or twice at the kitchen table. Most of the time, she comes to me, gorging on my rampion salad, swilling my dandelion wine, devouring most of the bread she brings to me so that I have almost nothing left when she departs. In truth, she hasn't been a very good friend. I do most of the giving.

The aunt says something to the baker that makes him rise swiftly from his chair and sends him out of the sitting room. She's obviously a woman used to giving commands and getting her way. I so dislike imperious people. From this different vantage point, I see the kitchen door open. Standing on the stoop, the baker bellows "Halloo there!" and soon the coachman emerges from the barn. No top hat now, no gloves. His waistcoat is unbuttoned. In the angling light of late afternoon, his hair shines a coppery red.

I am most likely too old for him.

He shuffles up to the baker and they talk briefly, then he goes off to fetch something from within the coach.

A present!

The aunt has brought my friend a present. Silvery ribbon and paper glint in the coachman's hand as he hands it over to the baker. Something for the baby, no doubt. Something expensive and impractical, while I have given the baker and his wife the greatest gift imaginable. I oughtn't to blame them for their ingratitude. How can they be grateful when they don't know how much I have done for them, how much they are forever in my debt?

Why haven't they sent for me?

In the sitting room, still seated at her aunt's knees, my friend removes the ribbon and paper … opens the box. What is it? Clothing of some kind. The baker's wife holds it up and displays it for her husband then for her aunt. I move closer to the window for a better look. It's white, I believe, and frilly. She clutches the gift to her breast and starts to weep – that way she always puts hand to mouth when the tears come. The baker's wife weeps at the drop of a hat, sometimes for no reason at all.

The baker draws near to the window and I withdraw in haste, my heart thumping in my chest. Has he seen me? He peers up at my bedroom window. Or perhaps he's only looking at the sky. He may be bored, listening to his wife's silly chatter and needless tears. He probably dislikes the aunt as much as I do and resents the way she orders him around.

He stretches his arms wide, as if to yawn, and in one swift decisive move, he draws the curtains together and closes them.

* * *

I don't think I'll place a curse of sickening on their well. A brief infestation of fleas might be more appropriate. The punishment should fit the crime, and hers is a comparatively small one. So far. If she comes to apologize tomorrow morning, I may overlook her rudeness. If sufficiently contrite, she might yet escape my wrath.

On the other hand, it's possible that the aunt is entirely to blame. My friend might have wanted to send for me but the aunt, accustomed to having her way in all things, said, "Even if she is your dearest friend in the world, I don't care to know her." She gives herself airs, that aunt. She believes herself above me. I might punish *her* instead. Lame her horse. Or blind her coachman.

But then she might stay even longer. Best to let her alone so she'll depart and leave us in peace.

It feels as if I've been sitting here for hours. Those curtains remain closed but I know the three are yet within because of fire and candlelight brightening the fabric edges. The coachman has brought the horses from the barn and put them once again in harness. He must be sitting in the kitchen now, waiting for his mistress to be ready. They wouldn't invite him into the sitting room. He's only a servant, after all.

The sky has gone fully dark and a shard of moon hangs over the barn. Such a wealth of stars! The way they flicker and blink makes me feel less alone, almost as if they are reaching out to me in my solitude. My teacher once told me that stars have a language all their own but that the art of understanding it has been lost. Sad, when you consider it. All those words floating through the cosmos with no one to comprehend them.

* * *

Waking with a start, I peer out the window. The coach has gone and the house across the lane is dark. I've missed the aunt's departure. How long did I sleep? One hour? Two hours? Now I'll have a hard time drifting off again.

She never sent for me.

Even with several rampion pickles to calm me down, I sleep poorly. Again and again, I awaken from rageful dreams I can't remember. I know they are rageful because they leave me exhausted and bereft, as if some tremendous machine of war has wreaked havoc upon my world. In the morning, my head feels thick and my body sluggish. A vague feeling of nausea.

I pour water into the basin on my washstand. Still groggy, I hang my head over the water and forget myself for a moment. Sleep briefly returns, my eyes close, and I'm falling, falling, falling. I jerk my head back as it drops toward the basin. Fully awake now, heart pounding. No reason to feel so afraid.

The reflection of my face, there in the still water beneath me. Red-rimmed eyes and hair bedraggled after a night of fitful sleep. Skin pitted and gray. I hate the old hag gaping back at me. I keep no looking glass in my house because I've always loathed my reflection. Even as a young woman, I was ugly. Never pretty and fresh like the baker's wife. More hideous even than that slattern, the carpenter's wife.

Of course she didn't send for me. Why would anyone care to be my friend?

I lave my face with cool water. This is not the first time I have felt this way, sick after consuming too many rampion pickles. I am pathetic and weak, unable to keep desire in check.

After dressing, I go downstairs to the kitchen. I probably ought to eat something wholesome but the idea of food only increases the nausea. It will pass. I know the discomfort will last a few hours at most. Black coffee will help. No cream and sugar, the way I usually enjoy it. The sharp and vaguely bitter taste of black coffee feels appropriate, as if I deserve no better.

Perhaps I will forgo all rampion today. Surely I can go one day without indulging myself. Cradling the big brown mug between my hands, I sit at the kitchen table and take tiny sips. I will finish my coffee and when the sick feeling passes, I will eat a slice of bread slathered with butter cheese.

My nails need trimming. So long that they have begun to curl inward. Almost like claws.

What are the baker and his wife doing at this moment? Probably loading dough into their massive oven, sliding loaves from wooden paddles onto those heated metal plates. They are always so busy in the early morning. They awaken much earlier than I do, in complete darkness, to knead the dough and let it rise. So hard does my friend work that she probably forgets all about me for hours at a time.

A knock at the door!

She has not forgotten. She has come to apologize, to sit at my kitchen table and tell me all about her aunt's visit. My eyes well up with tears ... so grateful that I am not entirely alone. I make myself walk slowly to the door and wait a few moments before opening it. I don't want it to seem as if I've been waiting for her knock.

The baker, not his wife. His hands and arms are powdery white. His apron, too. A smudge of flour upon his balding pate.

"I'm sorry to trouble you," he says. There are worry lines in his brow, worry creases at his eye corners.

"Is anything the matter?"

"It's my wife. She's unwell."

"Not the baby!" I cry. "It's far too early for the baby to come."

He shakes his head. "No, it's nothing like that. She complains of headache and fever. Sometimes the delirium takes over and she tells me her body will catch fire unless I do something to help her."

My friend has sent for me! She wants me at her side!

"I'll fetch my shawl," I say. "Give me a moment."

As I am turning away, he nearly shouts at me. "No, stop! She doesn't want you!" His words cut into me. I can see him struggling to calm himself. "What I mean is that she's far too unwell for visitors. She can bear to see no one."

He obviously wants to soften his tone but he can't hide the truth: he doesn't like me. He doesn't want to be here on my doorstep, asking for … what?

"Then why have you come knocking at my door? What do you want?"

He looks down at his slippers, the ones he no doubt wears in the kitchen when baking. So great was his haste that he didn't bother to change them before crossing the lane. He does not want to say what he has come to say.

"You know how women can sometimes be when they are with child. These senseless cravings will come over them." Now he looks up. "She insists that only your rampion will ease her suffering. She begs you to make her a salad and let me carry it back to her. I'll gladly pay whatever price you ask. Only hurry, please. I can't bear to see her in such agony."

I am not wanted. Only my rampion. She has never cared for me.

Now that her wealthy aunt has forgiven her, she will shut me out from her perfect little world and keep everything to herself – her home, her husband, and her baby. Even that isn't enough to satisfy her greed. She wants my rampion, too.

I could kill him now. My rage fills me up. I could kill them both.

But a death spell is not simple. A death spell takes time. He squirms under the glare of my hatred.

"I beseech you, please do what she asks. I will give you whatever you want in return."

"Anything?" I have thought of another way to hurt them.

"Anything within my power to give."

I smile down upon him in triumph. "Then give me your baby."

The shock of my words jolts his body. "What did you say?"

"I will give you the rampion you ask for, as much as you like and whenever you like. I am content to wait for payment. When the time comes and she is born, you will give me the baby. This is the price I set upon my rampion."

He struggles to hide his horror and disgust but can't help revealing what he feels. It's written there upon his face. "Have you gone mad?" he asks. "You cannot be serious. You can't think that we would ..."

"I am entirely serious. A simple exchange: my rampion for your baby. You can always have another one."

He scoffs at me and shakes his head. "You're an evil old woman and I've always thought so. My wife is more kind-hearted than I, but I've always distrusted your show of friendship." He turns away with a snort of disgust. "Good day."

Before he has taken three steps, I slam the door behind him.

Bid me to make her a salad, as if I were nothing more than a servant! How dare she!

* * *

What is this new feeling? I want it to stop.

* * *

The baker believes his wife to be like other women with child, beset by their cravings. He doesn't understand what the rampion has done to her. I understand because I have felt the same way, that time when I tried to give it up. I know precisely how much she suffers and I rejoice in it.

Pacing the floor of my kitchen, back and forth until the room feels too small to hold the vastness of my fury. Then I walk from place to place throughout the house, into the sitting room and up the stairs to my bedroom. The curtains across the lane are still drawn. I don't care. I no longer want to know what goes on within their squalid little house. To think I actually believed that she cared!

Once again I have deceived myself. It should come as no surprise. The baker's wife has proven herself to be as selfish and unfeeling as the others, driven like all people of her kind by greed.

Imbecile! To believe you would ever find a true friend, even one. No one will ever care for you.

Her agony, the lack of rampion – this will be my revenge. She has wounded me and now I can wound her in return.

Not enough, though. I want her baby. After all, I gave it to her. Now I'll take it back.

If he comes to me again, this time upon his knees, begging for my help, I will cackle in delight.

"Do you pledge me your child in payment?" I'll demand.

"Never!" he'll say. "You're mad!"

Once more I will slam the door and shut him out. My exultant laughter will follow him as he crawls across the lane to that hovel they call home.

Perhaps I'll have some rampion today after all. I'll make the salad she longs for and eat it alone at my table, all for me and none for her. With each bite I take, I will imagine how much she suffers.

* * *

Another night of fitful sleep. Each time I manage to drift off, I awaken with a start to the same thought – her flesh in agony, his helpless distress as he watches her writhe in pain. I ought not to imagine it, over and over. It appeases my anger but at the same time, makes it worse. Another rampion pickle, here in the middle of the night, is not what I need. I want it.

Downstairs in the pantry, gathering my tatty old robe around me, I count the jars remaining on the shelf. Will I have enough to last until I can harvest new roots from the first crop? Over and again I've counted the jars and reassured myself there will be enough, but the feeling of safety never seems to last more than a day or two.

Sometimes I wish I'd never begun enhancing the rampion. It weighs so on my mind. And yet, what pleasures would remain to me without my rampion bliss?

A noise! Out in my garden!

Some hungry animal must have scaled the high wall to pillage my greens, the unripe fruit on my trees, my berries. The spells I cast to keep the animals away last only so long. From time to time, I must renew them. This last spell must have been very weak, to fade so quickly. I'll frighten off the intruder and recast the spell tomorrow. Too tired tonight, too agitated and beset. The enchantment would surely fail. A witch must be clear of mind and thoroughly intent on her spells to work magic.

I light the big brass lantern and carry it outside. Must be a very large animal, to make so much noise. The lantern, lifted high in my hand, spreads light throughout the garden – across the rampion rows, past the quince tree, toward the trellis with clematis growing up the stone wall.

There!

The baker is halfway up the wall, using my trellis as ladder. A cloth satchel over his shoulder, stuffed with greens. Rampion leaves, of course. He has ravaged my garden. In the abrupt light, he holds himself perfectly still. Does he think I won't notice him there if he doesn't move?

With a groan and a crack, the trellis begins to pull away from the wall. The clematis clings to the stonework … it seems almost as if time has slowed down as the baker slips gradually backwards. The trellis vibrates gently, held in place by the vines; then the clematis lets go and the baker crashes onto the ground.

I draw close and hold the lantern above him so it spills watery light upon his face. The fall has knocked the wind out of him. His mouth agape, his body heaves like a fish stranded on land. He cannot draw breath.

How I relish his suffering! When I cackle in triumph, understanding makes his eyes grow wide in terror – that high-pitched evil sound only a true witch can make. Not just an old hag who lives across the lane. He fears my power and what I might do to him.

"Do you understand now why you have no choice but to give me your baby?" I say.

More heaving, still he can't breathe.

"Do you?!" I shout.

Finally, he nods his head. All at once, he gasps and the wind goes rushing in. One big hungry draught of air after another. He rolls himself gently onto his knees. The pain is slowly passing.

"I won't kill you for trespassing and theft," I say, "though I could easily do so. You know that now. I will allow you to leave and take my rampion with you, but first you must promise."

"I … p-promise," he wheezes.

"To make a pledge to a witch is the most binding of contracts. To break one would bring certain ruin upon you and your family. Do you understand?"

Sometimes a small lie is necessary to get the desired result. Sometimes you must terrify people before they will obey.

He nods his understanding. His breathing has almost returned to normal.

"Now you will make a binding pledge. You must say it in the correct form. Speak the words after me: 'I promise to give you our child when she is born.'"

He has recovered enough to glare hatred at me. "I promise to give you our child when she is born."

For effect, to seal the pledge and make it feel more weighty and binding, I throw my head back, cackling in triumph.

"You may go now, whenever you feel ready. Use the gate this time. And don't forget to take the rampion with you. After all, you've paid for it."

* * *

Whenever the baker's wife has finished gorging herself on rampion salad and there is none left, her husband knocks on my door and politely asks for more, his gaze downcast. He trembles on my stoop, unable to disguise his fear. Sometimes he waits days before asking while she struggles to break the rampion's hold upon her. I know because I can hear her wails of distress, high-pitched with an agony that carries. As the weeks have passed, I've made her portions smaller and smaller, giving him a tiny bit less each time he asks.

I haven't seen her in many weeks. Ever since the aunt's visit, the sitting room curtains have remained closed. She keeps to her bed, I expect. Fat and bloated with my baby growing inside of her, she has probably lost both her figure and her looks. Some women never shed the pounds they gain for their babies, remaining fat for life. Giving birth often leaves even the most beautiful women worn out and prematurely aged. Perhaps the baker's wife will die in childbirth. The baby coming forth might rip her body asunder; birth cries will mingle with one final piercing shriek as the mother succumbs.

The aunt comes to visit every few weeks. Each time, her coachman stows several boxes within the coach while his mistress takes tea. They think me an unobservant fool but I know what they are plotting. The baker and his greedy fat wife have no intention of delivering the baby into my arms, despite the promise he gave to me. With his meek manners, he may be the picture of submission, but I know they intend to slip away one night, never to return, taking my baby with them. What the aunt hasn't already removed in her coach, what they themselves can't carry, they will leave behind.

If men and a wagon were to come for the enormous oven, it would too clearly signal their departure, of course. They must have decided to abandon it as part of their wicked plot to deprive me of my child.

Maybe the wealthy aunt will take them in and allow the baker to renounce his trade. No longer will he have need of the oven. No longer will he and his wife rise each day before dawn and toil for hours in darkness. A life of ease and comfort may await them in some distant city.

Unless I kill them first. I certainly won't allow them to take my baby.

I am always on the lookout but even I have need of sleep. I've set the ravens to keep watch at night. I've bewitched the baker's dray. I permit him to continue taking his wares to market but should *she* ever climb onto the dray's bench …

* * *

With fall underway, even the second crop of rampion leaves has been exhausted and I've harvested the roots. Now I offer the baker a single rampion pickle when he comes begging. I give him the smallest ones from the jar to carry back to her, just large enough to slake the rampion thirst but not enough to fully satisfy her need for it, not enough to take the pain away entirely. I keep the biggest ones for myself.

I've finished setting up my baby's new room – the old closet where I used to keep my wheel before pain in my joints forced me to give up spinning. Fresh whitewash for the walls, an old crate with blankets for her bed, a rocking chair. No room for any other furnishings. Finding a wet nurse may be a problem. My old dugs have no milk, have never produced milk. I may need a spell of compulsion to make her stay. Not someone from the village nearby. Her people might come searching for her.

If the baker and his wife see me leave when I travel abroad in search of a wet nurse, they might try to slip away. Or break into my house and plunder my pantry. What if I were to return only to find my rampion stores exhausted? Then my own agonized screams might carry on the wind. I'm afraid to leave the house and travel far from my jars of rampion. But I must find a wet nurse for my baby before she is born.

Imbecile! Why didn't you think of it before? A summoning spell, of course.

But not yet. I'll wait until the baby comes. I can't abide strangers in my house and I won't have the wet nurse near me before I must. Some disheveled slut with enormous dugs, gorging on my food so she can make more milk. I'll put a lock on the pantry. I won't have her rooting about for herself and discovering my jars of rampion.

* * *

Winter.

Soon my baby will be born. Counting forward from the date on which I slipped the potion into her tea, it should be any day now. Two weeks at most if it was the second potion that made her fertile. I have decided to name my baby Rapunzel. It's the word my teacher used for rampion, what they call the plant in her native language. The name seems entirely fitting.

At night, I lie awake and imagine how it will feel to cradle her in my arms. I drift off to sleep in rampion bliss but often awaken in terror from a nightmare, the same nightmare again and again. Baby at my breast, enraged because no milk will come. Though newly born, she has large sharp teeth, almost like fangs, that sink into my saggy flesh. Sometimes it is the pain of teeth ripping in that awakens me.

Crack!

The sharp loud sound penetrates from outside. Then the frightened whinny of horses.

I know what has occurred. The baker and his wife have chosen this moonless night to make their escape, in the small hours hoping I would be asleep. Out in the barn, as quiet and stealthy as some rodent, he harnessed the horses and led the dray up to the house. She climbed onto the bench beside him, and as he urged the horses forward, it triggered my spell. Peering out the window, I can just make out the dray on its side, the axle broken. The baker helps his fat clumsy wife to her feet. As he calms the horses and frees them from their harness, she trudges back toward the house, one hand to the small of her back.

I wish I could hear the sound of her wretched tears.

I must be more fully on my guard from now on. They will try again. I should lame the horses so they can't ride away on their backs. Or I could poison their feed. You can't ride far on a dead horse. As much as I long to kill the baker and his wife right away, I don't want to harm my baby. Once she is born, we shall see. I might let them go, or I might not. It will depend on how much more trouble they give me. If they recognize now that they must comply and give me no further trouble, I might be generous.

* * *

The baker is coming less often to ask for pickles. Every other day, then every few days. Now and then, I hear her agonized wails but not so frequently as before. She is attempting to wean herself from rampion. The baker brings her the pickle I have given him, she breaks it in two and eats only half. The other half the following day. Then even smaller pieces with the next pickle. I have thought of trying this method before but could never bring myself to begin.

If she succeeds in breaking the rampion's hold, it will feel to me like a defeat. It will feel as if she has triumphed over me. The next time the baker comes, I give him one of the largest pickles. I generously offer him a second but he declines it.

* * *

Her screams awaken me from a shallow slumber. These days I always sleep lightly because I'm so worried they will try again to slip away under cover of darkness. She must have gobbled up that last big pickle and now her agonized body wants even more. The agony of craving, the fire in her limbs, the sweating. She is not stronger than I am after all. Her attempt to break free of the rampion was no more successful than my own.

These screams sound different. They come and they go. For a long while, I lie awake in my bed listening for the next scream, impatiently counting the seconds, willing it to come.

When it does, when I hear how much she suffers, I feel happy. The intervals between the screams seem to last about the same length of time though they're growing shorter.

Imbecile! The baby is coming!

Soon my little Rapunzel will be born, at long last. In the darkness, I raise my arms as if to reach out to her.

Come to Mother!

* * *

What is happening? Is this the end of me?

* * *

A different sort of screeching now – the first sounds of my Rapunzel as she begins life on this earth. I am so deeply moved. I never expected to be a mother. My arms ache to hold my little Rapunzel close, to comfort her, to quell her screaming. It's a very unpleasant sound and I wish it would stop.

I cannot bear the idea that the baker's wife is holding my little Rapunzel at this very moment and singing to her. With my windows shut tight against the winter cold, I cannot hear those songs but I know the baker's wife must be singing because it's what I long to do. I will sing to Rapunzel and the sound of my voice will calm her.

As I prepare my coffee and toast, I sing to myself instead, softly at first and then louder. I know only a few songs, and even those are half-remembered. I hum when I can't recall the words. In my own ears, my singing voice sounds like the grating noise of geese. Even though I hear the melodies in my head, I can't make my voice repeat them exactly. Never mind. Babies always find their mother's voice beautiful because they don't know any better. Of course my little Rapunzel will love me.

As soon as I knew my baby had been born, I chanted the summoning spell and now the wet nurse is on her way. On foot. She will arrive in a day or two, but I can't wait that long. I want my baby now.

I'll use this basket with my finest blanket inside. Rapunzel deserves the very best. My hand is sweaty on the basket's wicker handle as I knock. In my thin shawl, I'm shivering on the stoop of their cottage, elated and afraid at the thought of it – soon I will hold my baby.

The door opens narrowly and the baker peers out. His face is ugly with hatred.

"What do you want?" he hisses.

"My baby, of course. You've taken my rampion and now the time has come for you to fulfill your pledge."

"Get away, old woman. You're mad if you think I'd give you our baby. I'm not afraid of you." The door closes with an adamant thump.

"You should be," I say to the door.

Again I knock but now he won't answer. I continue knocking for long minutes, until my knuckles are swollen and painful.

"Be gone!" he finally shouts, the sound muffled as it comes to me through the wood.

I had hoped they would cooperate. I had hoped he would honor his pledge and save me the trouble of taking what is mine by force. I see now I have no alternative.

* * *

I could pile up my torments, week after week, until at last they realize the futility of resisting but I am impatient. I cannot wait that long. The cauldron is bubbling on the hearth and I have begun the lengthy process of brewing my potion. I'll be on my feet all the night long.

It seems a very great while since I took such satisfaction in my work. Consulting my spell and potion books gives me great pleasure, especially when I think that every moment of toil brings me closer to my daughter.

Rapunzel.

I whisper her name again and again as I stir the brew with my paddle.

I can't recall the last time I used some of these herbs. They have very specialized effects and you don't use them in your everyday potions. Balmony. Henbane. Knot Weed. When that lying old farmer tried to cheat my teacher out of payment, after she cured his flock of the bloat, she showed me how to make this very potion, one of her own devising, and I wrote the receipt into my potion book. When the villagers found him hanging from a tree, they believed he had succumbed to melancholia. His wife had died earlier that year, after all.

Teacher told me that you never know how the potion will affect people. You can predict the end result but not the method they will use to kill themselves. I wonder what the baker and his wife will do.

I'll have it ready by day's end then slip it into the well once night has fallen. If all unfolds according to plan, Rapunzel will be with me in time for the arrival of the wet nurse.

PART TWO

"Is there anything I might do for you, dearest Mother?" I always call her dearest Mother. It makes her happy to hear me say those words.

"I have everything that I need, my little Rapunzel."

Mother always calls me her little Rapunzel, even though I'm taller than she is. Now that my monthly blood has come, she says I'm a young woman, which must mean that I'm no longer little. The idea that I'm a young woman makes Mother unhappy.

Whenever she works on her plant drawings, she likes me to sit here in silence on the floor and play with my doll. She likes to see me brush its yarn-hair, long and yellow. She often says that the doll's hair looks just like mine only shorter.

My hair has grown so long now it reaches nearly to the floor. It's always snagging on drawer handles in the kitchen or getting caught in doorways. I want to cut it off but Mother won't allow it. After the weekly washing, she likes me to sit at her feet while she brushes and plaits it into one long braid. It hurts when she brushes through. Mother doesn't like me to complain so I don't speak of it. She ignores the silent tears slipping down my cheeks.

I hate this doll though I'm not allowed to say so. Mother becomes agitated if I say I don't like my old toys. Sometimes she weeps and tells me I mustn't grow up and leave her.

That scratching sound of her pen when she draws – it makes me want to scream.

I'd like to ask Mother why I must stand back from the window whenever a cart passes by. I asked her once before and

198

she told me that dangerous men roam the world and will do cruel things to little girls. Mother said that if the men saw me at the window, they might break in and hurt me. She tells me that all strangers are bad but I don't believe her. She cannot be the only good person alive.

And yet she is right about everything.

* * *

Never was there such a sweet, loving child. My little Rapunzel, brushing her doll's hair like a caring mother. Just like her own caring mother. That slight smile on her face ... the brushing of the doll's hair must remind her of me doing the same for her every week. Hour after hour, year after year. My little Rapunzel – how I adore her!

* * *

So many questions I long to ask!

Are there more than these two types of people, men and women?

Why is she old while I am young? Will I be ugly like her one day?

Are there ever any new people and where do they come from? Out of eggs like the chicks in our coop? Out of their mothers' bodies like our piglets? If I once grew inside Mother's body, how did I get there?

Do people die like our chickens do when they grow very old?

The idea that she might die and leave me alone one day ... it fills me with terror. All alone in this house.

Sometimes, though, I think I might prefer to be alone. I know that only a very bad person would feel that way. Uncaring. Ungrateful. Mother tells me I am uncaring and ungrateful whenever she flies into a rage. She must be right. Mother is always right, although I don't understand how I can be the most beautiful, loving, adorable girl in the world one day and a "hideous ingrate" the next.

The hurtful words are the more truthful ones.

Why am I so deeply curious about those men who drive carts along our lane? Not often, only once every few days. Lately I find I can think of little else. Even now, sitting here on the floor, passing the brush over my doll's yarn-hair, I see him – the young man who drove by here a few days ago. Broad shoulders and powerful hands. Reddish hair. I watched him from my window upstairs when Mother thought I was napping. As he drove his cart past our cottage, he pulled to a stop and stared for a long while at the empty old house across the lane. Though she insists that all men are ugly brutes, I did not find this one ugly.

I know better than to ask Mother why I want those big hands to touch me. She will tell me I am a disgusting slut. She has told me so before. I don't understand the full meaning of that word but I do know it means that I am very bad.

It is nearly time for her medicine. Every afternoon around this hour, she unlocks the pantry door and takes out a jar of rampion pickles. She counts three of them onto a plate, settles into her high-backed chair, and eats them slowly along with her tea. Always three and none for me. She insists they taste bad but I can see the relish upon her face. If I ask again whether I might try one, she'll tell me they are good for achy old women but harmful to little girls.

I am not a little girl!

I'd like to rip the yarn hair from my doll's wooden head.

Mother isn't ready yet for tea. She continues scratching away at her drawing. If that sound goes on much longer … I feel a scream rising in my throat.

"Would you tell me the story once more, dearest Mother, about the evil baker and his wife who once lived across the lane?" Even hearing this familiar old tale would come as a relief. Anything rather than the sound of her quill pen on paper.

"Perhaps later. For now, be silent until I've finished my work. Then we shall have our tea."

Along with the tea, I will eat one or two of those dry, flavorless cakes she always makes, the ones she refers to as my "favorites." I know better than to let her to know I hate them. Afterward, she will ask me to read aloud from one of her many books. When I was little, she refused to teach me how to read; she wouldn't explain why. As her eyesight grew worse, she thought better of it.

If I didn't have books, I think I might want to die.

I mustn't listen to the scratching sound of her pen or I might scream. I'll tell myself the story of the baker and his wife (I know it by heart) – here in my own thoughts where I can't be overheard. She won't mind as long as I don't say it aloud.

Once upon a time ...

Mother always begins the story in just that way, the very same words every time. When I once asked her to explain their meaning, she seemed irritated. "Long ago," she snapped. "That's what it means. Now hush and let me tell my story."

Mother doesn't like to be interrupted.

Once upon a time, a baker and his wife moved into the cottage across the lane. In those days, the cottage had not yet fallen into disrepair. So Mother has told me, again and again. In repulsive detail, she has described the slatternly wife who did nothing but lie around all day, growing fatter and fatter. The brutish husband who beat her at night. They had no children nor did they seem to want any. Mother pitied them in the beginning, until they stole from her.

Under a moonless sky, the husband scaled our high wall and plundered the garden. One time when telling the story long ago, Mother said he came after her quince; the next time she insisted it was the broccoli that lured him. In differing versions I've heard over the years, the greedy and brutish baker has ripped her lettuce from the ground, taken a knife to her leeks, and stripped apples from her tree. Awakened by all the noise he made clambering back over the wall, she came outside just in time to see him escaping with his plunder – the apples, the broccoli, or the quince.

In no version of the story did he escape with her rampion.

A week or so later, when they hadn't emerged from their cottage in days, with no smoke curling up from their chimney, Mother finally crossed the lane. They didn't answer her knock on the kitchen door and so she opened it. She found them dead on the floor in twin pools of drying blood, beside their enormous bread oven. They'd obviously slit their own throats – knives still clutched tight in their stiff dead hands.

Mother believes that remorse drove them to take their own lives. After the violence they'd done to her, they couldn't live with themselves. Even when I was still a little girl, this explanation made no sense to me. I could never imagine such people, the way Mother had described them, feeling so guilty for stealing a few plants that they would kill themselves.

And why all the other plants but never the rampion?

* * *

As she often does after her tea, Mother has fallen asleep in the high-backed chair. Her teacup is empty but half a rampion pickle lies uneaten on the plate beside her. It's not the first time she has drifted off before finishing the third one. I could cross the room now and take it. I could swallow it down before she awakens, before she has time to stop me. Stealing from Mother would be very bad. At the thought of it, I can hear the fearful beat of my heart in my ears. Sometimes the idea of my own badness excites me, though I know it is very wrong. This urge to steal from a sleeping old woman, one who has made such sacrifices for me my whole life – I must be very bad. I will sit here and finish eating these cakes. I will choke them down with mouthfuls of tea – my punishment.

* * *

I knew my little Rapunzel would pass the test. Even though she believes I am asleep, she would never take advantage of me.

She'd never steal the last piece of pickle for herself when I have told her again and again she must not eat them. Such a sweet, obedient child!

* * *

It isn't only the rampion pickles but the plant leaves, too – early in the season before she harvests the roots. I've watched unnoticed from the back door, pushing it ajar just wide enough to open a crack. The other morning, I saw her down on her knees, thinning the rampion shoots and stuffing the ones she'd plucked into her mouth. When she came back into the house, she seemed happy at first, then angered by a dirty pot in the kitchen sink. I have so many chores, I sometimes lose track of them all. The beds, the floors, the pots and pans. Other than baking those dry flavorless cakes, I do all the cooking.

Is this how my entire life will pass? Is there nothing more?

Every afternoon, she sends me upstairs for my nap, just as if I were still a little girl, but I almost never sleep. I do lie down upon my bed because when I least expect her, she may open my door to make sure I'm asleep. How does she sneak up, a fat old woman, so quietly that I never hear her before the door flies open? I keep my eyes closed and tell myself stories. I listen for the sound of carts or wagons along the road; if I actually hear something, I step carefully to the window, making sure to avoid the one creaky floorboard. That was how I saw the young man with reddish hair and broad shoulders the other day. I keep hoping he will come back again.

After enough time has passed, I go downstairs to the sitting room where I always find Mother waiting for me. I force a yawn and stretch my arms, as if I have just awakened.

"Did you sleep well, my little Rapunzel?"

This is what she always asks me, day after day. Today I tell her "Indeed I did." I don't add "dearest Mother" though I know she would like to hear me say it.

* * *

At breakfast, Mother complains of feeling unwell – not her usual complaints of vague pain or discomfort when she wants me to feel sorry for her. Her skin is a sickly shade of gray today. Her hand trembles when she tries to lift her teacup, and tiny sweat beads encrust the coarse hairs along her upper lip. I keep my gaze downcast at my own food. The sight of her face has killed my appetite.

"Is there anything I can do for you, dearest Mother? Fetch you some of your medicine, perhaps?"

She shoots me an angry glance. "More of the medicine will only make it worse!" she snaps.

Her words confuse me. It almost sounds as if the rampion pickles have caused her sickness, which makes no sense. After teatime, she always seems to feel better.

"Perhaps you should go back to bed, dearest Mother. What you need right now is rest."

"Don't talk to me as if I were a child!" she snarls. "And don't ever tell me what I need. What you *imagine* I need. Never! Do you understand?"

I've learned from experience that I must drop my eyes now and hold my tongue. I could force tears into my eyes, as if I am a poor innocent creature wounded by her words, but I'm too angry now to pretend. We sit in silence until she lifts herself from her chair and trudges off to her bedroom. I know she is going to take a nap, just as I suggested, but she won't tell me so. She won't let me believe I had something useful to say.

I mustn't indulge these feelings. It is only the illness that makes her behave this way. When she feels better, she will once again be my dearest loving Mother.

* * *

Out here in the garden, I can breathe. I'm not supposed to be here alone but sometimes, the air inside the house feels so thick and dusty I cannot bear it. Sunlight breaks through the clouds, filtering through tree branches, and falls upon my face, my bare arms, my hands. The warmth on my skin feels so good that I could weep. Why does pleasure so often seem half-sad?

Before I came outside, I heard Mother snoring through her bedroom door. I crept away and slipped into the garden as quietly as I could. Still, she might be awake now. Though she has no upstairs window from which to watch me, I feel her watching. I always feel her watching. Turning quickly toward the house, I half-expect to see her glaring at me from the stoop. She isn't there.

Her rampion plants need thinning again. She wouldn't want me to do it for her. I know this, even as I kneel down and go to work. I choose the shoots I think she won't miss, only a few. I brush away most of the soil and shove them into my mouth as my heartbeat goes racing. Fine grit between my teeth as I chew. My braid curling in the dirt.

It's a little sweet, something like spring lettuce, but nothing so delicious that Mother should want to keep it all for herself. Disappointment robs the sunlight of its warmth, makes the day seem thin and pointless. All the days of my life the same way. As I rise to my feet, the taste in my mouth turns bitter. Most things you look forward to eventually let you down this way. Now the sun above seems to be laughing at me.

Later, when I am scrubbing pots in the kitchen, my mood begins to shift. It comes on slowly. How beautiful the soapy bubbles! The colors that glint on their shiny surface, their perfect roundness. I plunge my hands down into the warm soapy water and leave them there. Pure pleasure, from my hands down to my feet, and a little throb of joy between my legs. No sadness now. The feeling throughout my body reminds me of the look on Mother's face at teatime after she has taken her medicine.

It's not the delicious flavor that she wants to keep from me.

* * *

At last!

It's the same wagon as before, the same sound of wheels rumbling along the road. Pulling back the curtains on my bedroom window, just enough so I can peer through, I see him standing beneath me in the middle of the road. The reddish color of his hair glints like copper. Why has he stopped? It must be the lingering effect of those rampion shoots that makes him seem so beautiful to me.

He is not alone. I didn't notice the other man at first but I see him now, yards away and peering through a crack in the boarded up window, the one that opens into the kitchen where Mother found the dead baker and his wife. The second man has reddish hair, too, though duller and shot through with gray. When he turns and speaks to the younger man, I see how much they look alike. The same full mouth and high cheekbones, their shoulders equally broad.

I look nothing like Mother.

What would she do if I were to go running downstairs and into the road? I'd fling wide the door so quickly she wouldn't have time to make me stop. What would I say to the men when I reached them, out of breath, the pulse of blood loud in my ears? I've never spoken to anyone, not a single person, other than Mother.

My name is Rapunzel and I am trapped in my mother's house.

I could never speak such words. Even to think them makes me feel that I am a very bad person. The rampion pleasure has begun to fade.

The two red-haired men, one old and one young, stand in the middle of the road and speak together. From time to time, one of them looks toward the abandoned house, or toward the barn out back with its caved-in roof timbers. How I long to hear what they are saying!

* * *

By the time I set our laden dinner plates on the table – boiled chicken and new potatoes – Mother is feeling much better. The pleasure unleashed in my body by those rampion shoots has passed and I'm wondering how I can have more of them without getting caught. I keep thinking about the red-haired men, too. Now and then the sound of Mother's chewing breaks through … moist smacking noises, her teeth scraping against the fork tines. There are bits of chicken visible in her open mouth.

My hand's grip around the handle of this knife is tightening. I could raise it high and drive it straight down hard into the withered flesh of her forearm. I could draw blood.

"You seem far away, my little Rapunzel. What are you thinking?"

I want to tell her that my thoughts are my own.

"What does it mean that you are my mother?" I ask instead. The wince of surprise and alarm on her face pleases me.

"What a very odd question. What do you mean?"

I hear her swallow hard but don't dare to look at her now. My grip on the knife handle grows ever tighter.

"Are you my mother the way our sow is mother to her piglets?"

"Whatever can you …?! Me like the sow! What an outlandish idea!"

In only a moment or two, surprise will become anger. She might slap me. She might hurl her plate against the kitchen wall and scream at me to clean it up.

"Was I born from your body? That is what I want to know. And if I was, how did I get there?"

Now I am looking up. I don't usually stare directly into her eyes this way, not for so long. Her gaze drops to the knife in my hand, my fingers livid from holding on so tight. When she glances back up, I know we both feel the danger. Mother doesn't thrill to it the way I do. Neither one of us is eating.

"Of course you were born from my body," she finally says. "You are my daughter." The fact that she answered means that something important has changed between us. This one time, I actually forced her to answer me.

"And how did I get there?" The younger man looked much like the older one, from his hair color to his cheekbones. "Men have something to do with it, don't they?"

Mother's body is shaking. Her eyes have taken on that wild look they sometimes get before she strikes me. She drops her gaze once again to the knife. A broad smile slowly spreads over her face and it doesn't at all match the feeling I can in her eyes.

"You came to life inside my womb because I so desperately wished for a daughter of my very own. Never did a mother so long for child!"

Liar.

I do not say it.

"You are everything to me, my little Rapunzel. You know that, don't you?"

"Yes, dearest Mother. I know."

* * *

It will be as it was before with the wet nurse, all over again – my little Rapunzel will find someone she loves better than me. A man this time. I know what she wants. A large hairy body on top of her, pushing in. She probably pictures it to herself, alone at night in her bed. She told me herself that she likes to put her hand there. Sometimes I wonder whether having a child is worth all the pain they bring to you. If only I could keep the men away from her forever! How much longer before she defies me?

There is always the tower.

* * *

"I don't care for any of those cakes today, dearest Mother. I'd rather have a rampion pickle with my tea."

We're together in the kitchen, with tealeaves bloating in the pot's hot water. She has already unlocked the pantry and placed the pickle jar on the counter alongside the cake tin.

Mother doesn't say what she usually says, that her medicine tastes bad and is better for achy old women than little girls. She knows the old reasons won't satisfy me. I told her this morning that I wanted to cut off my braid; rather than slapping my face, she said, "We'll see."

"Just one," I now say. "I think I'm old enough to decide for myself whether I like the taste."

Mother fusses with the plates and teacups.

"If you're worried that we'll run out," I add, "we could plant another crop. I could help you tend to it. Wouldn't that be nice, the two of us working together in the garden?"

I don't need to state it plainly: *the rampion could bring us closer, if only you'll share.* My dearest Mother is not stupid.

The pickle she finally places on my plate is smaller than any of the three she chooses for herself. "Don't think you're going to make a habit of it," she says. "Do I make myself clear?"

I don't need to answer back. Whatever she may say, she understands now that I will do as I like.

In the sitting room after our tea, we smile at one another across the room. Rather than settling onto the floor, I've taken the other high-backed chair, the one that matches her own. The afternoon sunlight streams into the room and my body feels aglow with a pleasure that seems a part of the light, a part of its warmth. From the look on Mother's face, I know she feels the same way. She doesn't look so ugly, now that the rampion has taken hold. Rampion pickles are far more powerful than the leaves!

* * *

She feels the same way I do. Perhaps this is how it will be from now on, forever after. Together.

* * *

We both hear it at the same moment. From the lane that passes by our cottage, wagon wheels rumbling toward us. I recognize the sound. The red haired young man has returned. Or maybe both of the men.

Mother's face has gone gray with fear. Now I understand that Mother is terrified I will leave her once I meet someone whose company I prefer. I've always known but not quite known it. I almost pity her.

The wagon has come to a stop out front, the way it did the last time. Faint voices and the sound of heavy objects dropping onto the ground. What could it mean?

I feel light on my feet, as light as a bubble floating past Mother on my way to the front door. She can do nothing to stop me now. I open the door before she has time to rise from her chair.

The two red-haired men who look alike, one older and one younger, have stopped their wagon in front of the cottage where the baker and his wife once lived. My heart beats faster at the sight of them. Matching brown caps with short bills and high fronts. They're unloading the bed of their wagon – lumber and tools mostly. They turn toward me as I come running up.

Does that look mean they're glad to see me? What will they think of me?

Breathless, stopping before them, I have no idea what to say. *Imbecile!* To have come running up this way without a thought beforehand. The older man drags the cap from his head and holds it over his belly.

"Good day, Miss." The rumble of his voice comes as a shock – so much deeper than Mother's or my own! Both men gaze at me with expectation lighting their faces. Heat has spread throughout my body and it needles me. I feel as ugly as Mother.

"Good day," I say, only because the older one already said it. I want desperately to run back into our house but my limbs won't listen.

"I'm Matthew," the older man says, "and this here is my son Thomas. He'll be your neighbor, once we make this run-down old barracks a fit place to live. Wants to raise hogs, he says. Wants to be his own master, he says. We shall see whether he can manage on his own. We shall see."

I'll have to save these words and think about them later when I'm alone. I'm so overwhelmed I don't understand half of what they mean, though the word "neighbor" jumps out. I want to clap my hands together and laugh.

The smile on the younger one's face, the one called Thomas ... my looks must please him. Mother has never gazed at me that way. I must not appear as ugly as I sometimes feel, at least not to Thomas. And I don't mind his crooked teeth. If he would keep smiling at me that way, I'd do almost anything for him.

"You must have the longest hair I've ever seen!" he says. I don't understand why my long hair makes him laugh.

"I am Rapunzel," I tell them. I reach back for my braid and hold it between my hands, tugging on it so my scalp hurts.

Matthew suddenly reaches out and knocks Thomas's cap from his head. "No manners! What would your mother say? Taught you better than to leave your cap on when a young lady is standing right in front of you."

Thomas bends down for his cap. Standing up, he holds it across his belly like his father.

"Begging your pardon, Miss." Thomas's voice is even deeper than Matthew's.

But why do they talk to me this way, as if I'm important? Matthew called me a "young lady," but in the stories, a lady is someone higher up, better than other people, a person who lives in a big house. They don't know who I am.

"I live over there," I tell them, pointing at our cottage.

"Course you do," says Matthew. "No other place out here."

Then why does he think I'm a lady? Talking to these strangers feels too complicated. I don't understand how to do it.

"I'm going now," I tell them. Before they have time to say anything more, I go running to Mother. I've hardly thought about her while talking to Matthew and Thomas.

"A pleasure to meet you, Rapunzel," one of them calls out. Thomas, I think. I'm almost certain the voice belongs to Thomas.

* * *

Of course she'll come back ... she's not ready yet to leave me. When she comes back, I must behave as if nothing has changed. I've always known this day would come and I'm ready for it. The tower is ready. The potion is ready.

* * *

When I tell Mother that we're to have neighbors, she smiles and says, "Wonderful news! So good for you to have someone else to talk with. Someone closer to your own age, not old and dull like your mother."

I expected her to be angry. I thought she'd scream at me for running outside and then tell me I must never again speak to strangers. I don't trust her smile but I'm glad she hasn't slapped me.

"You told me that all men are bad."

"Not all, certainly not all. We shall see."

"They didn't seem bad. They were kind to me."

"You must learn to judge for yourself, my little Rapunzel. I won't always be around to protect you."

When she's dead, perhaps I will go to live with Thomas in the house across the lane. Or maybe even before. Away from Mother but not too far away.

"And now," she says, "perhaps you'll read to me if it's not too much to ask. I'll even let you choose the book this time."

Why is her voice so full of kindness when I know she doesn't feel that way? Given everything she has ever said before, her tone must be lie.

"Any book?" I ask.

Mother hesitates. "Yes, any book. Even the ones that are forbidden to you." She doesn't know that I've already read them. "You're all grown up now."

That smile on her face frightens me. I don't want to show that I'm frightened. I make myself smile back.

"For being so very kind to me, dearest Mother, I will choose *your* favorite. The tale of ugly duckling. You've always done so very much for me, it's the least I can do for *you*."

* * *

I'm reading aloud to Mother but my thoughts are across the lane with Thomas and Matthew. If I were up in my room, I could watch from the window. Matthew said they were going to make the baker's old cottage a "fit place to live." They'll have to do something about that hole in the roof and the broken windows.

I hope it won't take them too long. I don't think I could bear to wait very long for Thomas to live across the lane from me. I can hardly bear for him to be out of my sight.

I'm coming to the end of the tale at long last. "'Then he rustled his feathers, curved his slender neck, and cried joyfully, from the depths of his heart, 'I never dreamed of such happiness as this, while I was an ugly duckling.'"

If I were to live across the lane, I wouldn't have to read this story ever again.

"Thank you, thank you, my little Rapunzel. You always read with such expression!"

"I think it must be time for my nap," I tell her, rising from my chair.

"You're too old for a nap," she says, the kindness gone from her voice. She understands the actual reason I want to be in my room.

"I'm very tired now. I'll rest for a while and then see to our supper."

* * *

Matthew draws the saw back and forth across planks of wood to cut them. He hands each one up to Thomas, who reaches down from the eaves. Thomas then carries the planks to the roof hole and fits them into place. While I was reading to Mother, they managed to block up half the hole. Maybe Thomas will move into the cottage tomorrow.

He suddenly breaks into song. The beauty of his deep voice reaches deep into my body. I can hear every word but there are many I don't understand. *Rapier, whiskey, dubloons.* Thomas sings while he hammers the board into place. Who is this Jenny? A woman, I think, and Thomas seems to care for her. I hate Jenny. But wait … she betrayed him and tried to steal his money. I think that's what happened. Poor Thomas. He no longer cares for Jenny and I am glad.

Matthew holds up another board to Thomas, who starts the song all over again. This time, Matthew joins in. When he sings the same words as Thomas, it occurs to me … the song is only a made-up story, like the stories I read to Mother. The ugly duckling didn't actually cry out in joy when he realized he was a swan because ducks can't speak. Jenny didn't actually steal from Thomas because she isn't real. Understanding this makes me happy.

When he lives across the lane, Thomas might teach me this song and all the other songs he knows. He'll explain to me about whiskey and dubloons. And he'll understand why I want his hands to touch me. It has something to do with the wetness down there and the same place on his body. Only it's not the same. Even from this far away, I can see that his body is different down there, not flat where I am flat.

He stops to wipe the sweat from his brow and looks over at our house. Is he thinking about me? If I wave to him now, will he see me and wave back?

Mother is downstairs … I'd forgotten all about her. If she knew I wanted to wave to Thomas from my window, she would scream at me.

* * *

I feel relieved, now that the time has come. No more worrying and wondering. I should have acted sooner, before the wish for other people took hold, but I've always hoped her devotion would last. My little Rapunzel is everything to me; why couldn't I be everything to her?

* * *

Mother and I don't speak during supper. We usually speak little but tonight the silence is deeper. I want the hours to pass quickly so the morning will come. How will I bear it if Thomas and Matthew don't return tomorrow? Today they didn't arrive until later in the day. Tomorrow afternoon seems very far off.

Once I've cleared up and washed the pots, I join Mother in the sitting room. Nowhere else to go in our little house. If I went up to my bedroom this early, she would be angry. I add another log to the fire and take the high-backed chair across from Mother. She has her knitting out. I could knit along with her but I don't want to. All I want is to sit here and gaze into the fire while thinking of Thomas. There's a red in the flames that is almost the color of his hair. I call up the words they spoke, and the sound of their voices, and the light in their eyes when they looked at me.

Matthew doesn't want Thomas to have a place of his own – I hear it now as I think over what he said. Matthew might have cut boards and handed them up to the roof, he might have joined in the song, but he doesn't believe Thomas can manage on his own. *We shall see*, he said. Mother says that sometimes when she means "no." What if Matthew convinces him that the cottage needs too much work and will never be a "fit place to live"? What if he makes Thomas doubt whether he truly does want to raise hogs?

All parents must be the same. They don't want their children to leave.

I couldn't bear my life if Thomas never came back. Only Mother and me alone in this little house, forever and ever. If I were to set off walking, she couldn't stop me. I could keep walking until the road took me to Thomas. If I met other people along the way, I could ask if they knew where to find him. My body shudders and my stomach goes tight.

Strangers.

Can you please take me to Thomas? He has red hair and crooked teeth.

What else could I say to them?

I didn't even notice that Mother had left the room but here she is, coming back from the kitchen. She stops before me and reaches for my hand. She places something on my palm and closes my fingers around it.

"My little Rapunzel," she whispers. Her eyes glisten with tears.

When she sits back down in her chair, I open my hand to see what she has placed there. A rampion pickle, a very large one.

Does she feel sorry for me? Has she sensed that the possibility of losing Thomas has upset me? Sometimes I wonder if Mother knows what goes on inside my head without my telling her. Sometimes I'm afraid to let a thought take shape because she'll hate me for thinking it. She doesn't hate me tonight. She seems different. I feel as if I don't know her and that idea scares me, too.

* * *

"I'll make the tea this afternoon, my little Rapunzel."

Thomas and Matthew have not yet returned and I am *distraught* – that's the word that describes how I feel. A woman in one of Mother's tales felt that way when she couldn't have children. I am also *beside myself*, like Rumpelstiltskin when the queen guessed his name. I will not have it so! If Thomas doesn't come back soon, I will tear myself in two like the angry little man. I have no idea how to do it.

Mother brings me tea; there are three rampion pickles on the saucer.

"So many!" I say.

Mother smiles. "You're not yourself today. The rampion will bring you peace of mind."

"You're very good to me, dearest Mother."

I gobble up the first one so quickly that a part of it lodges in my throat. I wash it down with a swallow from my cup.

"There's something different about the tea," I say.

"Nothing different," Mother tells me. "It's only the rampion that makes it seem that way."

The tea yesterday tasted as it has always tasted, even after I ate the pickle. But that pickle was much smaller. Perhaps it is only the larger pickles and not the smaller ones that alter the flavor of tea. After the second pickle, I no longer notice any difference. I nibble slowly on the third one.

Today, the rampion makes me hear sounds that aren't actually there. Each time I feel certain of rumbling wheels along the lane, I go to the window and peer out, only to find the familiar empty stretch of dirt between our house and the baker's cottage. No, now it is *Thomas's* cottage. Only if I think of it as Thomas's cottage and imagine him living there will it come to pass. I know I can't actually make it so with my thoughts but it feels true.

Perhaps I shouldn't have eaten all three pickles. Or I should have eaten them more slowly ... the room has begun to whirl around me. My stomach churns. Even when I hear more wagon wheels on the lane, I'm afraid to rise from my chair. I might fall down. I might vomit onto the carpet. The sound from outside grows louder and louder. This time I am sure – Thomas has come back at long last!

"Do you hear it, too?" I cry. My voice doesn't sound like me – thick and strangled somehow, as if my throat is closing off.

"Yes," Mother says. "I do believe our new neighbors have come back. I wonder if we should invite them in. Would you like to invite them in for tea, my little Rapunzel?"

I am falling.

* * *

When she awakens, she'll be glad to see familiar objects from home around her. The yarn-hair doll along with her brush, the counterpane from her old bed, a plate of her favorite cakes. On the curving wall of stone, I've tacked plant drawings from my collection, to remind her of me when I'm not here. I'll come every day without fail and she'll look forward to my visits. Alone here in this tower, she'll have little else to do but think of me and wonder when I'll be coming. I'll vary the times of my visits so she'll never be sure when to expect me.

* * *

Where am I?

Why does my head ache so? I can barely turn it upon this pillow. And the light from that window hurts my eyes. I'll lie here a while longer until the pain eases. My body feels heavy … weighted down by a thousand blankets.

What place is this? Curving walls … a round room. Those drawings belong to Mother. This counterpane used to cover my bed. Perhaps I can rise now onto my knees.

What has happened to my hair?! Already long before but now it has grown so much longer it's hard to lift my head up … the weight of it. I must have been asleep for years for it to grow so long. Twenty feet? Thirty feet? Much thicker than before. All in a single braid, so tight it pains my scalp.

Now I remember. We were having tea, Mother and I, and I heard the sound of Thomas's wagon outside. Then I fell asleep. How long ago? Maybe so many years that he has died by now. Am I old? Am I ancient and ugly like Mother? My hands fly to my face. Still smooth, not pitted and lined like Mother's.

Will I ever see Thomas again? The weight of my hair fills me with panic.

If I take hold of the braid further down and release the drag on my head … there, I'm on my feet. I revolve slowly to take in the room and the braid coils around my ankles. No door and only the one window, an immense metal hook driven into the stone beside it. A pallet on the floor under my feet, my rumpled counterpane, my old doll. A wooden table with a pitcher of water and a plate of those cakes I hate. A chamber pot. Nothing else.

She means me to stay here.

The shrieks shred my throat. On and on … I can't stop them. Terror floods up like blackness rising. The world goes dark.

* * *

When I awaken again, the pallet and my woolen dress are damp. I've wet myself. My stomach cramps with hunger but I won't eat those cakes. I'd rather starve to death than take a single bite. As I did before, I rise first onto my knees then release the braid's weight so I can stand. I drag it behind me to the window.

I'm high up in a tower, with outside walls so smooth they afford no toehold. If I tried to jump down, the fall would kill me. At least I have a way to end it if I need to. The tower rises within a small meadow, ringed by tall trees that close me in. No view of anything but grass and branches and a slight patch of sky above. The shrieks are rising up through my chest again but I push them down.

One by one, I tear down Mother's plant drawings and rip them into tiny pieces, as small as spring peas. It gives me something to do. I hurl the plate against the wall and stomp the dry old cakes into crumbs. I spin my doll by its yarn hair and fling it out the window. I would fling the chamber pot out, too, but I'll have need of it. Filling the tower with my own excrement will do nothing to hurt Mother.

Seated upon the window ledge, I call up pictures of Thomas, his coppery hair glinting from the rooftop while he and his father sang of Jenny. The tune is vivid in my head; when I start singing it aloud, I'm surprised that I remember the words, every one of them. The song parts come in pairs ending in words that rhyme, the way they do in some of Mother's books. *Sorrow-mor-*

row, forever-never. The longer I sing, the stronger my voice. The pleasant rumbly feeling in my chest distracts me from my groaning belly. Perhaps I should've saved those cakes.

As the day wears on, the sun lowers in the sky until it shines directly upon me at the window. Its heat against my flesh brings tears to my eyes. What will I do once the sun has gone? No candles. No hearth to light a fire. Alone in this tower, beset by darkness. And cold. I see myself shivering upon that thin pallet, with only my old counterpane to cover me. Does she intend me to starve or freeze to death, alone in this tower?

"Rapunzel, my little Rapunzel, let down your golden hair!"

Mother came up so quietly, I didn't hear her. She stands at the bottom of the tower, directly below the window, peering up with a basket hooked over her arm. If I took careful aim and surprised her, a blow to the head with the chamber pot might kill her.

But I am so hungry!

"I want to go home," I say.

"I've brought you food. Ham and cheese, a loaf of bread. And rampion pickles! I know how much you adore them."

I would spit on her but I want the ham. I want those pickles. "There's no door," I say.

"There's a large hook beside the window. Wrap your braid around it, the part closest to your head, and drop the rest down to me. I'll climb up."

"A fat old woman like you, climbing up the wall?" My laughter is full of hatred. "You'll never manage it."

"By now, my little Rapunzel, you should have realized I'm capable of many things that are beyond other people. Do as I tell you."

She continues smiling up at me but I know she is losing patience. The choice is mine: to let down my hair or go hungry. If she found a way to confine me up here in a tower room that has no door, she could force me to do whatever she wants.

Even with the full weight of her body hanging on my hair braid, I feel no pain in my scalp. What has she done to herself? She looks like a spider, as light as air, skittering up. Her feet and hands move swiftly between the folds in my hair. The dread of her deepens the closer she comes.

She is a witch.

Like one of those ugly crones from the tales she makes me read to her. How have I not understood this before now? You don't question what is right before you, day after day. You take it for granted.

Mother hops down from the window ledge like a toad. Smoothing her skirt, she smiles at the room around her. She keeps smiling even when she spots the piles of paper bits that are all that remain of her drawings. Then she places her basket on the table and unpacks it. Bread, ham, and cheese, already in slices. She knew better than to bring a sharp knife. Two water goblets. Last of all, she lays a saucer with rampion pickles upon the table. Six of them. Will she divide them evenly or take more for herself?

"Isn't this nice?" she says. "Just the two of us together, as ever."

"We have no tea," I point out. "You forgot to give me chairs."

"Yes, but it could be so much worse." That smile makes me shiver. "I think I'd like something to drink now," she says. "The climbing has given me quite a thirst."

When I pour water into glasses, the pitcher stays full. A magical pitcher that never empties. She can do so very much when she wants to. She can give or she can take away.

My hair … it was her magic and not time passing that made it this long.

I lay ham and cheese between slices of pumpernickel. "I would have liked some mustard," I tell her.

"Next time. I promise to bring some next time."

Thus it will be from now on – Mother spidering up my hair braid with food and pickles, day after day.

"If I promise to be good, will you let me come home? I'll do whatever you tell me."

"We won't talk about that now." She means we will never talk about it.

I grab three of the pickles from the saucer. "These are mine," I say.

"They're *all* for you, my little Rapunzel! As many as you like."

* * *

I've been lying here for weeks, it seems. I can't make myself move. What reason is there to move when I can go no further than the wall or to the window? Even the rampion pickles that Mother brings me every day don't make me feel better. They seem only to deepen the darkness. Mostly I try to sleep and hope that I don't awaken.

I will never again see Thomas. When I try to summon his face, I can't remember what he looked like, or the color of his hair. I recall that it was red but without flames to remind me, I've forgotten the exact hue.

Every afternoon, Mother calls to me from the bottom of the tower.

"Rapunzel, my little Rapunzel, let down your golden hair."

In the beginning, she came at a different hour every day but lately she comes in the afternoon so we can take tea together. Weeks ago, she finally brought me a teapot and a magic vessel that makes water boil when you fill it, but only if Mother is present. I can't have tea whenever I like. One morning, I woke up and there were two chairs, the high-backed chairs from our sitting room.

Every afternoon, I force myself to rise and unleash my braid out the window, but after she goes, I lie back down. Some day I will throw myself from the window. I will do it immediately after she calls up to me from below, so she can watch me die.

Lying exhausted one morning, unable to sleep, unable to move, I hear the cluttered sound of birds from outside. It has been there all morning but only now have I noticed. They're singing to one another …such joyful noise! Birdsong calls me to the window and I am finally able to rise from my pallet.

All around me in the trees, in flight across the meadow, hopping below me on the grass – birds everywhere! I gather up the sounds I hear them making – some thin and clear, others throaty – and piece them together within my thoughts. From the birdsong, I pick out sounds and make my own song, a song for Rapunzel, the lonely girl trapped in a tower. I put words to it and sing them aloud to the meadow.

* * *

My room never feels cold. Not warm either. I usually feel a slight chill so that I'm never truly comfortable, except at night when I'm warm enough under my counterpane. Each morning, I empty my chamber pot at the window. A thick brown pile has formed at the base of the tower with small red spots from the bloody rags I toss down there each month. I can't smell the pile up here but Mother makes sure to avoid it whenever I release my braid. She doesn't let my hair touch my excrement.

Whenever she's not here now, I spend hours seated on the window ledge, inventing songs. Living at home with Mother, I had no idea that I could do this. It seems almost like magic, the way a tune will come into my head. One moment my mind feels empty and I'm quietly waiting; the next, a piece of a song pops into it. A fragment. I spin it around and make it longer. I hum it aloud, adding different parts so it doesn't sound too simple. When I'm finished, I add words.

I am a songsmith.

I've lost track of the days but I must have been here for many months now because I've invented so many songs. I remember each one. The newer ones are mostly better than the earlier ones. As a songsmith, I'm improving. Many of the earliest songs were about Thomas but I no longer recall how he made me feel.

When Mother comes, she often hears me singing at the window. I stop at the sound of her voice her calling up to me.

"Rapunzel, my little Rapunzel, let down your golden hair."

She comes skittering up my braid with a basket, food and rampion pickles inside. I divide my days between inventing songs and the bliss that rampion brings. Sometimes when I sing after eating pickles, if the sky is clear and the lowering sun warms my body, tears will fill my eyes. Some day, I will invent a song about that feeling. Happy-sad.

"That was such a lovely song," Mother often says. "Would you sing it to me while I'm having my tea?"

"Perhaps some other time," I always tell her. My songs are my own and I won't share them, not with her.

She usually brings her knitting. After tea, we sit together while she knits. Alone in my thoughts, I run through my old songs and make plans for the ones I will invent after she has gone. Sometimes she brings her scratchy pens and works on her plant drawings. When lost in my song-thoughts, I can shut out the sound of her pen. We barely speak to one another. Living here alone in my tower, I have so little to say.

"When will you let me come home?" I always ask her.

"We won't talk about that now," she always answers.

* * *

One afternoon as I lie on my pallet, lost in rampion bliss, I hear a voice calling to me from outside the tower. "Rapunzel, my little Rapunzel, let down your golden hair." A man's voice. At the window, I look down and see him standing off to the side a little, avoiding the excrement pile. My face goes hot at the thought that he might smell it. He smiles up at me.

"There you are!" he says. He is young, about the same age as Thomas.

"Who are you?"

He throws his arms wide. "I am Cedric, a wandering prince in search of my true love and now I have found her."

He doesn't look like a prince. No fine clothes like the storybook princes, only leather breeches and a jerkin. Even from up here, his brown hair looks dirty and tangled. I like his face. I like the way he gazes up at me.

"What do you want?"

"I want you to let down your golden hair so I can climb up like the old woman does. I've been watching you, Rapunzel. And listening to your songs! It was your beautiful voice that first brought me here. Won't you lower your braid so I can climb up? I'd like to get to know you better."

Better than what? He doesn't know me at all.

When Cedric climbs, he doesn't skitter up like Mother. He struggles and grunts and curses. Even with my braid wrapped around the metal hook, the weight of his body makes the hair tug at my scalp. It hurts. He finally clambers through the window and rests his hands against his thighs, panting.

"The old woman … makes it look … so easy."

"What do you want?" I say again.

He comes upright and smiles. "Why just this, to meet the girl with the golden voice." He has straight white teeth, not crooked ones like Thomas's. "You're quite lovely, do you know that?" He takes a step closer.

"No, I am not."

"Indeed you are. But we won't argue about it. However did your hair grow so long?"

"Mother," I say. "She won't let me cut it."

I could tell him she's a witch but I don't know him.

"Even so, it would take a great many years. How old are you?"

"I don't know."

Cedric glances around him at the room. "It must be very lonely for you, living here in this tower with no one to keep you company but the old woman. Your mother, I presume. Why has she imprisoned you here?" He takes another step closer and it sets me trembling.

"Because I spoke to Thomas."

"A rival!" Why does Cedric think this is funny? How could he and Thomas be rivals?

"He was going to move into the cottage across the lane and I felt glad."

"I don't like the sound of that."

"So Mother put me here and won't let me out."

Another step closer and he stands inches away, still smiling at me. "Did you lie with him?"

I don't understand what he means. "I spoke to him only once, in the middle of the lane."

"Ah, that's good to hear. Have you ever been with any other man?"

"Only Thomas."

"And all you did was talk?"

"Yes."

"Good, very good." His hands suddenly reach out for the front of my dress. I slap them away.

"Don't!" I shout. I can only get the one word out, I'm trembling so.

"But I want to, very much."

He backs me into the wall and presses his body against me.

"Don't," I whisper.

"I'll be gentle, I promise. It's your first time, after all. I wouldn't want to hurt you."

His hands on my breasts frighten me at first. No one but Mother has ever touched me. But the warmth also makes me wet. It's what I've wanted for so long, a man's hands upon my body.

"Are you frightened?" he asks, still smiling. One hand stays on my breast and the other reaches under my dress.

"Yes." Fear is only part of what I feel.

"It's all right if you scream. No one will hear you."

I don't want to scream. When his hand touches me between my legs, it feels so good that I could weep.

He undoes his breeches and I see what lies beneath. It all makes sense to me now. He's very gentle with my braid, placing it behind me before he lowers me onto the pallet. He pushes inside and it feels as if he belongs there. Nothing has ever felt this good.

"So beautiful, so beautiful," he whispers. He puts his mouth over mine and my lips answer his. His breathing grows ragged and louder.

Perhaps Cedric meant what he said, that I am his "true love." He might have been listening to me sing for weeks now and has fallen in love with me. He moans my name and it sounds like love.

Afterwards when we lie together on the pallet, once his breathing has grown calm, I say, "Will you help me to escape?" He has his eyes closed.

"I'm not so sure I want you to escape. I like the idea that I'll always know where to find you."

"Please, Cedric. I can't bear to stay here."

"We'll see," he says.

* * *

My little Rapunzel has at last stopped begging me to free her. She took so long to make peace with her new life I sometimes wondered if I should withhold the pickles, to make clear why she could never leave me. For a few days only, just until the agony opened her eyes. Then I'd go back to indulging her. When we're alone together in her lovely tower room, when we share the rampion and sit together in silence, I feel as if we are one again, just as we used to be. I'm relieved I didn't have to make her suffer to help her understand.

* * *

In the beginning, I never knew when to expect Cedric. He might come several days in a row or he might disappear for long unbearable stretches. Lately, he has been coming almost every day. He says his love for me has grown so strong that being near to me is a physical need – like hunger, like thirst. He can't bear to be apart from me. He always waits for Mother to leave after tea then he struggles up my braid and makes me close my eyes while he undresses. I don't understand why he wants me to close them; I can see his body later as we lie together. He has skinny legs and pale white skin with many dark moles.

"Where do you go when you're not here with me?" I ask, beside him on the pallet one day after we have "played nug-a-nug," as he calls it. I've wanted to ask for so very long but I was afraid the question might anger him. Mother has never liked my questions.

"Attending to my princely duties, of course. I may not be king yet but I have many important responsibilities." Then he laughs. Cedric often laughs at the things he says.

"Tell me about them. I want to know what you do."

"Attend festivals, judge competitions, that sort of thing." When he has his eyes closed this way, I can study his face as long as I like and he won't mind. "Growing up so ignorant, my darling Rapunzel, you may not understand the crucial role I play in my kingdom."

"Do you live in a castle?"

"Where else would I live?"

"And you wear fine clothes and give banquets and go to fancy balls, the way princes do in the stories?"

"All of it, just as you say."

"And where are your fine clothes when you come to me? Why don't you wear them?"

"I'm in disguise, of course." This time, the sound of Cedric's laughter makes me wince with unfamiliar dislike. "You might think that a prince can do whatever he pleases, but only when I leave my finery behind am I truly free."

He answers so quickly and easily that what he says must be true. Why should I doubt him?

"How did you come by those scars on your back?" I ask. Long hard ridges that run from his shoulder blades nearly to his waist. My fingers run over them when he's on top on me.

I can feel the sudden tension in his body. He doesn't answer directly.

"It's a very sad story."

"Tell it to me."

"Perhaps some other time."

"Please, Cedric."

"I said *some other time.*"

I hear irritation in his voice. The sound matches the way I feel.

"You're never going to take me to live in your castle, are you?"

"There's the slight problem of your mother. After all, she *is* a witch." I've told him everything now, even about the rampion pickles though I didn't want to share them at first. "She might not take it very well if I were to steal you away from her."

"Then I'm to stay here forever."

"You must have patience. In time, I may think of a way."

"May?"

"I *will* think of a way. I promise, my darling Rapunzel. Now if you don't mind, would you move a little further away? Your braid is scratching my cheek."

* * *

My usual blood didn't come this month or last, I don't know why. And it feels as if strange changes are at work within my body. Sometimes when I awaken, my stomach churns and I vomit into the chamber pot. The rampion pickles have a bitter taste now that they never had before. I also pine for other foods – sweets and buns with raisins. I've asked Cedric to bring them to me but he always forgets. He slaps his forehead and says, "My princely cares drove it from my mind. Can you forgive me, my darling?"

I haven't spoken yet to Mother. I've wondered of late if she might have a potion to make the sick feeling go away but I don't like to need anything from her. There she is, sitting across from me with her knitting – I could ask her for a soothing potion but I won't. What I'd most like to do is stab her with one of those needles.

I'll work on my new song instead – not aloud so that Mother could listen but here in my head. This new song is about birds in flight, as if I, the singer, am one of them. The melody came to me easily, one day while lying beneath Cedric and wishing he would finish. I'm struggling with the words. All the rhymes seem too simple, too obvious. I want the words to rise up somehow, the way birds do when the wind carries them higher.

I spin words around in my head, sifting through the end pairs. Nothing sounds right. My thoughts keep jumping away from the frustration but I pull them back. I work so hard to keep the music present that I grind my top and bottom teeth together. I narrow my eyes.

"You've eaten only one of your pickles," Mother says. "Don't you want the others?"

I could scream at her for interrupting my thoughts, for taking me away from my song. "I'll save them for later."

"Why do you always save them for later?" Mother sounds hurt. "I want us to share them all."

I can see she feels sorry for herself. I'd like to slap her.

"Because," I tell her, "I enjoy them more when I'm alone than I do sitting here with an ugly old woman who doesn't know how to hold her tongue!"

The way she flinches and pulls her head back, it's as if I actually did slap her. Perhaps I will invent a song one day about the pleasures of cruelty. What a fine song that would be!

It occurs to me all of a sudden, the answer to my rhyming problem. The rhymes will come in the middle rather than at the end! Two lines in a pair will finish with the very same words and rhyme in their middles. If there is a songsmith rule that says rhymes must come at the end, I will break it.

My body drifts upward into the sky
My joy lifts me upward into the sky

Not quite good enough but something like that.

The idea makes me very happy. Inventing a good song feels better than rampion bliss, better even than playing nug-a-nug with Cedric once felt, back in the beginning. I am larger somehow, and happy with myself. I've never felt this way, so full of good feeling that I even find room to pity Mother, who has dropped her knitting and begun to weep.

Moving closer, I stand beside her chair and press her head against my belly. "There, there," I say, stroking her hair.

* * *

I felt a swelling at her waist, I'm sure of it!
And here at the bottom of the tower ... no bloody rags, not this month or last. And the sick from her curdled belly.
Who is he?

* * *

"Would you like to hear my new song?"

"Perhaps after nug-a-nug."

"I want to sing it for you first."

"Very well, if you must have things your own way. You used to be such a yielding maiden."

To sing for Cedric, I must turn my back and gaze out the window. I need to forget about him, as if I am singing only for myself.

My voice quavers at the outset, but as I go on, it grows stronger. The feeling of pride grows stronger, too. It is a very good song. The words and melody hold together as if they're of one piece, as if they belong together and no words but those would ever have suited that melody. The sensation of birds in flight comes through with so much power that I feel light on my feet, as if I am lifting skyward. I can almost believe my toes have left the floor and I am suspended above it. My braid is suddenly weightless, easing the drag on my head.

I did manage to forget about Cedric for the most part but now I want his praise. I want him to speak of the song's beauty and say he feels proud of me. When I turn around, he looks unhappy. He scowls at the empty plate that held the rampion pickles.

"Did you like it?" I ask.

"Yes."

"You don't *sound* as if you liked it."

"I could never write a such a good song."

"I am the songsmith. You are the prince."

He makes an ugly noise through his nose. I sense how much he doesn't want to look at me.

"You are free and I am trapped," I tell him. "All I have are my songs."

"Only your songs?"

"And you, of course. I'd die if you stopped coming." It's no longer true – I could survive on my songs – but I know he needs to hear it. At last he smiles up at me.

"Would you truly?"

"How can you doubt it, dearest Cedric? You know you're everything to me."

"It makes me very happy to hear you say it, my darling. And now I think I'm ready to play nug-a-nug."

* * *

The wind has come up and dark clouds have moved in while he lay on top of me. A powerful storm is brewing. Perhaps the rain will come down so hard and the wind blow so fiercely he'll have to stay overnight with me. I think I'd prefer to be alone.

Through the window, the clouds appear swollen and black – black like coal tar, black like the underside of a spider. Bloated angry spiders fill the sky.

"Listen to the wind," I whisper.

Cedric has fallen asleep and doesn't hear me. He doesn't hear the howling of wolves on the wind. No – worse than wolves. The high shriek of some monster from one of mother's books. Perhaps this is how dragons sound when fury catches fire in their throats. A thousand dragons rage against the darkening sky.

No ordinary storm.

The rain doesn't come. Wind spins round and round the tower, gaining speed. Louder and louder. For once, I'm grateful to live within a stone fortress. I am safe.

But now the chairs and table begin creeping toward the window … the suck of wind is drawing them out. My chamber pot suddenly hurtles through the opening and flies up into the spiral of clouds. The chairs break apart as they go through the window. Then the table, all in pieces.

Mother!

Cedric awakens with a jolt.

"What is happening?" he cries, holding tight to me. The wind tugs at his body. It wants to rip him from my arms. "Don't let go of me, Rapunzel! Please don't let me go! I don't want to die!"

The wind suddenly tears him from my arms. His head cracks against the stone lintel as he passes through the window. His neck must be broken. Even before the storm flings him to the ground, a thousand miles away, he will be dead.

Now I am sliding toward the window. I try lying flat and still but the wind comes under me. It lifts me up. With both hands, I grab for the giant hair hook as I am dragged through the opening. I hold on tight, my body pointing straight out from the tower. My braid whips around me, yanking on my head.

The wind slowly peels my fingers from the hook. Only seconds left … is this the end of me? It breaks my grip at last and spins me upward into the clouds, my braid going first.

Higher and higher.

I must be nearly to the top of the storm clouds because sunlight is breaking through. For one moment I am still, floating in place. Birds in flight must feel this way. With my wings, I reach for the sun.

Now I am falling.

The thought like a sob – when I die, all my songs will die along with me. No one will ever hear me sing them.

I will not have it so!

I sing out in loud defiance – my song of birds in flight, and I among the flock. All around me, the wind roars so fiercely I can't hear the sound of my own voice.

Ground rushes up to meet me.

* * *

What a fool! To have lavished years of love and affection on a worthless girl who wasn't even my daughter. I'm so much better off now without her, alone here in my cottage. No more trudging to the tower every afternoon, no need to share my pickles. Perhaps I'll have one now, even though it's not yet time for tea. I'm so exhausted from the cyclone spell – surely my greatest achievement! A good spell is sometimes like a work of art. I deserve an extra pickle.

I wonder if the wolves have found her broken body, wherever it landed. Perhaps their fangs are tearing in even now.

* * *

I am alive!

Was it this thicket that broke my fall? Or was it my song, my song of birds in flight that made me lighter, as light as Mother spidering up my braid?

Perhaps I, too, am a witch.

The End